ANGELS AROUND HER

BY

JENNIFER CUSUMANO
with KATHLEEN CUSUMANO

Copyright © 2011 by Jennifer Cusumano

Cover and interior design by Masha Shubin
Cover photos from BigStockPhoto.com. Beautiful Angel © Markus Gann. Winter in Central Park © Elzbieta Szpak. Roses © James Machin.

This is a work of fiction. The events described here are imaginary. The settings and characters are fictitious or used in a fictitious manner and do not represent specific places or living or dead people. Any resemblance is entirely coincidental.

All rights reserved. No part of this book may be reproduced or transmitted in any form or by any means whatsoever, including photocopying, recording or by any information storage and retrieval system, without written permission from the publisher and/or author. Contact Inkwater Press at 6750 SW Franklin Street, Suite A, Portland, OR 97223-2542. 503.968.6777

Publisher: Inkwater Press | www.inkwaterpress.com

Library of Congress Control Number: 2011934229

Paperback
ISBN-13 978-1-59299-639-1 | ISBN-10 1-59299-639-6

Kindle
ISBN-13 978-1-59299-640-7 | ISBN-10 1-59299-640-X

ePub
ISBN-13 978-1-59299-641-4 | ISBN-10 1-59299-641-8

Printed in the U.S.A.
All paper is acid free and meets all ANSI standards for archival quality paper.
3 5 7 9 10 8 6 4

DEDICATION

To our parents, who gave us wings.

ACKNOWLEDGMENTS

To all the talented people at Inkwater, especially Sean who first believed in the book, my editor Sandra Mardenfeld, my photographer Steven Lang, Arielle Eckstut and David Henry Sterry for their savvy advice and artistic encouragement, Bethany Siegler at UniqueThink, WBBC (you know who you are), friends and family for your feedback and support.

CHAPTER ONE

Bridge stood at the French doors looking out over the veranda and gardens below. She had hoped it would be sunny for the party. Ordinarily, the late afternoon sun cast such beautiful light into this room. But it was grey today. A layer of silver mist was descending upon the garden, quiet and somber, like her mood. Bridge had always enjoyed putting these parties together, decorating the rooms, and seeing to the myriad of details that made her Christmas Eve parties so spectacular. Lately, however, it all seemed so trivial, another elaborate affair produced more out of expectation than anything else. Looking up into the December skies, Bridge wondered if it might snow as dark clouds gathered over the house.

Behind her, the house was a flurry of activity. Caterers set up silver trays and florists arrived with Christmas centerpieces. Turning away from the threatening skies, Bridge glanced around the drawing room. The grace and grandeur of another time was so apparent in this room especially, with its fluted pilasters, floor-to-ceiling sash windows and detailed moldings. The crystal chandeliers cast the sparkle of rainbow refractions that danced about the room.

It was a beautiful house, but at Christmastime the Brookville estate was particularly magical. The gilded mirrors were draped with boughs of fresh pine and flowers. The marble fireplace mantle had dozens of silver candlesticks and fresh holly. Bridge had set a silver tea service on a stand in front of the silk couch, creating a cozy spot for conversation. She watched as the last of the candles about the room were lit, instantly adding an amber glow. As she took a last approving look around the room, Bridge wished she felt as warm and welcoming.

The house was Neal's prize possession, which he inherited from his family who were part of Long Island's Gold Coast society set. Although many of the old money coterie has disbanded and the nouveau riche has replaced some of the older homes with more modern compounds, privilege still prevailed here. Neal straddled both sets of society. Even though he was born into a family of significance, Neal made his own small fortune in various venture capital deals. He had a talent for befriending investors and courting the eccentric. They would all be here today.

Every Christmas Eve, Neal and Bridge had an open house. The black tie Christmas party seemed to be the one party they had that Bridge always enjoyed. For his part, Neal always had an agenda. The Christmas party just made it appear that Neal was simply doing something from his heart, in the spirit of the holidays. But Bridge always managed to plan these parties with the very best of intentions, especially where the children were concerned. Having no children of their own, Bridge lavished Claire's children with many gifts. This was the best part of the party for Bridge, but she could have done without the house full of guests who were little more than acquaintances. She had never let Neal's secret motives or petty obsessions ruin her mood before. And yet this year, this party, was different. Perhaps time had taken its toll.

As Claire and Jack drove up the long tree-lined drive towards the house, Jack let out a long sigh. Claire noticed he always did that when they arrived at her sister and Neal's house and wondered what he found so unbearable. Pulling up to the house beneath the limestone portico, the children were the first to run out of the car.

"Here we go," Jack sighed, rolling his eyes.

"Jack, please," Claire said. "Can you just try to have a good time?"

"God, I hate these things," Jack confessed. "You know I love your sister, but Neal and his friends always make me feel like an interloper."

"I know honey," Claire said. "But we're not here for Neal, we're here for Bridge."

As the children bounded through the front door, Bridge walked through the foyer to greet them. James and Olivia flung themselves into Bridge, throwing their arms around her neck and wrapping their legs around her waist. Bridge knelt down and cuddled both children in her arms.

"Kids!" Claire shouted. "Mind your Aunt's dress."

The children climbed off her, as Bridge stood up, not seeming to mind.

"Go see what Auntie has for you under the tree," Bridge whispered.

As Bridge embraced Claire, Claire adjusted a strap on Bridge's dress.

"Oh, let me fix this," Claire said. "I'm sorry, the kids are just so excited to see you."

"It's fine. No harm done," Bridge said as she embraced her brother-in-law. "Jack, it's so good to see you."

"Wow, you look great," Jack said, returning her embrace with his signature bear hug.

Bridge looked glamorous. Her silver, satin, long dress draped her tall, slender figure perfectly and when she walked, the small train trailing behind her moved from side to side. The color of the dress was off set only by the color of Bridge's light blue eyes and fair skin.

"She certainly does," Neal said, as he descended the last few stairs of the marble staircase. After adjusting his last cuff link, Neal extended his hand to Jack.

"What better time than the holidays to sport your finest," Neal said. Bridge stiffened ever so slightly.

"Still sticking with the penguin suit, Neal?" asked Jack, who always opted for a classic blazer. Neal looked particularly dapper in his tuxedo, but he certainly was not as good looking as Jack.

"I see you did not break from tradition either," Neal said, "but with your good looks, Jack, who needs a tuxedo? No matter. C'mon, let me pour you a drink."

As the two men headed for the drawing room, Claire held onto her sister's arm.

"Are you okay?" Claire asked.

Bridge waved her hand as if to suggest that it was nothing.

"It's just Neal always gets so obsessive before these parties, everything has to be so perfect. He's made me a bit edgy, I suppose."

With the sound of the doorbell chiming, Bridge shook off whatever doubts about this evening she had. She assumed her hostess role, donning a smile while greeting the arriving guests. Claire noticed the immediate change in Bridge as if her sister had slipped into a different character.

This persona, who had developed over her many years with Neal, was now effortless for Bridge. Claire sometimes wondered how Bridge managed to live with these two very distinct women within her—the one she had grown up with, the one loving the children wrapped around her neck, and this other woman created to be a part of Neal's world.

Milling around the grand foyer and drawing room, one could overhear various conversations, most punctuated with talk of success: deals made, trips taken, houses refurbished. In this crowd, one was either inspired, or nauseated by it all. And then there were those rare people like Claire, seemingly unaffected and unimpressed by any of it.

"So tell me, Mrs. Esterborough, what's your secret for staying so young?" Claire asked.

"Oh, my dear, you are a delight," said the white-haired matriarch of a whole family of guests. Her light eyes twinkled when she laughed and her skin was loose, but almost without a wrinkle. She was the kind of woman who had seen much of life and was all the more wiser and kinder because of it. She lived a privileged life, but had known harder times. The Esterboroughs were genuinely kind and giving people, and Bridge especially liked them more than any of the other guests.

As Bridge watched Claire talking to the Esterboroughs from across the room, she realized how glad she was that her sister was here. Claire could talk to anyone. She was a very attractive woman who never failed to turn the heads of Neal's friends. She was more petite than Bridge, but with the same fair skin and hair. Their only real difference was that Claire had her father's warm brown eyes, which smoldered tonight under some dramatic makeup. But Claire only had eyes for Jack, and as she mingled with the guests, she exchanged flirtatious glances with her husband across the room.

As Bridge joined Claire and the Esterboroughs, Charles was speaking about how important it was to have a hobby or interest that you love. For his wife, Marjorie, he believed it was gardening that kept her young.

"She dotes over that rose garden almost as much as me," he said. He talked about her funny little gardening hat and gloves, which he still found adorable on her. At that moment, they both exchanged an understanding, playful smile.

"You two are a delight," Claire said as she waved at Jack, motioning for him to join her. She knew he needed bailing out from Neal's circle and this gesture gave him reason to excuse himself.

Bridge was lost in her own thoughts for the moment, thinking how wonderful it must be to have a husband who appreciates all his wife's interests and idiosyncrasies. When they first met, Neal had seemed to love the fact that she was an aspiring designer. She now understood that it was only a feigned interest in order to win her. Back then, she was flattered by his interest in her and somewhat taken with his lifestyle. She lost herself in their whirlwind courtship. Now she saw that it was always about Neal and his interests. Everything was fine as long as he was in control of all the decisions.

"Jack, I'd like you to meet the Esterboroughs," Claire said.

"Pleased to meet you," Jack said as he extended both his hands.

"You have the most lovely wife," Marjorie said. Then leaning over to Claire in an aside, Marjorie commented on Jack's good looks. "He's very handsome, isn't he?"

"Yes, he is," Claire agreed.

With Jack's arrival, Bridge excused herself. She knew she should probably join the small gathering of women sitting around the tea service. Next to them was Helena McKay, who was on the board of Trustees of The Metropolitan Opera. Bridge had just seen her at a fund-raising gala for the Met a couple of weeks ago. Helena was already bending the ear of one of Neal's friends. She opted for the country club wives. As Bridge approached the group, their conversation became more discernable.

"She acts like she's really in love with this one."

"Do you suppose Edward knows?"

"Oh, he must."

"Well then, do you think he cares?"

"Edward's had his share of affairs, I'm sure."

"I don't know...I think Julia could leave Edward for him."

"Adelaide, don't be naive. Why search for a prince if you already live in the palace?"

"Oh, Carol, you're terrible."

Cutting in on their awful, forced laughter, Bridge felt her distaste for these women grow.

"Ladies, you appear to be enjoying yourselves," Bridge said, interrupting their conversation.

"Apparently not as much as Julia Baines," Carol joked, as more of their insidious laughter ensued.

"You're all wicked women," Adelaide said. "All I'm saying is, life is too short to waste on an unhappy marriage."

It was apparent that these women were only interested in shallow conversation, but Adelaide's words burned in Bridge's ears.

"Is there any hot tea left in that pot?" Bridge inquired,

as she walked over to the service and poured herself a cup. Just then, a flutter of children skipping through the room caused enough of an imbalance to tip the tea service in Bridge's hands, sending the hot liquid flowing down the front of Bridge's gown. Bridge let out a small gasp as the other women stood up quickly, drawing everyone's attention. The caterers immediately looked for a towel or something to help Bridge with her dress, but Neal launched into a small tirade.

"What's happened here?" Neal asked with restrained rage. "Look what they've done, they've ruined your dress!" The children stopped running nearby and looked about to cry.

"Neal, I did it to myself," Bridge explained as she patted the front of her dress.

"It was an accident," Claire interjected. "It's okay kids. Just slow it down."

"Why are there always accidents when children are involved?" Neal asked no one in particular. Then, Neal turned his attention to the caterers. "Just clean the mess off the floor so no one slips and breaks their necks."

Claire was the only one to move. The rest of the women stood there as though frozen.

"God, Bridge, did you burn yourself?" Claire asked with concern.

"No, I don't think so…well, I guess a change is in order," Bridge said, wiping the wetness from her fingers with a napkin.

"Oh, you poor dear," said Adelaide.

"Don't be silly! That's what a closet full of beautiful dresses is for, right?" Claire said, trying to lighten the mood, but glaring at Neal. "C'mon, let's get you changed."

When the sisters entered the master bedroom, Claire closed the door behind them and started at Bridge.

"What in the world is wrong with him?" Claire shouted. "He didn't even think to ask if you were OK."

"But, I'm fine…it wasn't that hot," Bridge said.

"That's not the point, Bridge," Claire continued. "Do you think his behavior is acceptable? The way he talked to you and to those young girls? Not to mention terrifying my kids."

"Claire you don't understand…," Bridge started. "There are certain social standards Neal expects me to uphold."

"Standards he obviously doesn't hold himself to!" Claire retorted. "Honestly, I don't know how you put up with him."

Bridge knew Claire was right. She had sacrificed so much of herself to be the wife Neal needed. In the beginning, the compromises were necessary, she told herself, in order to be a part of Neal's glamorous lifestyle. Her career aspirations, interests, and strong opinions were all watered down over the years as Neal's world made increasing demands on her time. Initially, she enjoyed certain freedoms that his money afforded her. The estate became a playground for her artistic whims and Neal let her redecorate as it fit her fancy. However, now the cost of all those compromises seemed to be exacting too big a toll.

As she sat on her majestic canopy bed, Bridge felt the denied truth of all those years come crushing down on her.

"Well, what are we going to put you in, now?" asked Claire, as she browsed through Bridge's closet.

"I don't care," Bridge said, somewhat deflated. "Pick something out…"

As Claire rummaged through years of acquired couture, Bridge sunk into contemplative thought. They were not new thoughts, just thoughts pushed away over the years--thoughts too uncomfortable to face. Bridge suddenly experienced a terrible sense of loss for the girl she was before meeting Neal, for the children she never had, for the heart still broken, never mended. She knew Neal was not the great love of her life when she married him, but they had been happy in those first few years as they settled into a comfortable, complementary relationship. Somewhere in the last couple of years, Bridge began to feel more and more dissatisfied with her role as Mrs. Hamilton and all the social responsibilities that came with the position. She was spending less time with Neal. All his activities, all his conversations were always about making money, or spending money, or how much money something or someone was worth. He seemed so shallow to her now. She had tried to connect with him on a different level, but Neal was disinterested in her pleasures, like accompanying her on her long walks. He was unmoved at the sunsets she described to him. He never lay in bed with her talking, or reading side by side. They couldn't be more different.

Recently, when she started to renew her interest in fashion, Neal had shown little support. Now, as Claire looked through her closet full of dresses, Bridge's emotions turned to anger. She had seen these clothes for years, but now she seemed not to recognize any of them as hers. But she did have one that was truly her own. She had made it years ago when she was still a design student in Paris. Bridge had kept it all these years, but tucked in the way back of the closet among the giveaway pile and the hopelessly out of date.

"Claire, grab the maroon velvet dress at the rear of the closet," said Bridge.

In a moment, Claire emerged looking somewhat confused with a dress covered in plastic wrap.

"You mean, this?" asked Claire.

"That's it," Bridge said, as she jumped off the bed. "I wonder if it still fits?"

It was a gorgeous gown. Bridge had been so happy when she conceived of the design and began shopping for material. It was hers; it was pure Bridge. Slipping the mounds of burgundy silk over her head, she felt defiant and strangely free beyond belief. The velvet halter top fell into place as if the dress had just been fitted to her.

"Hot damn!" Claire exclaimed. "How do you do it?"

The sisters shared an excited laugh.

"I always loved this dress," Bridge said. "I've never worn it..."

"Why not?"

But Bridge did not seem to hear her, or at least offered no response.

"Well, no matter," Claire continued. "You're wearing it now."

Bridge flew down the stairs with a renewed energy, much like a young girl, holding onto the skirt of her dress. Claire followed behind, amazed at her sister's quick change of mood. From downstairs the children called out to Claire.

"Are we staying Mommy?" Olivia asked.

"Can we go out back to the garden?" pleaded James.

"Alright," Claire said, "but keep your coats on if you go outside."

When Bridge entered the drawing room, she noticed that some new guests had arrived and had obviously been curious as to where their hostess might be. Of course, the other guests who had witnessed the incident surely filled them in on the details by now. It was the guests who had been here earlier that welcomed her back with the kind of applause and comments meant for someone who had recovered gracefully from an otherwise embarrassing moment.

"Bravo! Bravo!" shouted Helena McKay's escort, Felix, as if he were at the opera and Bridge had given a command performance. The ladies looked her over and the gentlemen smiled. Bridge looked radiant. Amid their clapping and comments, Bridge eyed Neal across the room. It was apparent that he was disappointed she had not selected one of the designer dresses that hung in her closet. Bridge was thoroughly enjoying the moment. In a playful gesture to appease her guests, Bridge took a long, theatrical bow.

As Neal began to approach her, Bridge made her way through the crowd, averting Neal's advances. As she walked through the room, she felt in command of her true persona for the first time in years. Looking around at the faces in this room, she realized that with the exception of Claire and Jack and the Esterboroughs, these people were not her friends. In more than fifteen years, she had not forged a single close relationship. Now she understood why. These were Neal's people and she was suddenly aware of a growing distaste for most of them.

The running of feet across the floor spun her around. Claire's children were upon her, each grabbing at her arms.

"Auntie Bridge, it's snowing, it's snowing."

"Yes, come see, come play with us."

It was a welcome distraction. "Okay, I'll tell you what," reasoned Bridge. "Let me get my coat and I'll come out with you."

As she made her way to the hallway, Neal caught Bridge by surprise.

"Where are you going now? You're not intending to disappear again, are you?"

"I'm getting my coat. The children want me to see the snow," Bridge said, as she reached into the closet and selected a long cape with a dramatic oversized hood.

"You're not serious!" Neal was growing impatient, but Bridge did not answer him. She pulled the hood up over her head.

"What about your guests?" Neal asked impatiently.

"What about them? They won't miss me," Bridge retorted as she began to walk away from him.

Out on the veranda, the children were already playing, but when Bridge emerged they led her by the hand, down the stairs and into the gardens. They ran in and out of the maze of hedges that led out to a clearing. Bridge looked up to the dark sky and felt almost dizzy with delight as she watched the millions of snowflakes that danced on the wind as they fell to the ground. The children's laughter seemed to fade into the background as she became lost in this dreamlike moment. The lights from within the house lit up the night and from where she stood she could see clearly inside. She fixated on the drawing room that glowed bright with candlelight. As she stood in the freshly snow powdered garden, the drawing room and all its fineries seemed to pale in comparison to the natural beauty of the garden and surrounding fields. The longer she watched the guests mill about the room, the further removed from them she felt.

The snap of the French doors opening interrupted her state of deep thought. Neal stepped out onto the veranda, followed by Claire. She knew Neal's presence alone was meant as a signal to her that it was beyond time for her to come in. He certainly would not call to her, so he had Claire call to the children, who were making snow angels. As the children ran to their mother, Bridge lingered in the garden, gazing down at the perfect angelic impressions left glistening on the ground. Bridge had long put away thoughts of angels at Christmas, but these child-like images of magical innocence only reminded her of what was missing in her life. She watched the children run up to the house, the place that once lured her into a lifestyle that she thought would make her life complete, important somehow. Now, she realized the lifestyle that once propelled her into the heights of society also had slowly stolen her very essence of being. She knew too that the man glaring at her from the veranda had not been her true love, but a means to an end. She was not without some blame in the matter with which she had married him. She was hurting and lonely and had made a hasty decision, not based on her true feelings, but on what Neal could offer her: comfort, prestige, security. As the haze of all these thoughts lifted, one distinct truth became clear; it was time to right all the wrongs.

A small, curious crowd had started to gather behind Neal. Then a more distinct voice approached.

"Is everything alright?" Jack asked, the concern in his voice palpable.

"No, everything is not alright," Neal whispered to Jack. He turned to Claire for some rationale of his wife's behavior, but was only more exasperated by the fact that Claire seemed perfectly calm, studying her sister.

"What's wrong with her? Why is she intent on embarrassing me?" Neal asked.

"I don't think that's her intent," Jack offered. "Honey, maybe you should go talk to her."

"No, I don't think so...," Claire said calmly. "She'll come in when she's ready."

Neal, seeing that Claire was not going to intercede on his part, began waving his arms in a motion that was meant for her to come back to the house.

"Bridge, your guests are waiting for you," he called out, trying to keep his tone polite.

Bridge smiled, looked down at the snow angels, and shook her head. Then she did something completely unexpected. She began to back away from the house, first slowly, step by slow step.

"Oh, this is absurd," snapped Neal. "What is she doing?" No one answered him, but kept their eyes fixed on Bridge. They wondered the same thing.

Then, with more intention in her step, Bridge turned her back on Neal and the life she was ready to leave behind. She ran past the gardens, descending the last set of stairs that led out into the open fields. Claire's expression conveyed that she understood what they did not.

"Where is she going? Is she having some sort of breakdown?" Neal asked in awe, as if this could be the only plausible rationale for her behavior.

"On the contrary Neal, I believe she is having a breakthrough," Claire said, with just the slightest hint of a knowing smile.

As Claire watched her sister running into the fields, the night wind blew back the hood of Bridge's cape, revealing her long tresses of caramel-colored hair. It reminded Claire of the curly, blonde-haired little girl with whom she had run through the fields surrounding their childhood home. In an instant, Claire was back to another Christmas long ago, when they had scurried about collecting pine cones. As girls, it seemed they were always outside playing or walking through the fields with their mother, who had a great appreciation for nature and the outdoors. Bridge, especially seemed to share this natural affinity with their mother. By the time she was nine years old, Bridge could name almost every wild flower and herb she had learned about from their frequent walks together.

It was a brisk, windy Saturday, the weekend before Christmas. Their father had asked them to go play outside. Dr. Baker was coming to visit their mother. Claire, only seven then, did not realize the severity of their mother's condition. They were told that their mother was sure to be out of bed by Christmas. Claire and Bridge, wanting to help in whatever way they could, collected pine cones and holly berries as Christmas decorations while their father went through the motions of putting up some simple ornaments around the house, a promise he had made to his wife. As they returned to the house, red-cheeked and out of breath, they could see the foil decoration that covered the entire front door. Their father opened the door, now covered with an angelic figure, and the girls entered slowly. They stared at the beautiful winged lady playing a harp and staring down on them with a soft, loving smile.

"She's so pretty," said Claire.

"She's an angel," instructed Bridge.

"I know. Christmas angels, right Daddy?" asked Claire.

"Well, yes Claire, that's right," their father said as he checked a string of colored lights.

"Can I be an angel?" asked Claire.

"No, silly. Angels only live in heaven," explained Bridge.

"Is that true Daddy?"

"Yes, it's true Claire, but angels are also about us working in mysterious ways to make wonderful things happen here on earth." As he spoke to them his voice faltered a bit as he was ever aware of his own wife's ill health.

Dr. Baker emerged from the bedroom with his medical bag, his stethoscope still hanging around his neck.

"Thomas, I'm going to move her to a hospital. She doesn't seem to be responding to the medication," he said.

Thomas hadn't expected this sudden turn for the worse. Surprise and concern washed over his face. The girls stood quietly with their coats still on, staring at the doctor.

"Is it...serious, Doctor?" Thomas asked.

"Yes, I'm afraid it is," Dr. Baker said grimly. "I've called the hospital already. She just wanted a moment with the girls."

Their father got down on his knee and spoke to the girls.

"Girls, Mommy is going to have to go with Dr. Baker to the hospital, but before she leaves why don't you go see her. That will make her feel better."

Ushering them over to her bedside, he was surprised to see her looking weaker than she had just a short time ago. She had been crying, but when she saw them standing in the doorway, she smiled and reached out her hand to them. Bridge immediately went to her, but Claire entered slowly behind her big sister.

"There's my beautiful girls," she said.

"We've been decorating the house for you, Mommy," Bridge said.

"Yes, and we have a pretty Christmas angel too," Claire added.

"You two are Mommy's little angels. Come here and sit with me."

Bridge sat in the bed snuggled up against her mother's shoulder, but Claire stood at the bedside.

"Now I want you to be good girls for Daddy while I'm gone. Bridge, you watch over your sister, OK?"

"How long are you going to be gone for, Mommy?" asked Bridge, sensing her mother's weakness.

"I'm not sure, honey, but whatever happens or however long it seems that I'm not here, I want you to know that your Mommy is always with you. You may not always be able to see me, or be with me, but I'll be there."

"Like the angels, Mommy?" asked Claire.

"Yes, darling, very much like the angels," she said looking over to her husband standing in the doorway, his hand cupped over his mouth, his eyes filling with tears.

"But if we can't see you Mommy, how do we know you're there?" asked Bridge.

Holding onto her children, their mother explained as best she could to her two young girls who could not totally understand what she was trying to prepare them for in case the worst happened.

"You'll know that Mommy is with you when you walk through the fields and the wind blows through your hair, or when the sunbeams fall on you and warm you like Mommy's hug, or when the snow flakes land on your cheeks. Think of it as Mommy blowing you kisses."

Just then Dr. Baker reluctantly interrupted. "The ambulance is here. We should go now."

"I'll meet you there Doctor, as soon as I get a neighbor to come stay with the girls," said Thomas. Bridge and Claire kissed their mother and slowly backed out of the room.

From their foggy living room window, the girls watched

the ambulance pull away, taking their mother away from them, forever.

Jack moved closer to Claire who was staring out at the empty fields, apparently lost in thought.

"C'mon honey, the party is obviously over," Jack said.

Turning away from the dark field, Claire took Jack's arm and they walked back to the house. In the drawing room, the children were quietly playing with toys under the tree.

"It doesn't look like it's going to be a very merry Christmas for everyone this year," Jack said.

As Claire watched the children playing she responded, "They're not always merry."

CHAPTER TWO

Once they were sure the children had fallen asleep in the back seat, Jack and Claire broke the silence on the ride home from Brookville to Manhattan. The snow that had fallen, combined with the heavy holiday traffic, made for a slow ride home. It was the kind of dreaded combination that earned the Long Island Expressway its nickname, "the parking lot."

"You're very quiet, are you thinking about Bridge?" Jack asked.

"I keep playing that whole scene tonight over in my mind," Claire said. "I knew there was something wrong with her, but I certainly didn't think it would come to this."

"Where do you think she went?" Jack asked.

"Probably not far," guessed Claire. "Just far enough to get away from Neal for a while."

"But surely, she had to come back to the house eventually?"

"Obviously, honey. The woman was wearing evening shoes in the snow."

"She must have really had it with Neal to pull a stunt like that," said Jack, a little amused.

"I think it must have been a long time coming," Claire responded. "And I think it was much more than Neal being difficult. I know she's been a bit unhappy lately. I guess it finally became too much tonight."

"Well, I'll be really surprised if she really leaves him," Jack said. "Give up that lifestyle after all these years?"

"You know Jack," Claire offered in her sister's defense, "you only know Bridge since she's been married to Neal. The Bridge I knew was strong and vibrant, with wonderful ideals and a mind of her own. I saw her reclaim some of that tonight."

Jack looked over at Claire, who was staring out her window. She was right; he didn't know Bridge as well as he thought. He never really understood how two sisters who seemed to be very different, were still as close as schoolgirls. Claire hardly had a mother, only for seven years, so it would be natural for her to be especially close with her only sister. He had been insensitive.

"It must have been difficult for you girls growing up without a mother," Jack said. He had a way of sensing her emotions, and he was trying to make up for his earlier flippant comments about Bridge.

"It was very painful losing our mother," Claire answered, "but it must have been harder on Bridge."

"Why would you say that? You were only seven."

"Yes, but I had Bridge, who really took on a mothering role. She was always there for me, but who was there for her?"

They both stared out into the endless flow of headlights, each absorbed in thought, then Claire began to explain Bridge's story, which Jack had never really been privy to:

"A short while after our mother died, our father moved us into Manhattan to accept the professorship at the University. The demands of work and the pressure to publish kept him conveniently busy. Even when he spent time at home, he always seemed so removed. Looking back now, he probably worked as hard as he did as a means of dealing with his grief over mother's death. Bridge, who was really still a child, had to mature quickly mainly because of me, I think. She was there to comfort me when I fell on my roller skates and scraped my hands and knees on the pavement. She would give me money from her allowance so I could buy more candy after spending all of mine. She doted on me, but she had no one older and wiser to confide in. My father, as you know, wasn't very progressive. Growing up in the eighties in Manhattan could not have been easy for a displaced rural girl without a mother. She chartered the unknown waters first. I learned from watching her..."

Jack smiled as he looked over at Claire. He had never heard Claire describe her sister in this way. They were memories Claire had not thought about for some time and as she reflected it seemed that she too was somehow changed by the night's events:

"I remember we'd take long walks in Central Park and sometimes Bridge would just stand still and turn her face towards the sun or feel the breeze blow though her hair, totally in tune with the elements. She loved to walk. She'd walk all the time, in different excursions around the city. In fact, it was on one of her outings where she first met Vincent."

"Vincent? Who's that?" Jack asked. "How come I never heard about him?"

"Ah...Vincent...," Claire reminisced. "We never bring it up because it was so painful for Bridge. But Vincent was great; we all loved him."

"Another rich business man?"

"No, no...Vincent was just a student when they met. But how he loved her..."

"So what happened?"

"Well, from what I remember there was some misunderstanding between them when Bridge went to study in Europe," Claire explained. "I'm ashamed to admit now, but I think I might have had a small part in her decision to break it off with him. After all, I had encouraged her to study abroad."

"People make their own decisions, honey," Jack said.

"I know, but when you're a teenager, you don't always realize the impact of some decisions," Claire said. "Bridge was young and confused and meeting all different kinds of people in Paris. Vincent waited faithfully for her, but he wanted a commitment. I guess she wasn't ready for that, so she set him free. I think she realized too late that she had lost her true love and was never quite the same afterwards."

"That's so sad," Jack said. "Makes me feel lucky I found you."

"Yes, we're very lucky."

"So when did Neal come on the scene?"

"After Vincent, Bridge threw herself into her work and that's where she met Neal. At the time we thought he was good for her. He was taking her out all the time to exclusive clubs, hobnobbing with the Manhattan elite. He was older and established. Of course, we were all a bit surprised when they announced their engagement so quickly. The rest you know..."

She had said her last words with a kind of dissatisfied finale, suggesting that "the rest" was not the best. As they crept across the 59th Street Bridge, Jack was quietly contemplating Bridge's story. Driving through the park, the white lights from Tavern on the Green put a festive hue on the quiet, Christmas Eve night. As they turned onto their street, Jack offered a thought:

"Well, maybe you're right. Perhaps this was a long time coming for your sister. Maybe it's not too late for her to find happiness again."

Jack found a rare spot not far from their apartment. The children woke with the momentum of the car coming to a standstill.

"Is it Christmas? Has Santa come yet?"

"No darling, not yet," Claire whispered to Olivia, as she bundled her up into her arms and carried her into the building, Jack and James close behind. "Go right back to sleep and tomorrow will come soon enough."

"Will Auntie Bridge be at grandfather's tomorrow?" James asked.

Claire and Jack exchanged a glance. "I guess we'll just have to wait and see, Champ," Jack said.

James put his head back on his father's shoulder and Jack commented to Claire as they entered the apartment. "Tomorrow should be interesting..."

CHAPTER THREE

As Thomas Adair made himself a second cup of tea, he heard car doors slam and the sound of familiar voices.

"That couldn't be them already," he said as he checked his wristwatch. He walked to the living room window to find his family trying to balance their packages as they made their way up the stairs.

"Grandpa, Grandpa," shouted Olivia and James as they came running through Thomas' already opened front door, she, dressed in a red velvet dress with white lace tights and he in a very grownup navy suit.

"There's my bunch," he said, picking up Olivia.

"Merry Christmas, Dad." Jack was carrying an armful of Christmas presents.

"Merry Christmas Jack," Thomas said, with a firm handshake.

Claire gave her father a kiss upon entering. "Good morning, Dad," Claire said, surprised to find her father still in his robe. "I hope we're not interrupting your breakfast, but the kids just couldn't wait."

"No, no, just having some more tea, kind of a late night," Thomas said, scratching his head. They moved into the living room, which Thomas decorated with the same fake Scotch pine tree, and the same ornaments placed in exactly the same spot every year.

"James, help Mommy with these bags," Claire instructed. "Put these boxes in Granddad's refrigerator."

"Here, let's put those packages under the tree with the others," Thomas suggested.

"Can we open these?" asked Olivia.

"No honey, not until after morning mass," Jack said.

"Auntie Bridge, I knew you'd come!" James shouted from the kitchen.

"Auntie Bridge? Where? Where?" asked an excited Olivia, as she went running into the kitchen after James.

Bridge emerged from the kitchen holding James' hand and a mug full of tea in the other. She was dressed in what was apparently a pair of her father's flannel pajamas and she looked as though she had not slept all night. With a weak smile on her face, she followed the children into the living room.

"Well, look who's here!" Jack said. "Back from your night flight, sis?"

"Very funny…" Bridge said with a half-smile.

"Bridge, I was so worried about you! Are you alright?" asked Claire, hugging her sister with a sigh of relief.

"It was a difficult night," Bridge said.

"I'll bet," Jack quipped .

"But I'm in the best place I could be right now," said Bridge leaning an arm on her father's shoulder.

"Showed up here I guess about…what was it dear? Just after midnight?"

"I kept Dad up most of the night, I'm afraid," Bridge said.

"Nonsense," Thomas responded with a flourish of his hand.

"Well, I'm glad you're here," Claire said. "You take it easy today and leave all the cooking to me."

"I know you girls will probably want to talk, so Jack and I will take the children to services," Thomas said.

"Oh, you're not going to come to mass with us Auntie Bridge?" asked James.

"James, your Aunt Bridge is really tired," explained Claire. "See, we've woken her up! She's still in her pajamas!" The children laughed and surrounded Bridge.

"Don't worry, we'll have all day together," said Bridge reassuring the children. "And when you return, we can open presents."

After the four left and the house was quiet, Bridge sat back down at the kitchen table and laid her head down on it.

"Ugh…" the moan came from under her mass of hair.

"What have you had to eat? Anything since yesterday?" asked Claire.

"Eat? Oh, some toast, I guess."

"Oh c'mon," Claire said. "I'll put up a pot of coffee and we can start in on a cheesecake I brought over."

"Well, I actually did it, Claire. I left Neal," Bridge said, raising her head from the table and running her hands through her hair as if trying to pull herself together.

"You 'left him' left him?" Claire asked, trying to clarify her sister's meaning. Bridge just nodded with her hand on her forehead.

"What happened?" Claire asked as she sat down across from her sister.

Bridge paused as if not sure where to begin:

"Neal and I have not been really happy for some time.

The last few years have become a comfortable arrangement for both of us. I'm embarrassed to say this, but I think the lifestyle kept me in the marriage more so than any feelings I had for him. Last night showed me the price I had paid for living without love for so long. I traded love for a standard of living and I had lost more in the trade than I ever suspected."

"Wow...that's honest...," offered Claire, somewhat surprised.

"Well, it's high time, isn't it?" asked Bridge. "You were right last night Claire. He's impossible."

"And pompous...," murmured Claire.

"Yes, I know! Pompous, and self-important, and angry..."

"Ok, ok...," interrupted Claire. "So you had this realization, and then what? You decide to make a big, dramatic exit?"

"Well, I hadn't planned it that way," explained Bridge. "Except that a strange thing happened to me as I stood in the garden. As I gazed upon the house from a distance, this house, which I had helped to make so grand, suddenly lost its appeal. It was not my home. I no longer felt like I belonged there, not with Neal, not with his crowd. The longer I stood there, the clearer everything became. It was as if a little distance was all that was needed for me to see the stark difference between myself and them."

"Finally...," Claire said, as if she had been waiting for this a long time.

"I know," Bridge conceded, as she reached for her sister's hand across the table. "I know you saw it long before I was ready."

"Well, I'm just glad you did...not at the most opportune time however..."

"No, it was exactly the right moment," Bridge said, a

little animation returning to her. "In the garden, I felt a strange resurgence of spirit and a sense that all would be right if I could take back what I had lost to Neal. The only way I could reclaim myself was by turning my back on the whole scene."

"From where we were standing, it was quite an obvious battle of wills," Claire said.

"You're right," Bridge agreed, "it definitely was that too. There was no way I was going to go back to that house and hand him another victory."

"You should have seen his face!" Claire exclaimed.

Then the two burst into laughter for a good moment.

"You know, he thought you were having a breakdown," Claire said as she handed Bridge one of the two forks she had put on the table.

"I'm sure," Bridge agreed. They both picked at the cheesecake, finding some humor now in a scene that they realized must have seemed bizarre to Neal and the guests.

"So where did you go?" Claire inquired.

"Well, after turning my back on Neal, I was temporarily exhilarated," Bridge explained. "It was like breaking free from a long chain. Then, after walking a few yards I thought, 'Now what am I going to do? It's cold and snowing, and my feet are frozen!' So I walked back to the greenhouse and stayed there for about an hour until I was sure everyone had gone! Can you believe it?" Bridge was partly laughing and partly astonished at her behavior.

"When I walked back to the house," Bridge continued, "Neal was sitting in his chair, drinking his cognac. He knew it was over. We had some words. I'm not even sure I heard him at all. I was so intent on getting away from it all. I put some things in a bag and drove to Dad's...but I forgot something to sleep in!"

"Yes, you look lovely in these old things," Claire said, tugging at the striped flannel top.

"I must look a sight," Bridge wondered out loud, exhausted.

"So, now what?" Claire asked.

"I'm not really sure...," Bridge said, gazing off to nowhere in particular.

"You're welcome to stay with us as long as you like," Claire offered.

"Thanks, but I think I'll stay here for a while," Bridge said. "It's quiet and I could use the time to think."

"Ok, if you're sure...?"

"Yeah, I am," Bridge said. "Plus, it will give me some time with Dad." Then, rising from her chair, Bridge tossed the forks into the sink and began to walk down the hall. "Right now though, I think I should go change before they return."

Just as many Christmas days come and go by so quickly, this one did as well. After the traditional turkey, there was the frenzied opening of presents, followed by the after-dinner drinks. As evening turned into night, Bridge started to tire, so Claire, Jack and the children left early. After seeing them off, Thomas returned to the living room to find Bridge gathering some of the empty glasses that lingered about.

"Come now, I think you've had quite a day," Thomas admonished Bridge lovingly. "Leave the rest of this cleaning to me. Why don't you turn in early and we will talk in the morning."

"Thanks Dad, I think I will," Bridge conceded without much coaxing.

Bridge disappeared down the long, dark hallway, its polished wood floors covered by the faded Oriental runner. In the harsh light of the fluorescent-lit bathroom, she went through her nightly ritual of putting her hair in a ponytail and washing her face. She stared at herself in the mirror, almost expecting to see a younger girl's reflection. After all, the last time she had slept at her father's house and went through this same nightly routine was before she had married Neal. Now, she looked at herself for several moments wondering if she could really reclaim the person she once was. She continued to brush her teeth and promised herself not to think about this until the morning when she would be much more lucid. Maybe a couple of aspirin would ensure a sound nights sleep. In the medicine cabinet, Bridge was surprised to see so many prescription bottles with her father's name on them. She looked at a couple, but the words had no meaning to her. One was long expired. Just like Dad, she thought. Half of these are probably old. Still, she would ask him about them in the morning.

She hadn't noticed much when she arrived here last night, but now she could see that almost everything in her old room was exactly the same as she had left it. Her father had barely changed a thing. The curtains she had made from the floral sheets that matched her comforter set, the pictures on the walls, the shag rug, all still there. The English lacquered jewelry box he had bought her remained on top of the dresser. Bridge climbed into the single bed; it was warm and soft and had a familiar feeling that enveloped her. Lying there, she looked around the room at the posters and drawings that covered the walls, mementos from a happier time, one that included Vincent. From the Van Gogh in Arles poster purchased at the Met, one of their first outings together, to the framed postcards that depicted works of new artists featured at local galleries in the Village. Strangely enough, this room and all its memories was a comfort to her now. She slept well.

The next morning, Bridge awoke to a sun-filled room. In the early morning light, she was almost happy before fully waking to the reality of all that had happened. She had dreamt of Vincent. For a moment, in her sleepy haze, it almost seemed as if she had been transported back in time, waking in her old room where she often thought of him. Had the last twenty years all been a dream?

It took a few seconds to figure out what was real. Looking over at the clock she could see it was still early, only seven. She had slept for over ten hours, but still felt worn from years of living a compromised life, without real love. Where did she go wrong? Somewhere in her heart of hearts she knew the answer to this question, but could not revisit the past and all its pain, not now. More awake now, Bridge stared at the ceiling wondering if she would ever be happy again the way she had been with Vincent? Or was it just the innocence and vitality of youth that made every experience and emotion seem so perfect, so intense and heartfelt? Perhaps. She knew she needed time to sort through it all; there was no point in trying to figure it all out today. She sat on the edge of the bed for a moment, then put on a robe and headed for the kitchen. Coffee would help.

Thomas was already dressed and reading the paper when she came into the kitchen. It was small but tidy, everything in its rightful place. The old, white metal cabinets with their chrome hand pulls were cold to the touch as she reached for a cup and saucer. The shelves were lined with new contact paper, but the dishes were the same old ones they had had for years.

"Hey Dad...you're up early. Why are you dressed as if you're going to work?"

"Because I am dear, a little later, but, oh yes, there's some work I could get a jump on."

"But Dad, it's only the day after Christmas...there's no school."

"Yes, precisely," Thomas answered as if Bridge had failed to understand his point. "It's very quiet and I can go over some papers I neglected to bring home. But that's later, here, sit down." He pulled out a chair for Bridge, who had poured herself some coffee from an old percolator pot, which made it too hot to drink immediately.

"How are you this morning?" he asked.

"Better than yesterday morning," Bridge said.

"So, are you still set on leaving Neal?"

"Yes, Dad," Bridge moaned. "Were you thinking I'd change my mind?"

"Well, to be honest dear, it all seems to have happened quite suddenly."

"It wasn't sudden, Dad," Bridge explained. "It's taken years for me to see how unhappy I'd become and more years to muster up the courage to do anything about it." Bridge stirred her coffee. Thomas did not want to press her any more so they sat a few seconds in silence.

"I wonder what Mom would have thought about one of her daughters getting divorced?" Bridge ruminated.

"No parent likes to see their children go through a divorce, or any kind of hurt for that matter," supposed Thomas. "Your mother always wanted you to be happy, so

I'm sure she would have supported any decision you make, as I do."

Bridge just nodded, looking down at the floor. The speckled linoleum flooring was in remarkably good shape. "God, Dad, doesn't this stuff ever wear out?"

"What? Oh, the floor?" he chuckled. "Yes, well I guess I've never had a need to replace much, living by myself and all."

Bridge wondered what it must be like living alone all these years and if that was to be her fate as well. "I guess I'll have to find my own attorney, I've always used Neal's."

"That's no problem, dear. I can make some inquiries," Thomas offered.

"Thanks Dad, I would appreciate that."

"So, what are your plans, Bridge? Have you given any thought to what you're going to do?"

"I thought I'd stay here for a while, if you don't mind," Bridge said.

"Of course you'll stay here. This will always be your home."

She wanted to hug him. It was evident that her father was eager to help. There was no hint of judgment or prying in his tone-there never was-only support and unconditional love.

Thomas Adair had always been a thoughtful and concerned father with his daughters, although his English reserve was ever present.

"You're sure, Dad? I won't be in your way?"

"No! It would be a delight," Thomas reassured her. He was concerned for Bridge, but he was glad to have her with him. It had been so long since they shared time like this.

Bridge was startled by the sound of the toast popping

up from the toaster. It made an extraordinarily long buzzing noise and it shook a little trying to expel the toast from its insides.

"OK, but if I'm going to stay here, we're going to have to do some serious shopping," said Bridge, as she wedged her almost burnt bread from the old metal toaster's insides, a less than appealing choice of breakfasts.

"Sure, sure," said Thomas. "Anything you want."

"You know, Dad," Bridge started, "there's an awful lot of pills in the medicine cabinet upstairs. Are you feeling alright?"

"Oh, I'm fine, Thomas reassured Bridge. "Just a little arrhythmia now and then."

"Are you sure that's all it is?" Bridge asked, wondering if he was being totally truthful with her.

"Yes, yes."

"You would tell me if it was something more serious, wouldn't you?"

"I'm telling you Bridge, I feel fine."

You know, you work too much," cautioned Bridge. "It wouldn't hurt to cut back on some of your hours at the University."

Thomas let this conversation die a natural death. He brought his cup over to the sink and rinsed it out. "So do you have any plans today? See your sister perhaps?"

"No plans, I just thought I'd stay around here, maybe walk to the market and get some things for dinner."

"Excellent. I'll be home early so I'll help you. I'll see you later, dear." Thomas patted Bridge on the shoulder as she stood over the sink, looking out the kitchen window.

"Sure, Dad. See you later."

After cleaning up a bit, Bridge prepared to spend a good

part of the day walking around town, a much-needed walk to clear her head and work off some nervous anxiety. She put on whatever clothes she had thought to grab from the house. While dressing, it occurred to her that she would have to go back to Brookville in a day or so to get her things. She would make sure Neal was not there when she went. But for now, this sweater outfit was warm and it was all she needed to be comfortable on a long walk through the park.

As she walked up 16th Street towards Fifth Avenue, the familiarity of these old city blocks returned. Of course, there were some new stores and boutiques along the avenue, which gave her an opportunity to window browse a bit before hailing a cab uptown. She got out at 59th Street intent on reacquainting herself with these familiar grounds.

She was surprised to see as many people as there were in the park the day after Christmas; mothers pushing strollers, and young couples walking arm in arm, sharing secret conversations, playfully lost in a world of their own. She remembered how Vincent used to walk with her. Sometimes they would share their thoughts and other times they would share a comfortable silence, just taking a moment to appreciate the landscape. It seemed as though for every place in the park she walked, there was a memory of Vincent.

After an hour or so, Bridge sat down at the nearest park bench. The walk through the park had tired her. Too many emotions from both the past and the present flooded her with sudden sadness. An old, familiar pain, which she had forced herself to bury when she met Neal, now revisited her. Why? Perhaps this walk was not such a help after all. She should not have come to the park. She felt more melancholy than ever.

Bridge very rarely cried. Sensitive as she was, she had

always been the strong, reliable one in the family. It was a habit she never learned to break. Who did she have to be strong for now? Perhaps it was time to let her family be strong for her. As she picked herself up off the bench and headed for home, Bridge realized she had walked longer than she thought. Her father would be back soon and she still needed to get some groceries. She hailed a cab to get her to the farmer's market at Union Square where she could get all the fresh ingredients for a home-cooked meal. It was a good day for soup.

CHAPTER FOUR

Bridge had forgotten how dark and cold the winters in Manhattan could be. The weather kept her from walking as often as she would have liked, the way she had at the Brookville estate. It was one of the things she missed about her former life. She missed the way the new snow dusted the barren branches of trees and blanketed the lawn. She missed walking those grounds in their serene perfection; it always made her feel so alive. In contrast, the blackened pilings on the city streets left her uninspired. Hopefully, now in March, there wouldn't be many more messy snowfalls.

Staying in a great deal this winter provided Bridge with an opportunity to read up on all the design news and trends. She had bought a new sketchpad and was drawing again; she still had that talent. Every so often there was some legal matter regarding the divorce proceedings she would have to deal with, but other than that, the separation had gone smoother than expected. Bridge and Claire had gone back to Brookville for all her things without incident. Neal appeared to have moved on with the same quick efficiency with which he approached any other business arrangement. It was time for Bridge to do the same.

Since she had moved in with Thomas, Bridge had been spending too much time alone. She knew she'd have to make more of an effort to get out on her own. But today was Saturday, a day that had become something of a new tradition for Bridge and her father. Thomas was usually out early in the mornings during the week, but on the weekends Bridge liked to make a big breakfast for her father where they would catch up, linger over the paper, and discuss what was happening around town and what their respective plans for the weekend might be. Sometimes they would select a restaurant they wanted to try. Occasionally, Thomas would have a friend over for a drink, or Bridge would take in a movie. But Bridge knew she needed more than Thomas or Claire as social companions. Still, she enjoyed these weekend mornings and it gave her a reason to dote on her father, a comfortable, old role she slipped right back into. It felt truer than the role she had been playing.

Claire arrived just after noon and was surprised to find her father not there.

"Where's Dad?" Claire asked while taking off her coat and scarf.

"He went to the school…something about finishing a lecture," Bridge answered.

"He couldn't do it here?" Claire wondered.

"I guess not. Maybe we bother him more than he lets on," Bridge supposed.

"Two women scared him off?"

"I guess so," said Bridge. They shared a laugh. "He's a bit of an odd bird that Dad of ours."

Claire noticed the paper on the table was opened to the classified section.

"What's this? You looking for a job?" Claire asked.

"I don't know…," Bridge sighed. "I've been checking

the papers, trying to get an idea what opportunities might exist for someone like me."

"You know, it's alright if you don't find a job," offered Claire. "It's not like you really need one. Your settlement is going to leave you a rather independent woman."

"That's just it, Claire," Bridge tried to explain. "I feel like I want to do something authentic with my life to be truly independent. All these years, I've been dependent, in one way or another, on someone. I just want something of my own."

Claire understood what Bridge meant. She herself had abandoned her career as a promising, young journalist when she and Jack started a family.

"I understand completely," Claire said. "I still think of myself as a journalist, even though I've been playing the June Cleaver role for a few years." Her sister always had a bit of sarcasm in her sense of humor, but Bridge detected the smack of real disappointment in her tone.

"Not that I don't absolutely love my children," added Claire. "...but I thought that at some point I might have some time to pursue my interests again."

"Claire, you're a wonderful mother! What's this all about?"

"...And I love being a mother," Claire interjected, "but I wouldn't mind being something else besides a mother."

"Who says you can't?" asked Bridge. "The kids will both be in school full time soon..."

Claire held up her hand to stop her sister. She knew where this was leading, there was just one small glitch.

"Jack wants to have another baby," disclosed Claire.

"Ah, I see...," Bridge said. "Have you told him how you feel?"

"Yes, but I don't think he quite gets it," explained Claire. "It would be another five or six years before I get the next one off to school, and I don't know if I'm willing to compromise my own needs for that long of a time."

"Funny, I had all those years with Neal and nothing but time on my hands," Bridge said. "How nice it would have been to have a little one to run after."

"Oh, I'm sorry Bridge; that was insensitive of me."

"No, not at all," Bridge reassured her sister. "I don't want you to feel that you can't talk about these things with me. Besides, I kind of accepted the fact that children seemed unlikely for me, given Neal's self-important lifestyle. I suppose I could have insisted on having a child, but who wants to bring a child into an already troubled marriage? At least I have my darling niece and nephew."

"You know, it's not too late for you," Claire nudged. "You still have a few more years left on the old egg timer. Who knows what your future might bring?"

"Or yours...?"

"Oh, now you've got me thinking of having another baby!" cried Claire.

"You and Jack have a great marriage! You'll make the right decision together."

"I guess...then maybe I'll finally get a good night's sleep."

"Why? You haven't been sleeping well?"

"Well no, I've been up at night wrestling with this dilemma," Claire confessed. "And I've been having these really strange dreams."

"You too?" Bridge asked.

"What do you mean, me too? Are you having strange dreams as well?" Claire asked.

"Yes, but they're quite wonderful actually," Bridge said. "What have you been dreaming about?"

"Well, I had this dream that I was baking in my kitchen," explained Claire, "but I couldn't really see myself. I was pulling cookie trays out of the oven. There was a woman sitting in the kitchen with me, but her face wasn't really clear. When I took the tray out, I turned to show her the cookies, and from the profile I could see that I was pregnant. That's not even the strangest part. When I woke up, I could swear I smelled cookies baking, and not just any cookies, those little almond cookies Mom used to make for us. Do you remember how they would smell up the whole house with that sweet, almond aroma?"

"You remember that? You were very young," Bridge said, somewhat surprised.

"You don't forget some things," Claire said with a touch of melancholy.

"How odd...," Bridge said. "Had you been baking, maybe?"

"No," Claire said. "But the smell seemed to linger so real, I actually went and checked the stove!"

"That's very strange..."

"I guess it was just some sensory memory triggered by the dream," suggested Claire. "So, what have you been dreaming about?"

"I've been dreaming about Vincent," said Bridge, thinking she'd shock her sister with a name from the past. But Claire never did shock easily.

"That doesn't surprise me," Claire said.

"It doesn't? Why not?" Bridge asked.

"After the emotional roller coaster you've been on lately, it's only natural that your thoughts would turn to a happier time from years ago," Claire supposed. "After all, unrequited love is always the most bittersweet in memory."

"Is that right, Dr. Freud?" joked Bridge.

"Well doesn't it make sense to you?"

"I don't know if it's that's simple. I've been dreaming about him a lot!"

"It must be staying in this house, in that old room of yours," reasoned Claire. "Why don't you stay with us? We've plenty of room and the kids would love it."

"Maybe you've got a point," mused Bridge. "But I like it here with Dad, we've settled into a nice little routine."

"Well, think about it," said Claire. "Now, what do you say we get a move on? I can't shop all day, I have kids to get back to."

When the phone rang, they hesitated before answering it.

"Should we get it?" Claire asked.

After considering for a moment, Bridge thought they should.

"I'll make it quick," she said picking up the receiver. "Hello? Yes? What? When?"

"What's the matter?" Claire shouted.

But Bridge did not answer her. She was intent on listening. Claire could tell by Bridge's expression that the news was serious.

"...Oh my God, where is he now? Yes, yes...thank you."

Bridge hung up the phone, stunned. "It's Dad...he's had a heart attack."

"Oh God! Is he OK?"

"I don't really know," said Bridge, dazed. "A woman at the University found him slumped over his desk. They took him to NYU Medical Center."

"Let's go. I'll call Jack when we get there."

When Jack burst through the emergency room doors, it didn't take him long to figure out that his worst fears were realized. One look at Claire and Bridge told the sad truth, that Thomas was gone. They were too late.

"Honey, I'm sorry," said Jack as he put his arms around Claire. "What happened?"

"He's gone Jack," sobbed Claire. "I don't understand. One day he's fine, the next he's gone."

"I knew he was taking some medication, but he told me it was nothing to worry about it," Bridge wondered aloud.

"Nothing to worry about?" shouted Claire. "That's so typical of him, minimizing everything!"

"Honey, calm down," Jack said.

"No, I will not calm down!" insisted Claire. "How could he be so irresponsible? If he knew he was sick, why didn't he tell us? Why didn't he take better care of himself? Whoever heard of a college professor working Saturdays?"

"You know he loved his work," Jack said. "It kept him young."

"He always put that damn work ahead of everything, including us!" Claire sobbed.

"Claire, Dad did the best he could, coping without Mom," Bridge offered gently.

"C'mon, let's get out of here," said Jack, walking Claire through the double swinging doors. Bridge followed quietly behind them, but she could hear her sister's painful, angry truth.

"I spent my whole life without a mother, and now I get to spend the rest of it without a father as well."

"We have each other Claire," Bridge said as a comfort, and then softer, as if to no one, "…and now they have each other, too."

CHAPTER FIVE

There was silence in the limousine as Bridge stared out at the long, black hearse driving ahead of them. She could see the flowers that were laid atop of the casket inside. Although she knew that the casket carried her father, it was hard to believe he was gone. One always accepts the death of a parent as inevitable, however she never anticipated how unprepared she would feel. Just the other day she had laughed with him over breakfast. She was just getting used to the routine they had established, and she was enjoying spending time with him. Now she would have to let him go.

The last few days were a blur of details and preparations that she had attended to in an almost perfunctory manner. It was as if she were making the arrangements for someone other than her father. Even now, after the service, after the condolences were offered from familiar faces and distant relatives, she felt oddly removed from it all; it was as if she were watching the scene unfold through someone else's eyes. Bridge looked at Claire, whose head was resting against Jack's shoulder, and wondered if she felt the same detached disbelief.

In the long seat facing opposite Bridge, James and Olivia slept. It had only taken fifteen or twenty minutes for them to fall asleep on the ride out to Long Island. Bridge looked at their sweet, sleeping faces and thought that James was just about as old as Claire was when they had lost their mother. She wondered if he understood what it meant that, "Grandad is gone to heaven." They knew enough that their mother was sad, and that it was important that they be especially good today.

"How are they doing?" asked Bridge with a nod towards the children.

"I think they're okay for now," Jack said. "It'll be harder in a few days when they figure out Tom's not around anymore."

Like the rest of us, thought Bridge.

"I don't want them to go to the grave site Jack," Claire stated with a sudden realization. "Maybe they should stay in the car?"

"Perhaps you should take them somewhere?" Bridge suggested.

"I am sure the driver won't mind taking Jack and the kids elsewhere for a few minutes," Claire said.

"Claire, do you think that horse farm is still there, near the old house?" Bridge asked.

"That's a good idea, the children would love that," said Claire. "It's right down Moriches Road, just past the old General Store."

"OK, I'm sure we can kill some time in there too," Jack agreed.

"I wonder if they still make those homemade molasses pops?" Bridge wondered.

"I'll be sure to get you one," Jack replied.

"Don't go overboard on the penny candy, Jack," Claire warned.

"Gosh," mused Bridge, "I used to love that place... remember Claire?"

They fell back into a comfortable silence, and into their own respective thoughts.

It was a brisk, clear day. The sun seemed brighter out here somehow. Perhaps it was the unobstructed views in this part of the Island that made the sunbeams seem to stream through the old, oak trees. As they drove along the scenic Route 25A, a one-lane, tree-lined main road of the North Shore, the landscape became all too familiar. Not much had changed since Bridge's childhood, except for a few restaurants and antique shops that have opened along the way. She passed some of the more distinctive old houses that dotted the drive, looking for ones that had been her favorites as a young girl. Wick's Nursery was still there, and remarkably busy for a weekday, Bridge thought to herself. She noticed gardeners were already buying flats of annuals and perennials in preparation for spring planting, and thought how she always looked forward to the spring as a time of rebirth. She wondered if she would still feel the same way this year.

"It was good of your Uncle Edward to come all the way from England on such short notice," Jack said.

"Yes, that was a surprise," Claire agreed. "It sounds funny though to hear you say uncle. We hardly know him."

"That's a shame, he seems like a really nice man," Jack said with a curious interest.

"Yes, he is," said Bridge. "It's strange how much he looks like Dad though, isn't it?"

They all agreed just as the children were waking up.

"Where are we, Mom?" asked James.

"We are near where your Aunt Bridge and I grew up as

little girls," Claire answered. Noticing the spire of St. James Episcopal Church in the near distance, Claire tried to divert their attention.

"Would you like to see horses and the house where Mommy lived?"

They both were excited to see a horse farm.

"Daddy is going to take you and I will see you in a little while," said Claire as they pulled into the parking lot.

"Why, where are you going Mommy?" asked James.

"I have to meet with some people, but I'll see you soon," Claire said firmly as she watched her children sit back in the limo, somewhat confused, somewhat concerned. In a moment, the car was out of her sight. Bridge, still standing by Claire's side, had turned to talk to the Reverend who had come out to greet them. Claire followed a bit behind as he discussed some small details about the service and burial at the gravesite.

"Do you want to go to the gravesite?" asked the Reverend. "So many families choose not to these days, but it is entirely up to you," he said.

Bridge and Claire shared only a quick glance to confirm that that was indeed their intention.

"Yes, our mother is buried here as well in a shared plot, so we would like to visit her grave."

"Of course," said the Reverend. "We'll just wait for the rest of the guests to arrive and we'll begin shortly."

Bridge and Claire began walking towards the area where their mother was buried. It was a lovely cemetery, small and private with old pine trees. Stanford White was buried here, as well as a host of other prominent families whose names bore witness to a legacy of local Long Island history. As Bridge and Claire walked among the headstones, they did not notice the handful of mourners who followed a few yards behind them. Instead, they were silently revisiting the familiar names along this path. There were more headstones now than before, but some they recognized as having been here for as long as they remembered. There were those really old stones that were illegible, worn with time, the unusual stones that held the mysteries of unknown stories; the ones they tried to piece together as young girls. They noticed the stones that bore the small flags for veterans and soldiers. In a small, shaded patch, Bridge could see the priest waiting near the already prepared site. Their mother's stone had not changed. It was not elaborate, but simple with a quiet allure. Their father had wanted it to somehow be a reflection of their mother's beauty. Remarkably, he seemed to capture her essence with a bouquet of wildflowers carved into the stone. Here, in this small spot, Bridge felt unusually calm. It was almost like coming home. They were all together again, if only in spirit.

A small crowd gathered round as the priest began. Bridge was aware of him speaking, but really did not hear a word. She was thinking of the times when she and her mother had walked the nearby fields; the days when a freshly picked wildflower bouquet was the highlight of her day. Simple days, with simple pleasures. They had been so happy.

Bridge was suddenly aware of Claire shivering next to her. It was much cooler here in the shade without the warmth of the sun. They must have been standing here at least fifteen minutes. Looking around the semi-circle of faces, Bridge came to settle on Uncle Edward who was wiping his face with a handkerchief. At first, Bridge thought it was an unusual display of emotion from an uncle they hardly knew. But as she continued to look upon him in his grief, she realized that his sorrow was unique in that there was no one there to comfort him. He was the last living sibling. The bond of brothers was now broken. Claire had also noticed Uncle Edward and was moved with sympathy. She put her arm through Bridge's arm and drew up closer to her sister.

When the service was over and the crowd started to disperse, Bridge and Claire went and stood beside Edward who remained at the grave.

"So much time lost...," Edward sighed. "My dear brother..."

It was the first time Bridge cried as she put her arms around her uncle. Claire began to gently lead him away, but he wanted to stay a moment longer, reassuring them that he was all right.

"It's very nice of you girls to console me, but I should be comforting you," he said taking each of their hands in his.

"You're beautiful girls, just like your mother, just like Olivia." Edward dried his face and smiled faintly as he composed himself. The three of them stood facing their mother's stone and a pile of fresh earth.

"You know, your father was devoted to your mother. She was all he ever needed. He would have gone anywhere to make her happy. But she wanted land and a home, things that weren't possible for them in Britain. She set her sights on America, and so they came, to this very place."

"Yes, we have very fond childhood memories here," Bridge said.

"And I have my memories of your father and myself when we were younger," Edward mused. "We were such rascals... you girls are lucky you have each other, hold onto one another," he said, patting their hands.

"We shall," Claire responded.

"You must miss your mother, she was taken too young," Edward cried.

"Yes, and part of our father died with her. He was never quite the same," Claire said.

"Death had parted them all those years ago, but now reunites them," Edward offered optimistically. "There's something happy in that, I suppose. Isn't there?"

Bridge knelt down and placed a basket of flowers in front of the graves. Touching the stone, she traced her mother's name with her fingertip. She thought of her uncle's words, finding some solace in them. She wanted to believe that what he had said was true. For if it were so, then there was indeed something happy in that. Bridge's heart was full; she was both pleased and sad in the same moment. She would miss her father, whom she only recently had built a new relationship with, and yet she was glad that his years of being alone had ended, if he was truly reunited with Olivia.

There was a tender touch patting her shoulder. It was Edward comforting her and she reached over and took his hand for steadying as she rose to her feet. The sun in the afternoon sky cast a warm glow over them, like a blanket of comfort from the cold shade.

The limousine had returned and was waiting for Bridge and Claire.

"The children are waiting. We'd better go," Claire suggested.

"You'll come back to the house, won't you Uncle?" asked Bridge.

"Yes, yes. I'll see you back there."

As Bridge and Claire walked to the car together, they looked back briefly on this place that held so many memories of happier days from long ago. As if unsure of whether or not they would return or when, they took a last mental picture of this pastoral, idyllic land of childhood pleasures.

CHAPTER SIX

It had been an exhausting, surreal and profoundly sad week. Friends and family had gone home, the caterers had cleaned up, and there were promises of visits to Uncle Edward's in the future. Now Bridge, Claire, Jack and the children were alone in the brownstone, collapsed on the comfortable, old sofa and wing chairs. It was strange that they were all gathered here without Thomas. Bridge looked about, her head swimming with details. It was all too overwhelming to think about right now; the closets to be cleaned out, memories to be put away, financial papers to review, lawyers to contact. There would be time enough to tackle all that in the days ahead.

"We should get these sleepy heads home," Jack suggested, stroking Olivia's blonde curly locks.

"You're right. Bridge, why don't you come back with us?" Claire asked.

"No, that's OK. All my things are here. I'll be fine."

"Ok. I'll come by tomorrow morning, help you sort through…everything," Claire offered reluctantly as she and her family walked slowly, absentmindedly towards the door.

Closing the door behind Claire and Jack, Bridge stood for a moment in the silence. She had never been alone in this house before, not totally alone. In fact, it occurred to her, that this was the first time she was ever really, truly alone. There had always been someone in her life—if not Thomas, then boyfriends, suitors, husbands. Someone had always been there for her.

Wandering around the familiar room, Bridge looked at sympathy cards and framed photos. She looked at it all with a strange uneasiness, as if not sure what to do with herself. Bridge thought about her mother, who would have made tea. She wondered what it was about tea that made people put on a pot when they needed some comfort or consoling. Thomas didn't have a big selection, but she found some chamomile and thought it the best choice.

Pulling out an old flannel blanket from the closet, Bridge curled up on the couch with her tea, and her cards, and her thoughts. Just a few short months ago, she had been a wife, with a privileged lifestyle. She was part of a family, however small. Now, her world was growing increasingly smaller by the day, it seemed. What else had the fates in store for her? Bridge knew her decision to leave Neal was the right one, but now her support system seemed to be diminished. Thomas had been such a help through it all, and good company too. She would miss him, and she would miss being someone's daughter.

The days ahead would be dark. There was still the matter of finalizing the divorce with Neal, and Bridge would have to find the strength to get through it on her own. But she was not ready to be strong. She wanted this time just to be able to grieve. Both her parents were now gone, and her dreams of having her own family had not been realized. She could feel herself descending into a deep abyss and did not know how she would make the long, upward climb out.

Bridge hadn't intended on spending the night on the

couch, but that's where she remained, too tired to manage the stairs. Staring at some of Thomas' pictures that lined the mantle, she focused on a photo of herself and her father from her wedding day. Her eyes closed and she drifted off to sleep.

In her dreams, she and Neal were young newlyweds dressing for some formal affair. He was complimenting her, but she was nervous, as though expecting something to go wrong. It was misty outside and Neal said he would bring the car around. Standing under the portico, Bridge looked about at the inclement weather. Just then, she thought she noticed a figure in the distance, in the woods. A man stood on the wooded knoll. Bridge could not help but be drawn to him. The closer she drew near, the more familiar his presence became. She knew this man. Her steps quickened as she rushed to him, her heart racing with the increasing surety of his identity. The closer she got, the more distant he became. She heard the car horn and turned her back on Vincent for a second to look at Neal, who was motioning to her to come back to the car. As she turned back, Vincent was gone. She had lost him again because of a moment's hesitation. She ran towards the spot he had been, searching desperately between the tall oak trees. Still the horn blew persistently, but now nothing else mattered. She was still searching in the eerie mist of her dreams when a car horn from outside awakened her, blending reality for just seconds.

Bridge woke with a strange, haunting feeling. The disturbing dream was still with her, and she thought about its meaning. "Why am I having these dreams about Vincent?" she asked herself. At first, she believed as Claire did, that it was just a reaction to being in her old room again. But now the dreams were becoming more intense and significant.

Deep down, she knew what these dreams meant. She was trying to reconcile with the one decision that had plagued her all these years. But she also knew that she couldn't turn back the hands of time.

Throwing off the blanket, she realized she was still in her clothes from the night before. She reached for a jacket, and headed out the front door. A good, strong cup of coffee was needed to meet this day head on. The morning air was cool, and a little damp. It felt good on her face and she inhaled deeply trying to shake off the unsettling feelings left over from the dream. The scent of fresh citrus from the Korean grocer mingled with the assortment of early spring flowers he had on display.

At the coffee shop, Bridge ordered a double cappuccino and a raspberry brioche. She had not eaten very much recently and was suddenly hungry. She thought she'd stay and enjoy her warm breakfast. There was an available stool at the bar, which faced the front window. She sat there, sipping her coffee and watching the passers by, wondering about their lives. As the bar started to get more crowded with the morning influx of business people, Bridge felt the need to move on. She finished the rest of her coffee on the walk back home.

As Bridge arrived back at the brownstone, the woman who lived next door was just leaving.

"Good morning," said Bridge.

"Oh, hello," said the woman. Bridge had seen her a couple of times over the past few months, but only to exchange a quick greeting. Now she stopped Bridge with a look of concern on her face.

"Excuse me, I don't mean to pry...," she started, as Bridge suddenly realized they had not thought to tell any of Thomas' neighbors, or invite them to the funeral for that matter. They had not known him to be close to any of them.

"...I couldn't help but notice the cars and the commotion...is everything alright?"

"I'm sorry," Bridge said apologetically. "I should have introduced myself sooner. I'm Bridge Hamilton, Thomas Adair's daughter."

"Nice to meet you, my name is Ester," she said. "Is he alright?"

"Uhm...I'm afraid my father's passed away," said Bridge, surprising herself by getting choked up on the strange words that she'd only just uttered for the first time.

"Oh, I'm so sorry...," Ester replied sincerely.

"Thank you," Bridge felt the need to explain. "I hope you're not offended. We didn't think about neighbors..."

Ester reached out her hand, and held Bridge's arm.

"It's OK," Ester reassured her. "I didn't know your father that well, except to say hello now and then. He was a quiet sort...but I was concerned."

"Yes, he was...," agreed Bridge.

"Well, if you need anything," said Ester, "I hope you'll knock on my door. Are you staying here now?"

"Yes, at least for a while...," said Bridge, unsure of exactly what she was going to be doing.

"Again, I'm so sorry..."

"Thank you. It was nice to finally meet you," Bridge said.

"Yes, the same here, although I wish it had been under different circumstances."

When Bridge got inside she opened a few windows, hoping the dead air would somehow vanish. She brought her terrycloth robe into the bath and took a long, hot shower until her skin was pink and her fingers wrinkled. She was glad that the mirror was too steamed up to see her image. There was no one to see today, no need for blow dryers or makeup. She towel dried her hair into a wavy mass and let a headband hold the front pieces away from her face. She dressed, then sat on the bed wondering if she should call Claire, or the lawyers. Her head was not entirely clear, and her thoughts kept drifting back to that dream. She couldn't shake it. It had hold of her. She went to the closet and dug out the shoe box she knew was there, had always been there, but stuffed in the back in its own sort of resting place. She took it out and returned to the bed, placing it in the middle. The cover was a little dusty, but otherwise exactly as she had left it. The first thing Bridge knew she would see was a stack of envelopes, letters tied up neatly with string. Underneath were photographs, small gift boxes, ticket stubs, and cards. This was her life with Vincent.

As she untied the package, Bridge looked at the familiar handwriting on the envelopes. It was neat and exact, with strong, bold accents, and a deep imprint that comes from a firm hand holding the pen. She dumped the contents of the box onto the bed. An antique brass bookmark with a satin ribbon caught Bridge's eye. She reached for it, holding it in her hand, gently caressing the metal as she recalled the day it was given to her. Bridge stared at it for a long time, as if it were a touchstone enabling her to see the past with vivid recall. They had been out enjoying the bright spring day, combing through shops in the antique district, something Bridge had always loved to do. As they browsed through yesterday's treasures, they tried to imagine the former owners of these trinkets, who they were and what their lives were like. Everything seemed to fascinate them. They were in love, and the day seemed perfect. Vincent wanted to give her something to remember the day by. He had noticed her admiring a unique bookmark. When she had moved to the back of the store, spellbound by some new find, he quickly purchased the bookmark and later surprised her with it. It had meant so much to her because she knew that, although small and relatively inexpensive, for Vincent it was an extravagance he couldn't really afford. His only concern was that it made her happy.

As she removed the letters and cards from their respective envelopes, she scattered them across the bed. They were relatively still in the order they had been received and stored, but now Bridge was randomly sifting through the heap of paper. As she began reading the letters she could still hear his voice in her memory. She read for hours…

JENNIFER CUSUMANO

December 24, 1982

Dear Bridge,

You have made Christmas magical for me.
   I chose these hairpins for you because they were so unique and beautiful, much like yourself, although I could never find anything that remotely compares to the beauty I see every time I gaze into those crystal clear blue eyes. These last few weeks with you have been the most amazing weeks of my life and I hope they never end.

Merry Christmas!
Vincent

June 12, 1983

My Dearest Bridge,

I don't know why I must write this letters after spending an hour on the phone with you tonight, I guess I still feel like I left something unsaid.

I think just telling you how much I love you seems inadequate. I can't even find the words to express exactly how I feel for you, and no matter how hard I try, I can not think of anything that can accurately describe the intensity of my love for you.

I believe I fell in love with you the day I found your journal in the Cloisters. I thought such a pure heart could not exist, but then there you were! From the moment I first met you, I knew it was our destiny to be together forever.

Someday I will find the words to truly explain how much I love you.

Vincent

JENNIFER CUSUMANO

March 24, 1984

To My One and Only Love,

I heard something beautiful the other day and it reminded me of you. It was a story of a young man journeying through the desert where he happened upon an old man who seemed to be very wise. The young man asked the elder if he knew how big the desert was, and the old man said yes, that he thought he knew. The old man went on to say that the desert was as big as the architecture of thought, and as small as the universe when viewed through the eye of the smallest living creature on the face of the earth. To me, when I thought about it - that little parable comes close to explaining how vast my feelings are for you. Bridge you are my universe, you are my whole reason for being, for my existence, and you have certainly taught me what it means to be alive on this earth, to feel and to love with every ounce of strength I hold in my heart. To me, you are happiness, you are life and you are the meaning of love.
I love you more and more with each passing moment.

Yours Forever,
Vincent

December 24, 1984

Beautiful Bridge,

I wanted to write this letter before I saw you tonight, in case I don't say everything I wanted to, have wanted to for a long time.
 With every passing year, it becomes clearer to me that our destinies are forever intertwined. Your love is the greatest gift I could ever receive and I am constantly in awe that you choose to give it to me! Let this humble ring be a reminder to you that I believe in our future together, I believe in our love, and I believe in you. Wear it with the knowledge that I give it with all my being. My heart is yours-

Vincent

JENNIFER CUSUMANO

August 15, 1985

My Darling Love,

I walked to the park tonight and sat there alone, dazed and bewildered for a couple of hours.

I keep turning our conversation over and over in my mind. I find myself here pitifully alone. I miss you terribly already.

You have been the best part of my life for a long time and I have many beautiful memories of us, but I don't want to be left with those memories, I want us together for the rest of our lives. I want to grow old with you, watch our children grow and have their own children. I want you by my side for the rest of our lives and I thought that was what you wanted too.

You said that if I truly loved you I would understand why you thought it would be best for us to date other people. Perhaps I am not being fair to you, but I know that for me there could be no other, and I don't need to test our relationship to be sure of that. I know in my heart it is true. It saddens me that you need to tempt fate.

You tell me that you love me, but you owe it to yourself and to us to date others. You say you don't want to marry me because I am the only one you have ever known. You need time to grow and if you find your way back to me than you can always be confident in our love. It is something you need to do in order to prove your love for me. If you truly mean that, you have my blessing, I only wish I could believe that things will work out. It is just every fiber of my being is terrified of inevitably losing you someday. This fear drives my jealousy, and it is hard for me to control myself. The thought of you with someone else makes my blood boil, I can't stand it for a minute.

I will give you your time and I will promise to love you always, but I can not do both. When you know it is me that you want, I will be here for you. There will never be anyone else for me, you alone will have my heart forever. I hope you find the happiness you're looking for and rightly deserve. I will wait for you always and I can only hope and pray that you will find your way back to me.

I will love you forever,
Vincent

JENNIFER CUSUMANO

Bridge,

It's November 30th about 4:20 in the evening. Today I am 23 years old. I am sitting in this empty apartment watching the sun set as this pain grows in my gut. I received your card last night when I walked in from work. I can think of nothing to say but how much I love you and will always love you.

Bridge, I never meant to cause you any pain- and what I would give to see your face and hear your beautiful voice right now goes without saying. But a lot has passed between us and although I love you with all my heart and all my soul- I've become so confused in the past month or so that I just don't know what to want, or to think, or to even hope for anymore.

The bells of the church just rang and they seem only to haunt this place with memories of you.

Trying to forget you or what we had would be trying to forget the happiest and most fulfilling moments of my life. No my love, I could never forget you, that is something that is impossible, something that I would rather die than do.

It is pitch black outside now and I can barely see what I am writing. I want only the best for you and I wish you only happiness for the future. I will carry you inside my heart always.

Vincent

December 10, 1986

Bridge,

Why I am allowing myself to show my feelings again, I don't know. I don't really know much of anything these days except for how I feel inside, how I constantly hurt, no matter where I am. I writhe and toss in bed before exhaustion overtakes me and I sleep
   only for a few hours to dream of you. I know how twisted and broken my heart feels and how empty my soul has been over the last several months. I know how bitter my pain is and how bitter I have become. I wonder if you ever truly loved me. Are you trying to keep what I feel for you alive until you finally decide what and who it is you really want?
   I know I told myself I would never allow myself to be so open again, but, my darling you leave me with no choice. I'd much rather ride out this period of uncertainty with you, than to ruin any chance we may have for our future. For doing without you is like a living death, I am merely going through the motions. I yearn to look at you and hold you again.
   I believe these days and weeks ahead will be a trial by fire, and fire is what I am willing to walk through if I am to spend the rest of my life with you…
   I honestly do not know how I am going to fight these jealous demons, but I will work it out some way.
   Besides I can't imagine spending Christmas without you.

Vincent

Bridge sifted through the box as tears ran down her face. The red velvet square box contained the hair pins, the smaller, black velvet box held the ring, which once had so much promise. She picked up some of the old photos. Looking down through tear-filled eyes, she reminisced over the Polaroids. They had made a handsome couple. Photos of smiles and stolen moments someone happened to capture, occasions they had dressed up for and recorded for posterity's sake. Bridge felt her throat tighten with emotion, so much emotion. Love, passion, anger, longing, sadness. It was all recorded in the letters. As she read them, she could envision each memory. She could still see every detail of his face. She could still hear the way he laughed.

The phone rang, but Bridge lingered for a moment, bothered by the intrusion upon her visit to the past where she had thoroughly immersed herself, heart, mind and soul. When the machine picked up she could hear Claire's voice. She reluctantly, but dutifully, picked up the phone.

"Hi, I thought I missed you," Claire said in the receiver.

"No, no I'm here."

"How are you doing?"

"I'm OK, I guess. Tired."

"Me too, but I thought I'd come by in a little while so we could…"

"Claire, you know what…I'm really not up for it today. I think I'd like to just stay in and sort some things out."

"Well, I'll help. You don't have to go through all Dad's things by yourself."

"No, that's not what I mean. Sort some things out for myself."

"Are you alright, Bridge? You sound upset."

"I'm…I'm just so…lost. I'd really just prefer to be alone today."

"OK, maybe tomorrow then?"

"Yes, maybe tomorrow."

Bridge moved lethargically about the house, from one room to another. The sun had come out and was helping to warm up the rooms some. The morning sun was always brightest towards the rear of the house. She reluctantly entered Thomas' study. She had always remembered it as a small, dark room, but then Thomas would use it only at night, when the sun had set and lamps were needed.

It was bright this morning. Bridge sat in an old wing chair by the window and let the sun warm her back. She stared at her father's large, wooden desk. Papers and notes, unfinished work still lay on its well-worn top. Two of the walls were lined with bookcases, filled to capacity with various works of literature, essays, and tomes by noted writers of both prose and poetry. Some texts were the work of former colleagues and some were by Thomas himself. "All this work," she thought. The years he had spent locked away in this room, researching and writing. Bridge had always thought it was an escape from the loneliness that drove Thomas to work so fervently. Looking about the room, Bridge came to understand that this was not work produced for its own sake, but work that was borne of inspiration. Thomas clearly had a passion for it and the work he produced had lasting importance.

Bridge walked over to Thomas' desk and sat in the tufted leather chair. She closed her eyes and ran her hands over the armrests. She sunk into the imprint left in the chair, created from years of use by the same form. It was almost like sitting in her father's lap. Oh that she could extract some of that energy, some of his passion, from this chair. It had been years since she had been passionate about her work, or anything in her life. Reading those letters had brought it all back, all the emotion, all the excitement and wonder. Where had it all gone? Had she buried it all along with her memories of Vincent?

Opening her eyes, Bridge noticed the long, white beams of light that were streaming into the room through the pane window. She hadn't noticed it before. The sun must have shifted overhead. She stared into the streaky haze with its particles of dust that seemed to dance within the ray of light. It seemed very ethereal to her, and she wondered if this was what heaven was like. She walked over to the window, first moving her hand in and out of the light beam, then turning her face towards the pane of glass. The sun was bright and burned her eyes a bit. She remembered her mother telling her as a child to never stare into the sun. Bridge smiled as the sun warmed her face. The memory of her mother seemed to gently comfort her. Bridge wished Olivia were with her now. Basking in the sun's glow, Bridge recalled her mother's last words to her. As a girl she had always derived some solace from those words and after all these years she found that they still had the same effect.

Bridge stood at the window for a while, wondering how she could move forward with her life, when she seemed so drawn to the past. There was more rediscovering to be done, more lessons to be learned. She needed to reconnect with the passion she once possessed, the enthusiasm she left behind. She knew it was time to mend her past with her present, but where to begin?

Her eyes looked about the room. So far this day seemed full of ghosts. Even here, in this room, there were answers to be found; she suddenly felt sure of that. Thomas' desk was laden with work. Bridge began searching, for exactly what she did not know. Rummaging through the top drawer of the desk, she found a legal pad and Thomas' favorite Mont Blanc. She sat at the desk for a long while, her mind a flood of memories and emotions. Decisions made and opportunities lost. There was supposed to be wisdom in hindsight, wasn't there? There was supposed to be lessons learned, nagging questions answered. For Bridge, there was just regret so far. She knew there had to be more, a way to make it all okay. These thoughts needed recording, she thought. Maybe that would bring some peace, some clarity. Her father certainly found purpose through writing, maybe she would too. Bridge began making notes on the pad.

Soon, ideas were springing forth onto the pages-ramblings at first, questions mostly. Then, suppositions about life, peppered with details about her own past, who she had been, whom she had loved, decisions she had made. The writing was easy for her; she must have inherited some of her father's skill. She filled page after page, stopping after a long while to see what she had accomplished. She read what she wrote and was pleased. What started out as sporadic thoughts had taken on a loose form. She continued to write on and the day passed into evening, as if some other force was compelling her to write.

Late into the evening, exhaustion finally overtook her.

CHAPTER SEVEN

The next morning, Bridge woke with an unexpected amount of energy. After a quick shower, she put on a comfortable pair of old jeans and an oversized sweater. A big bowl of cornflakes and half a pot of coffee would give her the fuel she knew she would need to continue working on her project. She didn't know how else to think about this undertaking that had become so important to her suddenly. After her second cup of coffee the phone rang. She decided not to answer it.

Back in her father's study, Bridge collected all the pieces of paper she had written. Before sitting down to write again, she tidied up a bit, putting all Thomas' papers in a neatly stacked pile off to the side of the desk. Reviewing her hand-written pages, she was surprised to learn she had written more than she thought. She pondered over the last few lines. "…it was a love I would never forget, or find again. But how was I to know that at so young an age…?" Reading her own insights now, Bridge thought that losing Vincent was particularly sad because it had been through her own volition, a cruel trick of fate on a young woman's beliefs. It occurred to Bridge that she could not be the only woman, or man for that matter, to have made a decision that they painfully regretted. She felt she should explore these notions further.

Bridge started on a new writing pad and began writing with purpose now. She made notes in the margins of the papers, and reorganized pages and paragraphs. A renewed clarity overtook her as she began filling up page after page with her writing. After an hour or so, the phone rang again. Bridge let the machine pick it up, but the caller did not leave a message. It couldn't have been too important, she thought. By the third interruption, Bridge promptly rose from her chair and yanked the phone from the wall. For good measure, she turned her cell off too. She wrote for another solid hour until the doorbell rang. This time, she could not ignore it.

She walked out of the study, down the long, narrow hall to the front door. She inquired on the intercom who was calling and as she expected it was Claire. She buzzed her in.

"Hi, so you are here? I've been trying to reach you," Claire said as she took off her coat and walked towards the kitchen.

"I've been here, but I was working on something and I just did not want to be distracted," Bridge replied.

Claire threw her coat over a kitchen chair and opened the refrigerator. She noticed that none of the food from the funeral had been unwrapped or even touched.

"How come you haven't eaten any of this food?"

"I guess I haven't been very hungry," Bridge said.

Bridge's answer concerned her sister. Claire noticed now how distracted Bridge looked.

"Well, it's lunch time," Claire insisted. "Will you at least have a sandwich and share some of these salads with me?"

"Sure," said Bridge reluctantly, running her hands through her hair.

Claire felt as if she was imposing.

"So, how are you holding up?" asked Claire. She took out two plates and set each up with a serving of sandwich and salad.

"It's difficult…"

"Yes, I would imagine it's especially difficult staying in Dad's house."

"Hmm, there is still so much of his presence here," Bridge said quietly, looking about the room.

"I don't think it is a good idea for you to remain here," Claire said in a concerned way. "Why do you insist on staying on here?"

"I feel that this is the only remaining connection I have to the past," said Bridge. "This is our home Claire, and I am not quite ready to leave it just yet."

"I would think after everything you've been through these past few months that you would want to start over, leave the past behind," Claire reasoned.

"I'm coming to realize," Bridge started to explain, "that you can't move forward until you come to terms with the past." Bridge rose and brought her plate to the sink. She stared out the small window for a moment.

"Well, if you need a change of scenery, you are always welcome to stay at our home for as long as you like," Claire offered.

"I know that, thanks."

"Let me help clean out some of Dad's old things?" asked Claire. "I think it will help make the place feel more like your own, cheer things a bit."

"Do you mind if we didn't, I don't think I am up to it,"

said Bridge. "You see, I've started this project and I just don't want to divert my attention from it."

"It sounds important," Claire asked. "Is it a job lead?"

"No, nothing like that," Bridge hedged a bit. "It's a kind of writing project."

"Really? What sort of writing project?"

"Therapeutic mostly," explained Bridge. "A sort of reconciling of all the events from my past until now."

"Hmm, that's interesting," Claire said pensively as she ate her sandwich. "I'm guessing that includes Vincent?"

"Yes, he is certainly part of it...," Bridge answered somewhat evasively.

Bridge knew Claire didn't understand and she wasn't sure if she could or wanted to try to explain. Instead, she just ran her hands over her face as Claire questioned her sister's actions.

"You know, most people find it helpful to put the past in perspective so they can get on with the rest of their lives," Claire suggested. "Why do you keep going backwards when you should be making a fresh start?"

"What do you think all those years with Neal were about?" Bridge retorted. "I tried forgetting the past and what I had with Vincent. I changed everything about my life that was remotely associated with him. But I found the more I tried to change my life, the more of a stranger I became within it."

Claire knew her well-meaning advice had sounded too simplistic and a bit hard edged. She also knew it was totally inappropriate for Bridge's sensitivities. Bridge had always been that way; she felt more than most people, loved more than most people, gave more than most people. She had a pure heart and it caused her to experience life differently, on a deeper level somehow.

"So, is this writing project some kind of exercise in closure?" Claire asked.

"It's funny, it feels more like the start of something," Bridge explained. "You see Claire, you think I'm living in the past as some sort of attempt at comforting myself. But I know that for me to really live again, I have to reconnect with that part of myself that I buried back there. It's about keeping a part of myself alive--maybe the best part."

Bridge began putting the food away and cleared away Claire's plate. Claire thought for a long while about what her sister had said. She had pushed enough for one day. Although she still had concerns about her sister's behavior, she sensed that Bridge had renewed strength and was certainly up for her new endeavor.

"OK, do what you feel you must, but don't neglect yourself in the process," Claire admonished lovingly. "I need to pick the children up from school. Would you like to join me? They would love the surprise of seeing you and I think the fresh air would do you much good."

"Thanks, but I really want to keep writing," said Bridge as she walked Claire out.

"OK then, I'll talk to you soon."

"Send the children my love," Bridge said.

As soon as Bridge closed the door behind Claire, she retreated into the study and continued writing. She wrote late into that evening, and then the next. Days passed into nights. Bridge was compelled to continue writing. There was a story to be told and she was determined to do it. Why writing this story had become such an obsession, she was not quite sure. All she knew was that she felt this overwhelming force willing her to complete it. It took precedent over all aspects of her life, from kickstarting her career again, to visiting with her niece and nephew. All of her energy was directed towards finishing the story.

In the weeks that followed, Bridge allowed Claire to distract her with other activities from time to time just to prove to Claire that she was not losing her sanity. They managed to finally pack away some of their father's belongings and gave the rest to charity. Bridge had worked out a very comfortable schedule for herself. In the mornings, she exercised a bit, walked around the neighborhood, sometimes stopping for groceries, sometimes getting the paper and a few of the design trade journals. But the weekday afternoons and most of the evenings were spent writing.

One evening, the Mont Blanc finally ran out of ink. Miraculously, it was with Bridge's final words; a poignant statement that took her all these weeks and three legal pads to unearth. But there it was. She read it and knew she was done. Bridge felt a great weight lift from her chest. She didn't know if she should cry or celebrate. So she did a little of both. After wiping her face, she put her papers in a manila folder and placed them square in the middle of the desk. Bridge brushed her hair, put on a light-colored lipstick and black blazer. She deserved a really great meal and she knew just where to go. Tocqueville was a private and elegant French restaurant in Gramercy Park that she liked to frequent when she was feeling especially decadent.

It was a beautiful evening to walk. The late May sun was setting later these days, inviting people to linger longer outdoors. Bridge had become quite comfortable with her surrounds these past few months. She walked down Third Avenue, past the gated park and noticed a few of the older men talking in front of it. She wondered if they were key holders. In the distance, the white facade of the clock tower stood out in the bright, setting sun that bathed these treed streets in evening's amber glow. Turning onto 15th Street, she passed a group of boys and girls with their heads together over some handheld gadget, watching a YouTube video no doubt. Men and women, still dressed in their business suits, were still walking home from work. Couples were leaving restaurants arm in arm. As she approached the restaurant, Bridge caught a glimpse of herself in the glass panes of the entrance. For a brief moment, she saw a confident, chic woman who moved with an assured grace. It was good to be out.

The restaurant had a charming lounge where patrons could order cocktails and enjoy small, delectable morsels, but Bridge had come for a special dinner. She didn't mind dining alone and when she was seated in the dining room, Bridge told the maître d that she wouldn't need a menu. She knew exactly what she came for. She ordered her favorite white wine, the Chassagne-Montrachet, an appetizer of fennel salad with caramelized pear and hazelnut, and the sautéed lobster.

While she relaxed with her wine, Bridge thought about the past few weeks. She still wondered at what exactly had compelled her to write, how she had made Thomas' study her own, and how that pen had died a most timely death, as if done with its purpose in life. It was all very odd, but apparently very necessary. She felt different somehow, like her life could go forward now with a new sense of purpose. She had uncovered treasured gifts from the past, and pieces of herself that had been missing these past many years. From this point on, she would live a truer existence. She would recognize true love next time. She would pursue her passions. She would trust her heart.

When the waiter arrived with her lobster, Bridge was thrilled. She anticipated its arrival from the minute she started her walk here. Each bite seemed liked heaven, as if she had not tasted anything for weeks. In fact, Bridge could not remember the last time she was this elated, and over food no less! The dining room was not crowded tonight; a couple of businessmen still lingered in the lounge. Bridge noticed one of the men who faced her from a table across the room was staring a bit, hoping to catch her eye. He was handsome, impeccably dressed and probably in his mid-to late thirties. Then there was an older couple who were dressed as if they might have come from some sort of an affair. The only other table was a young couple dining with the young man's parents, or so it seemed. This was obviously the first time the young woman had ever met them. She seemed self conscious as she frequently changed positions in her seat and fussed with her hair, tucking loose pieces behind her ear. She had a nervous laugh and smiled the entire time. Bridge remembered meeting Neal's mother for the first time and how she probably seemed just as silly with her same eagerness to please. How refreshing it is to not be so young. The present had afforded her much more comfort and self assurance.

After Bridge had finished, the waiter came to her table with a petite cordial glass.

"Compliments of the gentleman in the blue suit, Madam."

"Oh? Which one, please?"

"The light-haired gentleman with the impish grin," he retorted wryly.

"Ah yes…I see," Bridge said.

It was the same man who had been staring at her. She was not overly surprised at the gesture. He was looking for an invitation to join her. As he raised his own glass to acknowledge her, she smiled at him.

"I suppose asking him to join me would be in order now?" Bridge asked.

"Whatever you desire, Madam,"

Bridge thought for a moment. She couldn't decide at first if she was put off by the intrusion into her private celebration, or flattered.

"Why, not…please ask him to join me, thank you," said Bridge.

"As you wish."

Bridge watched as the waiter whispered something into the man's ear. His smile was a bit too self-assured, as he excused himself from his party and approached her table.

"Good evening," he said, pulling out the other chair from her table. "May I…"

"Please, sit down," said Bridge.

He extended his hand as he introduced himself.

"I'm Jeff Danvers."

"Pleased to meet you Jeff, Bridge Hamilton."

"I assure you the pleasure is all mine," Jeff said with a winning, Hollywood perfect smile. Bridge couldn't decide which was brighter, the pearly whites or the ice blue eyes that seemed to light up more when he smiled.

"I can't begin to tell you how refreshing it is to lose those guys," Jeff said jokingly.

"Well, I am glad to be of service," answered Bridge. They shared a laugh.

"Ah, beautiful and witty."

"Good looking and full of compliments," retorted Bridge. "Should I be concerned?"

"Concerned? No, you should be flattered."

Bridge sipped her wine without comment.

"Tell me, how is it that someone who looks the way you do is dining alone?" he asked.

"Actually, I was treating myself to something of a congratulatory dinner," Bridge revealed. "What about you? Business?"

"Yes, an out-of-town client," Jeff said, "but business is done, they're just running up my tab now."

"Oh, I see," said Bridge. "So my drink here is on the company tab, actually."

"And so is our dessert, if you will allow me to order us some."

"I'll just stick with the cordial," she remarked. "Besides, don't you need to get back to your party?"

"No, my partner will take care of them," Jeff reassured her.

Intrigued, Jeff drew closer to her, leaning his large shoulders over the table.

"You're not trying to politely end this conversation already, are you?"

"Just wondering...," Bridge answered.

Say, are you sure you don't want dessert?" Jeff asked. "The soufflés here are not to be believed!"

"Yes, I know," Bridge agreed. "But...no." Bridge smiled as she stared at him . She studied his handsome face, his square jaw and hollow cheeks. His light, straight hair was cut tight on the sides, in keeping with his well-manicured appearance. It played against his boy-like charm.

"You must live around here then?" Jeff inquired, subtly changing the direction of the conversation.

"Well, not here exactly, but a few blocks away," Bridge revealed.

"Great neighborhood," he said, revealing little of where he lived. Was he local?

"Yes it is," Bridge parried back, without offering too much herself.

"You live alone...?" he inquired gingerly.

Bridge knew where this conversation was going. She had averted the topic earlier, but now she supposed she must give him an answer.

"I'm divorced, if that's what you mean," Bridge responded matter of factly.

"Divorced? What fool would let you go?"

"It's a long story..."

"They always are," he said cynically.

"Are you...?" started Bridge.

"Available?" finished Jeff. "Let's just say no one is waiting up for me."

"Really? I'll bet you've broken many a young girl's heart."

"Now, that's true," he said with a cocky humor. "And I'll bet there's a guy or two in this city whose heart has never mended."

Bridge was suddenly serious and noticing he had touched a nerve, Jeff tried to recover quickly and save the rest of the evening. He talked about his plans to entertain his clients and they made small talk about the must-see shows, clubs and hot spots that usually please most. When they were finished with their drinks and the dining room had grown quiet, the conversation, although fun and witty, was starting to grow thin

"It's a great night for walking...let's walk," suggested Jeff.

"I should probably be getting home," said Bridge.

"Then let me walk you home."

Hmm...a potentially dodgy situation, Bridge thought. She reluctantly agreed.

They walked through the breezy night. The streets were well lit in the now dark. Jeff was surprisingly easy to be with away from the intimacy of the restaurant. He joked with her and had an energetic gait. Bridge was more reserved, but was feeling younger and more carefree than she had in a long while. It had been years since she had been with anyone her own age and it felt right. Jeff took her hand in his as they walked, looking at her to see if she was okay with the move. Neil was not a hand holder. They continued on, and she purposefully took him the longer way around to her street.

"This is it, right up here," said Bridge as they approached the house.

Jeff put his arms around her waist and pulled her close to him. He looked into her eyes for a few seconds before he kissed her. He was a good kisser, very good. It felt incredible, and yet she couldn't quite trust it. Bridge pulled away slowly and returned his long look. She looked in his eyes, not sure what she was seeing. They were hard-to-read eyes. She kissed him again, slowly, and felt that unusual tingle down her neck and spine, the kind that only happens on a first date or first kiss.

"That was nice...," said Bridge.

"Yes, it was," said Jeff, still holding her close, "an

interesting little appetizer, but there's so much more on that menu."

"Ah! What a shame," Bridge pouted. "I've already had my dinner."

"Yes, but no dessert…!" Jeff reminded her as they played with innuendo.

"True…," said Bridge, "but a girl has to be careful with dessert. One can't always indulge one's appetites." She gave him a playful smile.

"No? Why not?" Jeff asked with feigned seriousness.

"Because that would make one gluttonous. One of the seven deadly sins…?"

"Really? Seriously…" Jeff moved to advance this witty repartee. "Aren't you going to invite me in?"

"Don't you think it's a bit soon to have a perfect stranger up?" said Bridge as she took one step back from his embrace.

"You got the perfect part right. I'm still working on getting past the stranger," said Jeff with that same confident humor. He was laughing, but somehow Bridge didn't think it was so funny anymore.

"How else am I supposed to get to know you better?" he continued.

"Now let me see," Bridge said sarcastically, putting a finger to her chin. "I've got it! We could go out on a date?"

"Uh-huh, definitely, definitely go out on a date," agreed Jeff quickly. "And we could also go upstairs…"

"For coffee? And conversation?" Bridge played on.

"Sure, for coffee," Jeff responded, taking a step closer. "And for that dessert we never got."

"You're persistent, I'll give you that," said Bridge shaking her head a bit in disbelief.

"Good night, Jeff Danvers. Thank you for walking me home." Bridge started to head for the stairs.

"Really?" Jeff asked in disbelief. "Bridge, you're killing me here."

"You'll live Romeo," Bridge promised.

"C'mon…?"

"Goodnight…," she said, as she opened the door and waved goodbye.

As she took her coat off and undressed for the night, Bridge was amused by the evening's events. She may have been out of the dating circuit for a good number of years, but some things, like some men, never changed. Jeff was charming and fun to be with. And Bridge was sure she would have had a wonderful night of passion with him. Just as sure as she was that she would have never seen or heard from him again. Well, maybe a few more times. In fact, now that she thought about it, he hadn't even bothered to ask for her number. She was right to be concerned after all. Who needed that? No, she had decided that from now on she would not waste any more time on inauthentic relationships or circumstances that made her feel compromised.

CHAPTER EIGHT

The next day, Bridge started her day much the same way she had for these last few weeks. Except today, she noticed that she hadn't felt this good in a long time. Maybe it was finishing the manuscript (at least that was how she had come to think of it), or maybe her fun flirtations with Jeff, but she felt as though her senses were keener than ever, as though a part of her personality that had previously been suffocated had a new life.

Having finished one project, Bridge thought it was time to turn her attention to the future. She had settled most of her legal concerns and had taken her belongings from Neal's to storage. Except her clothes, which were considerable, and were now taking up way too much space in Thomas' small closets. Bridge knew she wanted to give most of these clothes away and the time seemed right to sort through them all and be done with yet another chore that would give her even more closure so she could really focus on her next venture.

Bridge sorted through years of expensive dresses and outfits knowing she would likely never wear any of them ever again. Although she still appreciated great fashion, most of these things seemed impractical now. As she dropped dress after dress into plastic bags headed for the local charities, she hoped someone would appreciate them. Of course, there were a few dresses she could not part with, and these she laid on the bed, knowing that every woman needs a few fabulous dresses for that rare occasion.

When the doorbell rang, Bridge assumed it might be Claire stopping by, but she was surprised to see her neighbor, Ester, smiling back at her when she opened the door.

"Oh, hello," said Bridge.

"Is this an OK time?" Ester asked. "I'm not bothering you?" Ester had a bakery box in her hand and Bridge knew she should ask her in.

"No, no...please, come in," Bridge insisted.

"You're sure?" Ester asked before stepping inside. "I can just leave this with you if it's a bad time."

"No, really," Bridge assured Ester, "it's a fine time."

"I thought I'd just be neighborly and see how you were doing," Ester said. "I haven't seen you come out at all and I wondered how you were getting along."

"Oh, you know...," Bridge started explaining. "It's always hard to lose someone, but then the settling of the estate and packing things away..."

"I know, I know...," Ester said sincerely. "Such tough stuff. Have you had any help?"

"Yes, I have a sister who is nearby."

"Oh yes, the one with the kids...I've seen her before," Ester said. "But still...

"Would you like coffee or tea?" Bridge offered.

"Whatever is easiest," Ester said, throwing up her hands. "I got a chocolate babka, if that helps you decide."

"Coffee then I think, right?" Bridge guessed.

"Oh good, I was hoping you'd say that," Ester said, relieved. "I hate tea." She was odd, Bridge thought, but very likable. Ester was an older woman with soft, silver curls that fell loosely around her round, friendly face.

"I have to apologize for this old coffee maker," Bridge said. "My father wasn't one to buy many new things."

"I can see that," said Ester looking about the kitchen. She laughed in the sort of good-natured way that made you feel comfortable, not embarrassed.

"I know...," said Bridge, laughing a bit too. "It's pretty dated around here."

"Do you have any plans to stay or sell?" Ester inquired.

"I'm planning on staying for a while," Bridge said. "But, I'm not really sure. I guess I should think about updating this place a bit. Right now I'm just sorting through all these clothes."

"Oh, your father's?" Ester asked.

"No, we did that already," Bridge said sadly. "Mine, actually. I had moved them from my former..." Bridge broke off. It was too much to explain. She rose and motioned to Ester to come see for herself, as if the sight of the abandoned wardrobe would say more than she could.

"Wow," said Ester. "That's a lot of clothes. And such beautiful things!"

"Yes, another life...," Bridge said.

"Looks like it was a nice life?" commented Ester.

"Hmm..., nice things," Bridge said, choosing her words carefully.

"Ah," Ester said knowingly. "I see..." Ester looked through some of the clothes. "Halston, Armani...Phew!" Ester clearly knew her designers too.

"Yeah, pretty dated, but..."

"Still beautiful," said Ester. "I know fashion...I grew up in the garment district practically. My father was a pattern maker and, of course, I could sew, make things. I was going to follow in his footsteps but...I went another way. Long story."

"I sew too," Bridge revealed. "Well, I used to, I was a designer once..."

"Oh, really?"

"Well, I was going to be. I studied in France and worked a bit before getting married..."

Ester, a woman with considerable history herself, could sense that Bridge had a story, too. Who didn't? Instead of prying, she deflected Bridge's comment with a compliment.

"Well, I can see you have extraordinary taste," Ester stated as they made their way back to the kitchen. As Bridge poured two cups of coffee and Ester cut the cake, the conversation turned towards the future once again.

"I was hoping to maybe get back into something related to fashion or designing," said Bridge. "But so much time has passed, I'm not sure what I could do."

"There was a time I could maybe help you with that," Ester said, "but it's been a lifetime since I worked in that industry. I'm sure all my contacts are gone."

"That's okay," said Bridge. "I'm still trying to figure out exactly what it is that I want to do."

"We should all be so lucky," Ester commented. As she sipped her coffee, Bridge realized that she was lucky in some ways; luckier than most women in that she had the time and the means to be selective in pursuing work that would be meaningful and fulfilling for her. She wondered what Ester's experiences had been.

"There's always retail sales?" suggested Ester.

"I guess...," said Bridge unenthused.

"Some little couture boutique, perhaps?" continued

Ester. "Heck, you have enough clothes there to start a little boutique of your own," joked Ester.

"Second-hand glamour," joined Bridge.

"You know, that's not half bad," Ester said. "Thrifty chic is very big today. Recyclable and sustainable are the words my daughter uses."

"Hmm...maybe you're onto something," Bridge mused.

"See, I've helped already," Ester said as she rose from the table. 'Now I should let you go."

"I really enjoyed this," Bridge said. "We should have dinner some time."

"I'm free tonight?" offered Ester. Bridge was a bit surprised, but their conversation had seemed so natural she thought, why not?

"Uh...Ok!" said Bridge. What time should we go?"

"It's Saturday," said Ester, "without a reservation we should probably go early. Six?"

"Ok, what do you like to eat?" Bridge asked.

"I eat it all," Ester stated enthusiastically. "We'll find a place. Come knock on my door, I'll be ready."

Bridge spent the rest of the day thinking about what Ester had said. Maybe Ester had inadvertently hit on an idea? Bridge turned a more careful eye to the process of sorting through her clothes and when she felt she was done, had two large bags to show for it. She then started on Thomas' old appliances, plates, linens, and anything else she thought someone in need could use. Bridge had collected so many items, she needed someone from the church's community thrift store to help her carry the bags back to St. Xavier's, who Bridge knew helped the community with food, clothes and appliances.

When she returned to the house, Bridge put the rest of

her clothes in a separate closet, one that she had already cleaned out of Thomas' room. She didn't know exactly what she would do with them yet, but she was starting to learn to trust her instincts again and they were telling her to wait and consider all possibilities. There was no rush.

At six o'clock, Bridge rang her neighbor's bell. Ester emerged looking rather elegant. She wore a loose, silk black pantsuit that had wide, flowing legs and a long top piece that fell over her hips. Bridge thought Ester must have had a great figure in her day, and still had a nice shape, but a bit round in all the usual spots for a woman of her age. She still had great taste in clothes and wore them well; they seemed to be as free flowing as her spirit. Around her neck hung a pair of half-rimmed reading glasses, which she used to look at close details and printed materials.

They walked through the neighborhood and settled on Pipa, a trendy tapas bar on E. 19th Street known for its exotic décor, innovative menu and drinks. Plus, the restaurant had been recommended to Ester by a friend of hers, Sherman, who raved about the food.

Over dinner, Bridge and Ester shared the abbreviated versions of their respective life stories, as women do. At 65, Ester had had two husbands, three careers, and her share of heartache. She had seen friends and trends come and go, neighborhoods change, and fashions make comeback after comeback. Her story was not unlike many women her age who had been born at a time when the world had certain expectations of women, but then the world changed, and women changed.

Ester had married young, a neighborhood boy named Avi, and gave birth to a baby girl, Leah, a few months later. But as the years passed, his traditional ideas about home and "a woman's place" proved too frustrating for Ester who wanted to do more than just sew dresses for Leah. She knew how to pattern dresses and wanted to work with her father, but her father told her that she had a husband and child to care for and that should be enough. When it wasn't enough any more, she defied her family's traditional values and left.

Ester's second husband, Douglas, was twenty years her senior. She met him at a high-end custom clothing store where Ester was working. A handsome attorney at the top of his game, Douglas adored Ester. Her passions and interests made Douglas feel alive, and in return he taught her how to live well. They maintained a very nice lifestyle on the Upper East Side until his unexpected heart attack left Ester alone again, but more surprisingly, with very little money. Although always good to Ester and Leah while he was alive, Douglas left most of his assets to his own children. Having long abandoned her job, Ester was left with their joint checking and savings accounts, Leah's college fund, and her jewelry, all of which she promptly liquidated and moved to a smaller place downtown. A friend of Douglas's knew someone in publishing who needed some help reading manuscripts. He knew Ester to be a voracious reader, and on his recommendation, she got the job. Ester continued working, reached a prominent position, and bought the place next to Thomas Adair some years ago. She never married again, although she sometimes took lovers, some much younger than herself. These days, she was mostly content to live alone.

After Bridge told Ester about Neal, Ester's tone took on a kind of well-intended admonishment, something one might have heard from a grandmother as a young girl.

"Never give up your own dreams for a man," she said,

shaking a pointed finger in Bridge's direction. "If he's anything, he'll love you more because of them. Right?"

Bridge just smiled demurely and nodded in agreement. She hadn't expected this brazen advice, but Ester had a good point, one Bridge had learned for herself the hard way.

CHAPTER NINE

Over the next few months, Bridge and Ester became fast friends. Ester thought Bridge had an old soul and that was the reason they had such an easy time getting on. As for Bridge, Ester was someone with whom she could relate, despite their age difference. She was so full of life and easy to talk to. Some nights they would go out for drinks, or do a little shopping. Often, they would take some groceries and wine back to Ester's eclectic apartment and prepare dinner together.

By September, Bridge and Ester had worked out a plan for Bridge's new business. Bridge was starting to collect elegant, designer clothing to sell cheaply to people who liked beautiful things, but who couldn't ordinarily afford them. She contacted all her old Brookville neighbors and pressed them for donations of clothing, which she knew they could not refuse given Bridge's long and generous history of giving to their many causes and fundraisers. Bridge would also identify people, organizations, theatres, designers whom she could contact for donations of clothes. She understood the industry a bit and knew where all the toss-off and trunk sale items ended up. The one detail Bridge didn't have worked out yet, was a small space in which to showcase her high-end, low-cost inventory.

Ester had been a good confidante in developing the idea

and delighted at seeing Bridge get excited about her own business. She wished she would get excited about some of the men she had tried to introduce her to. Ester still maintained a healthy social life, but was concerned that Bridge didn't seem to date much. At first, Ester, chalked it up to the divorce, but after a while Ester began to take matters into her own hands.

"He's a good-looking attorney!" she insisted.

"No, no more attorneys, thank you very much!" Bridge answered emphatically.

"But I know this boy," argued Ester. "His mother used to be a neighbor of mine."

"Ester, I wish you would not offer my companionship to sons of all your old friends."

"You never go out. What's wrong?" Ester asked.

"I go out…," Bridge responded. "I'm just selective. And I like to select them myself!"

"You're too picky, that's what's the matter with you."

"I should be more like you?" Bridge asked with a sarcastic, playful tone.

"You know, you're starting to sound like me," warned Ester. "You should spend more time with people your own age."

Bridge knew Ester was right, of course. She hadn't expanded her social circle much. She was content to stay at home, reading or researching for the new business. Some evenings she would sit in the study, typing up the handwritten manuscript on the new laptop Bridge had bought for herself. Bridge hadn't thought much about what she would do with the manuscript, if anything, but she liked seeing it printed out on paper, a more finished version from her original penned piece.

The day before Thanksgiving was particularly hectic.

Bridge had agreed to cook Thanksgiving dinner this year and was busy shopping and starting to prepare certain dishes ahead of time. In the evening, Bridge called Ester who was expecting Leah to arrive from the airport.

"Ester, has Leah's plane landed yet?"

"Change of plans, honey." Ester sounded disappointed. "Leah got stuck at the hospital, covering for somebody I think."

"Oh, no!" Bridge exclaimed. "And you were so looking forward to seeing her."

"Oh, I'll see her, just not until Saturday."

"Well, you must come over for dinner tomorrow," Bridge declared.

"No, honey, I don't think so...," Ester said.

"Why not?" Bridge asked.

"You have your family there...it'll be hectic."

"Don't be silly!" exclaimed Bridge. "It's just Claire and Jack and the kids, besides I'd love for you to meet them."

"Well...," Ester hesitated.

"It's settled then, you're coming," Bridge stated.

"Can I bring anything?" Ester asked. "Something from Zabar's?"

"Bring anything you want, just come!"

The next day, Ester had just come over when Claire, Jack and the kids arrived just after 1:00 o'clock.

"Auntie Bridge, Auntie Bridge..."

Olivia and James were so excited to tell Bridge everything they had seen at the parade.

"We saw Santa Claus!" exclaimed Livy.

"You did?" said Bridge as she picked up the beautiful, blonde little girl. "You're frozen! Your hands are so cold. Would you and your brother like a cup of hot cocoa?"

"Yes, yes."

As Ester chatted with Claire and Jack, she noticed how Bridge doted on the children and how much they loved her back.

"Look at her, how good she is with them," Ester commented to Claire.

"I know, she'd make a great mother."

"Perhaps it's not too late? I keep trying to introduce her to nice young gentlemen, but…"

"Nothing?" Claire asked.

"No, nothing," Ester said. "You know, I had a long period in my life where I didn't have a man in it. Didn't want one either, at the time. But then, of course, at least I had my Leah already."

"I heard she couldn't make it into town today. I'm sorry," Claire said.

"Don't be sorry, it's alright," Ester replied. "Besides I got to come here and meet you nice people and these gorgeous kids!"

Claire and Ester got on as well as Bridge had expected. By dinnertime, it was like they were all old friends and everyone pitched in, working like a well-oiled team to whip the potatoes, baste the bird, and set the table. Jack opened the wine and kept the children out from under foot by busying them with games. By the time dinner was ready, however, it seemed to Jack that the women were slightly giddy, or, in very good spirits. Ester certainly made the day come alive with often-outrageous humor, even breaking the silence during an awkward moment. James had found the wishbone and wanted to share it with someone so that he could make a wish.

"I think it would be polite if you offered the other half to your sister, James," Claire suggested.

"Oh, I have to share everything with her though," he complained.

"Gimme, I wanna wish too," whined Livy.

"Children, you will behave properly at the table," admonished Claire, shaking her head a little to hide a smile.

Like all older brothers, James did concede to share his wishbone with his sister, but made sure he had the better, meatier side, and with a better grip. He snapped off the bigger half easily.

"SNAP"

"I won, I won," exclaimed James.

"What did you wish for Olivia?" asked Bridge to keep the girl from feeling too bad.

"I wished for a puppy," said the little girl.

"I wished for a baby brother," said James.

It was the first time all day there was a moment of complete silence in the room as all eyes fell on Claire and Jack, who looked at each other, then looked down. Ester rang in with a diversion.

"What's the matter? You don't like playing with your sister?"

"She's OK, but she's a girl," James tried to explain.

"And girls, they can't play like boys?" Ester said to James. "I always played with the boys in my neighborhood. And I was the best stickball player on my block!"

"You were?" asked James, impressed by this fact.

"I was!" maintained Ester. "At least you have a sister!" said Ester. "I didn't have a sister or a brother, just friends."

"I have a lot of friends at school," said James.

"I bet you do."

After dinner, while they cleaned up, the children watched the time-honored classic "March of the Wooden Soldiers," which thoroughly conked them out by movie's end. Soon, it was time for Claire and Jack to take the children home, and after a very warm goodbye to Ester, the family was on its way.

"I guess I should go soon, too," said Ester.

"No, stay, it's early, besides, you don't have to work tomorrow."

"Okay, I'll stay, but I'm going to need some more pie."

"I'll make a fresh pot of that coffee you brought," said Bridge. "It's so good."

"It's the best!" agreed Ester. "Sure I'll have another cup." Ester walked around the living room looking at some of the pictures.

From the kitchen, Bridge told Ester about all the dresses she had been able to collect thus far and how much fun she was having in the process. Bridge asked Ester to go into the back rooms and take a look at all the clothes she had accumulated. After a couple of minutes, Bridge laid out a tray with coffee and pie on it, and Ester came out of the study with a perplexed look on her face.

"Did you see them all?" Bridge asked.

"I did," Ester said. "You've got a nice little collection going there." Ester was holding another stack of papers in her hand, which she held up to Bridge.

"What's this?" she asked.

"Oh, that's just something I wrote…," Bridge said, a little embarrassed.

"You never told me you wrote."

"Well, it's kind of private…"

"Oh, excuse me," Ester said. "I didn't mean to intrude."

"That's OK, I just wrote it because I had some ideas that had to be sorted out on paper, so I did it in a story, sort of way…"

"May I?" asked Ester as she flipped through the pages, pacing as she read.

"Go ahead. You know, it's odd," explained Bridge to her only half-listening friend, "when I was writing that, I was so focused and full of purpose, but now I'm not sure why it was so important."

"And you never thought to mention it to me, your friend the senior editor?"

"Honestly, no," said Bridge. "It was more therapy for me than anything else, I think."

Bridge paused as if trying to remember a feeling she couldn't quite connect with at the moment. Ester paced around the room, reading. Bridge sat quietly, feeling a little strange that someone was reading her work. After a while, Ester interrupted Bridge's thoughts.

"Can I tell you something? It's very good."

"You don't have to say that," offered Bridge.

"No, I'm not kidding," Ester persisted. "I haven't read much, but what I did was very stirring. You should show this to Sherman."

"Oh, Ester, I don't think so," Bridge replied.

"I'm telling you, this is publishable."

"That wasn't my intention when I wrote it," Bridge argued.

"Maybe not, but like you said before…that purpose you said you felt writing it? Perhaps getting it published was part of that purpose on some level. You know, there's a reason for the things we do--a reason for everything," Ester asserted. "Would you object to me having Sherman read this He's always looking for new material."

"But I'm really not a writer," Bridge maintained.

"Well, you may not think so, but something possessed you to write this. I can't believe you never told me about it?"

Bridge giggled.

"May I show it to him?" Ester asked rather insistently.

"I guess so…," agreed Bridge reluctantly.

"Good," said Ester. She put the manuscript into her large, leather bag. She had an almost smug look about her that made Bridge laugh.

"What?" asked Ester, moving into the kitchen. Bridge followed close behind her.

"What's with that face?" asked Bridge, as she watched Ester serve up two big slices of pie, topping each with a large scoop of Cool Whip.

"What face? I don't know what you mean."

Ester ignored Bridge's question. It was as if she had made her up mind that she was going to make things happen for this girl she had come to care for like a daughter.

"Here," said Ester, passing the plate to Bridge, "Eat, you're too thin."

CHAPTER TEN

A year had passed and it was a new holiday season in Manhattan. The city glittered with millions of small white lights that adorned barren trees and store fronts. Tourists lined up and down Fifth Avenue to view the more famous windows of Lord & Taylor and Saks. The promenade of Rockefeller Center filled daily, despite the late November winds that whipped all around the slow-moving tourists, causing them to turn up their coat collars and huddle together. For New Yorkers, there were the old, familiar decorations that made their yearly appearance: Cartier, with its signature red bow wrapped around the entirety of the building; Radio City Music Hall, with its toy soldiers atop the roof; the rows of recently imported pine trees that line the median of Park Avenue; the heavy pine roping around the facade of the Helmsley Building; the donated toys that flood the lobbies of office buildings, some for up to a full city block.

 Bridge had pursued her business idea of making fine clothing available to the less fortunate. She had networked, and built a website, and had gotten herself established as a non-profit organization. The only thing left to do was to find a modest space in which to showcase her low-cost offerings. Ester and Claire had been great help, even collecting items from some of their friends. It was also because of Ester, to a large degree, that Bridge was, as of this day, a published author! Sherman, an agent with great flair for marketing, saw an opportunity to package Bridge's story, into a quasi-Christmas book and sell it to a publisher he knew was looking for just that kind of commercial appeal. Not a Christmas story per se, but the kind of story that people like to read around the holidays—the kind that warms your heart. With a few clever changes, and a priority production status, Sherman managed to get *Vincent's Gifts* on the shelves of bookstores just in time for the holiday buying rush. He liked the title when he first read it, but now it seemed even more apropos. Sherman had the pulse of the female book buying market, and knew it was the right time for stories of this genre. In several seasons of best sellers whose focus was either contemporary dating advice or cynical women in bad relationships, this book seemed to offer a refreshing perspective for the romantic optimist. The packaging was just as appealing as the story, a pretty little hardcover, priced just right.

When Sherman first told Bridge he liked the manuscript and thought it publishable, she was flattered of course, but didn't really believe it would ever come to fruition. In fact, she didn't even bother mentioning it to Claire. It occurred to her that perhaps Sherman was just being polite because he worked with Ester. However, when he sent her a contract, it suddenly became very real. Even so, Bridge thought of all the published authors whose books fill the stores with stories that people never even notice, much less purchase. Just because her work was being published, didn't necessarily mean it would sell. Still, it was just nice to know that someone thought her writing good enough to print, and perhaps it would touch a few lovelorn souls. Bridge's memories were now tangible, something that could be passed on. She had immortalized a love she would never share, but one that would now be shared with others. It was a comforting idea for Bridge to think that her ruminations on love and healing were part of a much bigger, universal truth shared by all women alike, whether they had her experience or not.

Today, however, Bridge had her first inkling that she might have more than just a little, unknown story on her hands. Returning to the brownstone after work, she looked for the mail first, as usual. Here it was, a package from Sherman. Bridge knew it would be the book, her first copy. Opening the package, Bridge was elated. It was beautiful. She loved everything about it; the way it looked, the way it smelled, the way it felt in her hands. After her initial excitement, she glanced at the rest of the mail. This letter looked important. It was from the publisher congratulating her and saying that they were anticipating the book selling well over the next few weeks.

Bridge took the letter, folded it, then put it in her pocketbook. It nestled between her wallet and her precious new book. With the book now available in stores, it suddenly occurred to Bridge that she needed to tell Claire right away. Bridge had wanted to surprise her sister, whom she knew had worried about her obsessive writing all those months ago. Now it seemed silly that she had kept this secret from Claire for so long, when she could have been enjoying her good news with her family. Today, she would finally let herself celebrate.

Bridged hailed a cab to take her to Lincoln Center. At the Metropolitan Opera House box office, she looked over the fall program and saw that one of her favorite operas was playing next week. Even though Puccini's *LaBoheme* was a romantic tragedy, Bridge thought it would be a festive way to get into the holiday spirit since the story was set in Paris' Latin Quarter during Christmas.

"Do you have any seats for Friday night's *La Boheme*?"

"Let's see...for how many?"

"Just two seats."

"The only seats I have together are a pair in family circle, a pair in dress circle and a pair in the front grand tier."

Bridge took the two seats in the grand tier.

"Here you go ma'am..."

As he passed her the tickets through the ticket window, she checked the seats approvingly and then noticed the date stamped on them, November 30th. It was Vincent's birthday.

Outside the box office, street vendors selling fresh-cut flowers caught Bridge's eyes.

Settling on a bouquet of mini roses, she headed over to Claire's place. It wasn't a far walk to Claire's apartment on Seventy-first Street. Bridge couldn't contain her excitement as she walked briskly uptown. The further uptown she walked, the people began to thin and she found herself almost sprinting the last several blocks.

She reached Claire's building and swung open one of the heavy glass double doors. Entering the lobby, Bridge exchanged a courteous glance with the attendant behind the desk. He gave her a nod as he picked up the phone to announce her and she smiled back at him as she made her way to the elevator. Claire was waiting outside the open door to her apartment.

"This is an unexpected visit," Claire exclaimed.

"These are for you," Bridge said, handing Claire the bouquet of flowers.

"What's all this for?" Claire asked.

"I just wanted to thank you for all your support with the business," Bridge explained while fishing around in her bag.

"You came all the way up here to give me flowers?" Claire asked.

"Well, the flowers and this," Bridge pulled the book out from her bag and handed it to Claire.

"What's this?" Claire wondered, looking at the book and then back at Bridge.

"Look at it more closely," Bridge gently gestured with her finger towards the book.

As Claire read the title, Bridge watched her expression slowly change. As her eyes dropped to the author's name, they widened with surprise. A slow grin came across Claire's face as her eyes met Bridge's.

"Oh, my!" Claire let out a scream, then Bridge let out a scream, and they both began jumping up and down in the hall, embracing each other. A neighbor opened the door to see what the commotion was all about, but soon discovered that all was fine.

"How did this all happen?" Claire asked in a hush.

"I honestly believe by sheer luck," answered Bridge.

"I didn't know you were planning to do anything with it?" Claire questioned, excited but a little confused.

"Neither did I really…or, maybe I did on some level. I don't know…," Bridge's answer trailed off a bit.

"Why didn't you say anything?"

"It was all so haphazard," Bridge explained. "I wasn't sure anything would come of it at first."

"It's beautiful," Claire remarked as she looked over the book. "I still can't believe it."

"It's so strange the way everything has happened," Bridge continued. "Dad dying, me moving back here, then writing that, meeting Ester and then Sherman…"

"*Vincent's Gifts*, huh?" Claire observed. "Interesting title."

"Naturally, I am anxious to hear what you think of it," Bridge said.

"I'm going to read it just as soon as I get some time alone," said Claire.

"No rush, I know you have your hands full," said Bridge. "Now, I must go."

As Bridge began to head down the hall, she remembered their celebration.

"Oh, clear your schedule for November 30th."

"Why, what's November 30th?" asked Claire.

"We're going to the opera."

"We are? OK…," said Claire as she watched her sister enter the elevator.

"Bye love," Bridge said with a quick wave.

"Oh, Bridge…congratulations! I'm so proud of you."

Bridge blew a kiss from the elevator as the doors closed.

Claire walked back into the apartment marveling over the book. She briefly read over the jacket description on the rear cover and was even more intrigued, although not especially surprised. She had suspected Bridge had been writing something about her time with Vincent, but not a story, and certainly not of such magnitude. Claire could wait no longer. She picked up the phone and called one of the other women in the school carpool.

"Janice, hi it's Claire..," she started. "I'm glad I caught

you. Would you mind getting the kids today and I'll pick them up tomorrow? Great, thanks…no, everything's fine. Just need a little time for a project. Thanks again. Bye, bye."

The kids wouldn't be home for an hour. It was certainly enough time to get through a couple of chapters. She opened a box of chocolates that she hid away from the children. With box and book in hand, Claire nestled into the oversized chaise by the window and began *Vincent's Gifts*:

Foreword

"If you love something, set it free. If it comes back to you, it is yours; if it doesn't, it never was."
-Author Anonymous

I remember when I first heard that now popular quote as a young girl. It sounded so right to me at the time, but of course, such idealism would appeal to the optimism of youth. As for me, I don't believe in fate anymore, especially not where love is concerned. I do believe that love, when you find it, needs holding on to, needs to be cultivated and cared for with patience, understanding, and above all, honesty. Time has taught me this. Time has given me the advantage of hindsight, and time will give me the opportunity to recognize love again. I write this story for all who have loved, are in love, or who hope to love again.

Chapter One

I first met Vincent on a cold, but sunny afternoon in late November. I had gone uptown to the Cloisters, a massive castle-like structure whose passageways and galleries are a study in medieval architecture, art, and artifacts. Ever since my father had brought me there as a young girl, I had thought of the Cloisters as a mystical place, with its dark corridors and stained glass windows. It was a sanctuary in which you could immerse yourself in reverence and serenity. Occasionally, I would go there to escape, to lose myself in thought, or to write in my journal. On this particular day, I had been admiring the unicorn tapestries. I was reflecting on their meaning and the care and skill that had gone into their making. I moved to an area known as the Bonnefont Cloister, a square of columns that create a covered walkway, which surrounds a large garden, where I found a bench to sit. Since I was very much alone there, I took great pause in simply staring out at the garden, considering how some of the themes represented in those tapestries applied to life today. Like the unicorn in captivity. The guide had said one interpretation was that it symbolized the quest for love, with a lover finally capturing her adored, elusive mate. It seemed so sad to me and an affront to my ideals about love being free and boundless.

After writing down some of the philosophical questions that ran through my brain, questions that my 18-year-old mind could never offer answers to, I put my journal aside to button my coat and put on my hat and gloves, which I had been carrying all the time I was indoors. But now I moved out into a garden area that had a most alluring scent. After searching around a bit and investigating the curious plants, I found, in the middle of the garden, a series of small quince trees. Despite the fact it was almost December, the trees still had fruit on them, albeit, somewhat overripe and perhaps even frozen. They filled the air with a heavenly fragrance, something close to the crisp smell of apples mingled with the sweet nectar of pear.

I was about to leave when I realized I didn't have my journal with me. I hurried back to the bench only to find a young man leafing through its pages. Ordinarily, I would have been more than upset by such an inexcusable intrusion, except for the fact that he was one of the most stunning men I had ever seen. I stood there, frozen for a moment, studying his features, his sharp, angular jaw line and long, straight nose. He had dark short hair and tight, flawless skin.

He was obviously a Marine, trying to blend into civilian life, but his "high and tight" haircut gave him away. Under his denim jacket, one could tell he had a lean, muscular build, probably the result of years of physical training.

When he finally became aware of me staring at him, he offered me a sheepish, boyish grin. He guessed the journal was mine and that he had been caught in the act. He stood to explain himself.

"I was just trying to see who this belonged to," he said.

I said nothing.

"I thought I might return it to..."

He took several steps forward, then held the book out for me to reclaim.

"I didn't read that much, really...," he said with a charming smile. He had perfect white teeth.

"It's very rude to read someone else's journal," I said as I looked down, pretending to check the book, but I knew it was just to avert his gaze. As he stepped closer, I could see his warm, light brown eyes had an intensity and depth to them. It felt as though he were looking through me, right down to my soul.

"I'm sorry...I couldn't help myself. The passages were so interesting. But now I see that they were written by an angel," he said, as he flashed a smile, hoping the compliment would get him off the hook. I couldn't think of a witty response, but he was not as inarticulate.

"My name is Vincent Valez," he said holding out his hand.

"Bridge Adair," I said.

"It's a pleasure to meet you, Bridge. Is this your first time here? Maybe we can tour it together?" he asked. He had a very slight accent, the kind that suggests that English was probably not his first language. It was charming, romantic, I thought, and it only added to his already intense presence.

"I've been here before," I said.

"Oh, maybe you could show me around then?"

"Well, have you been upstairs yet? There's a great view of the Hudson from up there."

"Lead the way," he said.

Vincent and I stood on the balcony looking out at the scenic view across the Hudson. From here, the city below us seemed far removed. Standing here with this handsome stranger, I felt oddly at ease. Was it just the sereneness of this place? No, it was more than that, and Vincent felt it too. He was quiet at first, savoring the panorama before him. He didn't try to fill what should have been an awkward silence with nervous conversation. He was comfortable with the silence, contemplative, and appreciative of the moment.

"It's pretty up here, isn't it?" I asked.

"I was just trying to imagine how much prettier this would be in the spring, when the trees are green again," he said. "I love the spring, everything is new, you know?"

"I think it's my favorite season, as well."

"Did you know that John D. Rockefeller purchased that part of the Palisades Parkway just to have this unobstructed view?"

"Really? How do you know that?"

"I just heard it from a passing tour guide before," he said, with a joking grin.

"Have you ever taken the tour?"

"No, I just came here to marvel at the architecture," he said. "How about you? Why do you come here?"

I had to think about it for a moment. What could I tell him? The truth? That I come here out of some need to connect with my dead mother?

"To think mostly," I said.

"That's nice...I mean, I can see why you come. It's so peaceful." He stared at me, as if he knew me a little better.

"So, you're interested in architecture?"

"Yeah, I'm going to be starting the spring semester at Cooper Union."

"Wow, impressive. Don't you need like 1600 on your SAT's to even apply there?"

"Do you? I guess so..."

Modest too, and smart! He told me how he had always been interested in architecture and design, but had joined the Marines instead at seventeen. He didn't elaborate on his reasons for joining, but now I can tell you that it was because Vincent was something of a patriot. His parents had come from Cuba and taught their children to cherish their freedom. Plus, at seventeen, Vincent had something to prove. It was a quick way to get out of the crowded apartment and start contributing to the family. He wanted to make his parents proud, to make it on his own, and build a better life for himself.

Now Vincent was looking forward to a new start. Since CU was a full scholarship school, he was going to use the money he had saved from his Marine pay to get an apartment of his own. I was intrigued by what seemed to be a unique blending of personalities-- on the surface, a street smart soldier, and yet, sensitive and charming. Vincent was unlike most of the young men of the time. He was a throwback of sorts, someone out of time with the new values of the greed decade.

I told him it was my first semester at Parsons School of Design and he commented on how much we had in common already. When it got too cold to stand there any longer, I told him I should probably go.

"No, don't go. Come have coffee with me."

"It's getting late..."

"Late? It's only three o'clock. And besides, it's my birthday today. Really, it's my birthday today," he said laughing at my skepticism.

"How do I know it's really your birthday?" I asked coyly.

"Here, look at my driver's license."

His license was very recent, but the date was accurate. He was telling the truth, but even if he wasn't, I probably would have had coffee with him anyway.

"OK, coffee it is. Where would you like to go?"

"Anywhere, you decide."

"No, it's your birthday, you should choose," I said, not having any idea where to go. There were a million places you could get coffee in Manhattan, even before the Starbucks revolution. But what kind of place did he have in mind? A cafe? A luncheonette? A restaurant?

"Well, I tell you what, I don't know this area too well..."

"Me neither. I live downtown."

"So do I. Where do you live?

"I live on West 16th Street...with my Dad and my sister. Where do you live?"

"Well, right now I'm looking for a place of my own near school. So, why don't we take the train back downtown. There's some great places we can go, get a table, maybe get to know each other a little more?" He was smiling again.

"That sounds really nice, Vincent."

We found a small cafe in Union Square. At a sunny, window

table we talked for two hours as the world outside passed by without our noticing. Vincent captured my total attention. He was a lot to take in all at once; he was a man who commanded respect just by the way he held himself, and yet, sitting across from me, he had that boyish grin and almost silly sense of humor. He was serious and mature beyond his 20 years, and then, he was suddenly light, and playful. He toyed with the small plate of pastries, opening and closing the lid of a cream puff, doing his best Senior Wencez impersonation.

"Hello Bridge…please don't let Vincent eat me…oh no, no…"

I couldn't help but laugh as he ate the cream puff, its puffy pastry filling his cheeks.

This was Vincent. Complex. Funny. Charming. And all this from our first date, if you call coffee a date. I hoped there would be more.

It was nearly dinnertime and I knew I should get home. I offered to get the bill since it was his birthday, but Vincent insisted on paying.

"I was brought up to believe that a gentleman never allows a woman to pay," he said.

"Ever?" I asked, slightly playing with his traditional values.

He smiled and looked up at me as he took money out of his wallet.

"Not if he can help it," said Vincent. He rose from his chair then took my coat off the back of my chair to help me on with it. I couldn't resist pressing the issue.

"Not even if they're together fifty years?" I asked as we headed towards the door.

He didn't answer.

"Not even if you lost your wallet…?"

"Ok, Ok…,"he said.

"What if both your hands are broken and you physically can't handle the money...?"

"Alright, that's enough..."

By the time we reached my door, I knew I wanted to see Vincent again; couldn't wait to see him again. Apparently he felt the same, promising to call the next day. I wasn't sure then what we were starting, but I was sure that whatever it turned into, it would be extraordinary, for Vincent was unlike anyone I had ever known, or would know again.

Over the next few weeks, Vincent and I spent as much time together as we possibly could, every spare moment away from school. Like most couples just dating, we looked for reasons to stay together, even if it was just to run errands. Christmas shopping became whole-day events, as Vincent turned even the most mundane tasks into romantic adventures. After all, shopping was not just shopping, it was learning about the other person, their likes and dislikes, interests, the thought that each one of us put into a gift. Although I was fairly accustomed to shopping in different areas in Manhattan, with Vincent, I saw it all differently, all new through his eyes. As we made our way up Fifth Avenue, Vincent pointed out historic buildings, explaining what made them so significant or who was responsible for its structure. From the few remaining original Lalique windows of the Coty Building, which now housed Bendels, to the more famous residents who inhabited certain homes in Gramercy Park, to unique cupolas atop other buildings, he was a walking tour guide of information, and I loved listening to him and learning from him.

Of course, these expeditions almost always consisted of a stop or two at a local eatery, always the best part of the day for me. We couldn't afford much, but wherever we ate, just sitting across from one another became an intimate experience. We were so focused on each other, it was as if we both trying to absorb the very essence of the other. It was all very intense, until Vincent would pretend to wipe the side of my mouth with his napkin, while actually wiping ketchup or mayonnaise onto my face. It was his way of making me laugh, which he thoroughly enjoyed watching. He would sit back and smile as he watched me try to come up with my own devious retaliatory plans. Sometimes he would kiss away the mess on my face, unaware of people's gazes at this obvious display of new love, infatuation and increasing desires.

"Here, let me get it," he would say, kissing the side of my mouth.

"Vincent..."

"Uh oh, you got a little more here..." kissing the other side.

"Vincent, people are staring..."

"That's because they're jealous."

He'd only stopped because he didn't want me to feel embarrassed.

The connection between us grew stronger every day. I worried that since he was a few years older than myself and much more independent and experienced, that perhaps we would find out that we were really on different maturity levels intellectually, and physically, which of course, we were. But Vincent was patient and respectful. He seemed to instinctively know when to pull back from me. He listened to my ideas and took in what he perceived my values to be with a quiet acceptance. Although, I must have sounded very young and inexperienced in at least some of my conversations, he never showed it or questioned it. We were allowing each other to be ourselves and to grow, to open up to the other without fear of judgment or rejection.

The week before Christmas was hectic and thrilling. Vincent had found a tiny, studio apartment near school and was thrilled that we would have a place of our own to be together. It also happened to be the week of my first college final exams. I had never prepared for finals before and was nervous about what to expect. Some were written exams and others were in the form of design projects. I was splitting my time between helping Vincent set up house and staying at the library studying. Vincent had a much better plan, however. With the excuse that I was going to school to study all day, I'd actually meet Vincent at his apartment, where he would cook us something while I studied or worked on projects. He would help me by asking me questions from my textbook, sometimes for hours. We'd take breaks by going out and buying odds and ends for the new place, or groceries. They were wonderful days.

On the day of my last final exam, I surprised Vincent with a small tabletop Christmas tree. I let myself in with a spare key he had given me, though I rarely used it. I had prepared dinner with some groceries I had borrowed from my father's freezer and a bottle of red wine I found in the kitchen. While dinner was in the oven, I decorated the tree with tiny lights and miniature decorations, even using a small, tin silver star for the top. I placed it on a small table just under the window and turned out all the lights. At five thirty, the only light in the apartment came from the glowing little tree. I was quite proud of myself.

Vincent arrived right on time to find his very own first Christmas tree, and dinner on the table. I knew he would be surprised and I expected him to break into one of his boyish grins, but instead was visibly moved. He came to me and held me for a very long time. I think it was in that moment that I must have decided to love this man, and probably would have made love to him then and there. But it was Vincent who shook off his emotions, and the moment, probably for fear of pursuing me too soon. Instead, he made impressive comments about my cooking and selection of wine.

"Look at this beautiful spread! Ooh, and wine?"

"I just threw this together."

"You just threw this together? It must have taken you hours?"

"I had the time..."

"How did your final go?"

"I think I aced it!"

"I knew you would. C'mere gorgeous."

He kissed me and then held me away from him to look into my eyes.

"Thank you for all this, really..." he said.

"You are welcome."

"Nobody has ever done anything like this for me before."

"I want to do things like this for you all the time," I confessed.

"Well, maybe when you're a big, successful designer, but you shouldn't be spending your money on me."

"I stole the wine and food from the house!" I explained with a naughty grin.

"Oh, no! You're kidding?" He laughed. "Didn't your father ask you where you were going with all his food?"

"That's the best part...Dad went to some collegiate conference, or seminar or something...I'm not sure, but he's not coming home tonight, so you don't have to take the midnight run with me tonight back to the brownstone."

"Oh really...?" said Vincent as he raised an unexpected eyebrow.

"Of course, if you prefer me to leave..." I said playing with him.

"No, no, no...are you kidding? This is a celebration, let's toast," he said opening up the wine.

"Alright, what shall we toast?"

"You...the stars...ahh...that conference!"

"Here, here," I said as we finished the wine in our glasses. We went on toasting and drinking until we were practically too giddy to carve the roast. We ate, but left the food and dishes on the table, as we moved to the floor to finish our drinks. We sat in the middle of the apartment, on an old soft rug, finishing the wine and talking about everything. Out of wine and conversation, we moved closer to each other, each of us knowing the time was right, we could wait no more. There was no need for words, only kisses. We made love by the light of our little tree, and later, when I picked my head up from his chest to look at my lover's face, it was wet with tears.

The next morning Vincent woke me by moving the hair away from my face.

"Morning...," I said lazily.

"You have such beautiful hair..."

"What time is it?"

"I don't know, early."

"I'm starving."

"You're hungry? Well then we should get some breakfast."

"Eggs benedict?" I asked.

"Whatever you want."

Vincent caught me in his arms to slow me down. He wasn't quite ready to leave the night behind, but just as eager to please me.

"Hold on there," he said. "What do you want to do today?"

"I don't know, why?"

"I want to do something special with you."

"Can we talk about it over breakfast?"

"OK, sure," he conceded.

"I do have to get back home some time today. Besides, I want to shower and get new clothes."

Over breakfast Vincent thought it would be great to get tickets to Handel's Messiah at Carnegie Hall. But it was the day before Christmas Eve and I doubted if we would be able to get tickets. But he was optimistic. We ran over there and were able to get two relatively inexpensive seats for that evening's performance. We decided to get together later in the day. I had to get home and he had some things to do too.

When Vincent came to pick me up, I met him wearing one of my final projects for school. It was a burgundy wool hooded cape and I was a little uncertain of wearing it. But as I came out of the door, he allayed my fears.

"Wow. You look beautiful."

"You're sure this is OK?"

" It's amazing. I can't believe you made that."

It was just the start of what would be a most memorable evening. Vincent had told me on the ride uptown that he had never been to Carnegie Hall and he was thankful he was sharing the experience with me. Upon entering Carnegie Hall, Vincent stopped to admire all the detail in the construction of the building. He had read about it, but never had the opportunity to see it firsthand. It was magical for both of us.

Throughout the performance, Vincent and I shared glances that acknowledged we were both impressed. He held my hand and squeezed it just a little when he was particularly moved.

I remember his face was filled with delight and awe, staring straight ahead at the stage. Watching him, seeing his face, was the best part of being there with him. Afterward, as we started walking in a downtown direction, Vincent was alive with holiday energy, humming as we walked and talked about the performance. To make the night even more magical, it had begun snowing lightly.

By the time we reached Rockefeller Center, the snow blew softly through the nighttime sky. I don't remember ever seeing a prettier night or feeling as special as I did. It was as if Vincent had made it all to happen on cue to celebrate our love. The lifesize white angels strung with lights that lined the promenade of

Rockefeller Center, seemed to dance under the falling snow. The huge tree in the background ablaze with thousands of colored lights flooded the ice of the skating rink with a rainbow of color. The roping and bows turned the whole area into a winter wonderland. We sat on a bench in the promenade for a while, not wanting the night to end. When I was suddenly quiet, Vincent asked me what I was thinking about.

"I was just thinking about angels..."

"What about angels?"

"When I was a little girl I used to think my mother was an angel. And that's why she had to go back to heaven. I know it's silly, but to this day, when I see an angel, I can't help but think of her, especially at Christmas."

I hadn't meant to upset him, but as I talked Vincent stared at me with soulful eyes. I tried to change the subject, not wanting to bring us down from our special night, but instead Vincent pulled me towards him and kissed me on my head. He held me for a while trying to take away that nagging sadness.

"I'm OK," I said. "I just miss her sometimes..."

"Sure you do, it's Christmas..."

"But you know what? I don't feel as lonely this Christmas."

"Oh yeah, why not?"

"Because I have you in my life."

"Those words are the best present I could ever hope for, Bridge. But now, I have something for you."

"You do? But it's not Christmas yet?"

"I know, but it's been such a perfect night. Besides they've been burning a whole in my pocket."

"What's this?" I asked as he handed me a small box.

"Just something I thought you should have."

I opened the wrapping and lifted the lid to the small jeweler's box. Inside, fixed to the velvet, were two antique hairpins, studded with tiny gemstones that sparkled in the light.

"Oh Vincent, they're beautiful..."

"I thought they'd look great in your hair."

"I'll treasure them always, thank you."

We kissed for a while, then he helped put the hairpins in my hair. He ran his hands through my hair and gazed at me adoringly. We had fallen in love and it was clear for anyone to see.

Claire jumped off the chaise when the children burst through the door. She grabbed a nearby piece of paper to use as a book mark, then closed the book and stored it for safe keeping. Until tomorrow...

CHAPTER ELEVEN

The early morning mist seeped through the dense, silver fog that hung over the park. From Vincent's balcony windows, he could normally see the top of the Plaza, but not on this November day, only some patchy areas of the park below. Vincent stood for a while, looking out on the early morning scene: dog walkers, joggers, the early morning bunch cloaked in their trench coats, newspapers under the arm that held a briefcase, paper cups of coffee in their free hand. Vincent had made something of a morning ritual for himself from this view. He enjoyed having his coffee in the morning and taking a few moments to gaze out at the city; a few moments of morning solitude when the day was new and full of possibilities. Some days he would make plans in his head for the future, other days he would just enjoy the view. Since he and Anne had bought this place a few years ago, he never took his good fortune for granted, and he never stopped appreciating this view.

But today, Vincent could not see his future. He had accomplished pretty much what he had wanted to over the years. Now, as he looked back over the whirlwind pace he had kept and the successes he had achieved, he wondered what else lay ahead for him. What was missing in his life? Why this malaise? He told himself that perhaps it was just part of an early mid-life crisis, this empty feeling, a longing he sometimes let himself feel when he stood here in the early morning, quiet, wondering. He told himself it was just the grey day. He told himself that it was just because it was his birthday today.

At 45 years old, Vincent Valez was the quintessential picture of Manhattan success. His natural good looks were obviously cared for with the same attention to detail Vincent put into most things. The black, straight, shiny hair was cut to perfection, every dark strand falling into its stylish place. The tight, flawless skin that covered his sharp jaw line and straight nose barely had a wrinkle. Only around the corners of his beautiful, almond-shaped eyes could you see the signs of time when he laughed or smiled.

As Anne came out of the bedroom, she noticed her husband by the window, seemingly lost in thought. She poured herself a cup of coffee and watched him for a few seconds. He was looking straight ahead, chin up, shoulders back. Vincent had always maintained an exercise regiment; his V-shape physique still filled out the starched, white dress shirt. Anne walked over to him, slipping her arms around his waist.

"Happy birthday, darling," she said.

Vincent smiled and looked over his shoulder at his wife. He only nodded as he continued looking out on the park. "Thanks," he said.

"What's the matter? You're not upset because you're another year older, are you?"

"I don't know," said Vincent.

Anne kissed him quickly on the cheek, then turned back into the kitchen, looking for a quick nibble as she offered some understanding from across the room.

"Well, when I turned forty," said Anne, "I thought my life would change somehow, I'd suddenly feel different, older, but that's not the case at all. I think I'm in better shape today than I was when I was twenty-five and I have just as much energy. Besides, you look amazing, Vincent."

The fog had begun rising and Vincent could see through the patchy, dispersing clouds. Below, people seemed to fade in and out of sight. A spot of color moved in the distance. A woman in a dark red, wool cape moved briskly through the park. Vincent focused on her. He could see her long, wavy hair moving in the wind, but her face was not clear from this height. For a moment, he was back in time. Then, as sure as he had seen her, he lost her, disappearing from his line of sight.

"...I mean, I think this is probably the best time in our lives. We can do just about anything we want, go anywhere we want...don't you agree, Vincent?"

Anne had been speaking, but Vincent had hardly heard a word. She came and sat down at the table, bringing a biscuit and the pot of coffee with her.

"You are preoccupied this morning, aren't you?" she asked.

Turning away from the window, Vincent joined Anne at the table. Leaning forward, he grabbed Anne's hand.

"You're right, we have a great life," Vincent said. "You know what would make it even better?"

"Oh Vincent...," Anne said, pulling away and sitting back in her seat. "Not this again."

"Listen Annie, we've done everything we wanted to do with our careers. Don't you think it's about time we slowed down and enjoyed the life we worked so hard to build?"

"Exactly," Anne agreed quickly. "I do want to enjoy our

lives. I don't want to complicate it with the demands of parenting. I thought we agreed on this a long time ago?"

"We agreed to hold off on having kids until after we had both accomplished our professional and financial goals. We've done that, so what's stopping us now?"

"I didn't think that was something we wanted anymore," Anne said.

Vincent leaned back his chair and folded his hands in his lap. He stared at his hands because he knew if he looked at his wife, she would see the disappointment he knew had to be reflected in his eyes. He realized now that there was no point in pushing the issue any further; it was something he would have to live with.

When Vincent met Anne, they were both just starting their careers. A young associate from the architectural firm, Sammy, introduced Vincent to Anne. She was a friend of Sammy's then girlfriend, Lisa. Sammy had thought Anne was just as ambitious as Vincent and that they would make a good pair. Besides, Sammy knew Vincent needed to start dating again. He knew Vincent had been torn up over a breakup with a long-time girlfriend, and felt it was his male duty to put his buddy back in the saddle again.

Anne was instantly attracted to Vincent. She was one of the first yuppies of the eighties, working and living in the city, making all the right connections and spending almost all of her paycheck on living the lifestyle people moved to Manhattan for, the trendy nightclubs, restaurants, new shows, the most expensive gyms. And Anne had no trouble moving from one role to another. She was an attractive woman, though not especially pretty, who always managed to look the part. It was Anne's idea that they move in together, and Vincent agreed. It wasn't long however, that

Vincent's traditional values prevailed and they married. He was enamored with the fact that Anne was so focused on him, insisting that they were a great team.

"I can't have this conversation with you now," Anne said curtly, as she rose from the table. "I have a bear of a day ahead of me. I'd better finish dressing."

As Anne disappeared behind the bedroom doors, Vincent poured a second cup of coffee and sat at the table staring into the cup, with a million vague thoughts running through his head. From the bedroom, Anne was calling out to him.

"Remember, we're going to the opera tonight with Sammy and Lisa for your birthday. We should probably meet them by 7:30."

Vincent sipped his coffee. "Ok," said Vincent, almost to himself as if resigned to the idea.

"What?" yelled Anne from the bedroom.

"I said OK," Vincent said a little louder as Anne came back out with a new black suit on. "What are we seeing anyway?" Vincent asked.

"One of your favorites, *LaBoheme*," Anne answered, grabbing her lawyer's brief from the sofa. "See you later, darling," she said as she kissed him and made her way out the door.

In the quiet, Vincent was once again alone with his thoughts. He stood and walked back over to the balcony. He looked below, but all he could see was grey.

The rest of Vincent's day was much like any other of his days. On the surface, he was just as focused and attentive to client job specs. But those who knew him well, like Sammy, could detect that Vincent was not quite himself today. He was just a little quieter than usual, a little distant.

Sammy always knew when Vincent was troubled by something. After nearly twenty years together, day in and day out, Sammy was more than Vincent's business partner, he was his best friend. They had seen each other through the hungry years, been best man at each others' weddings, Vincent even taught Sammy's kids to ride bikes and play ball. They had shared disappointments, successes and confidences. In some ways, they shared more with each other than with their wives. Today, there was no lively gait in Vincent's step, no mischievous grin that was so often his usual way. Something weighed heavily on his friend's mind.

Returning from a client meeting, Vincent and Sammy walked the short distance from the Avenue of the Americas to Madison, cutting through Rockefeller Center, which was more hectic than usual today since the Christmas tree had been delivered this morning and a crew was working on putting up all the topiary displays and angels that line the promenade.

"That went well," Vincent remarked about the meeting.

"Yeah, I think you sold them on that last design," Sammy said.

"I hope so. These guys are hard to read...hey, you want to get a pretzel?" Vincent asked.

"You're still hungry after that lunch?"

"Not really, but I know we won't be eating until late tonight," Vincent said.

"Oh, right, good point," Sammy agreed.

Just along the sidewalk stood a pretzel and chestnut vendor. It was a clear indication of the impending holiday season when they started roasting chestnuts. Vincent ordered two pretzels. While the vendor heated them over the coals, Vincent watched the workmen set the angels into place. For a moment, he thought back to Christmases spent with Bridge and how they had fallen in love in this very place. He could not help but think of her every time he saw these angels.

"...You gonna pay the man, Vincent?" Sammy teased, breaking into his thought.

"Oh, geez, I'm sorry," Vincent said absentmindedly, taking out his wallet.

"Man, where are you today?" Sammy asked.

"I don't know...," Vincent said quietly, as he put the change back in his pocket. Sammy grabbed the two pretzels and they began walking off.

"Here," Sammy said, handing Vincent his pretzel. "You know, you always get like this right before the holidays."

"Get like what?" Vincent asked.

"I don't know," said Sammy, taking another bite of his pretzel. "Like this...kind of distant, a little melancholy..."

"No, I don't," Vincent protested.

Sammy laughed. "Yes, you do! It happens every year."

"What are you talking about?" Vincent asked, bewildered. "I like the holidays..."

"Really?" said Sammy, "because you could've fooled me and everyone else around the office. I mean, you're great to my kids and everything, but..."

"Well, the holidays are for kids, I suppose," Vincent reasoned. "They don't mean that much to me anymore." Then changing the subject, Vincent looked down at his half-eaten pretzel.

"This is disgusting," said Vincent. "I hate when they overcook it." Walking further into the promenade, Vincent looked for a trash receptacle in which to deposit his pretzel. There was one right under one of the angels.

As he tossed the pretzel into the can, the promenade of angels suddenly became illuminated with hundreds of white lights. It stopped him in his tracks. He looked up. Staring down at him, the faceless, white round head blinked back at him with her twinkling electric light.

Vincent paused, smiled for a second.

"You comin'?" Sammy shouted.

"Yes, I'm coming," Vincent said as he hurried to catch up with his friend. Sammy thought he saw Vincent's quick step and familiar gait return.

Behind them, the workers were satisfied with their test run.

"Ok, Charlie, they're all still working," said the electrician, as he disconnected the power and the angelic lights went out.

CHAPTER TWELVE

Claire put the kids into their slickers and sent them off with the rainy day car pool. It was a good day to stay in and read. She put up a pot of coffee and then returned to her bed with some toast, propping herself up with several pillows and pulling a comforter up to her chest. As she progressed through the pages, Claire had to remind herself that she was reading her sister's book. She was so enjoying the way it was written, she sometimes forgot that this was Bridge's life she was absorbing and not that of some unknown, fictional heroine. Although Claire had lived through those years, she hadn't really known everything that went on between Bridge and Vincent. Now, Claire was able to experience the story from a much more intimate perspective, learning about romantic weekends on the East End of Long Island, and summer block parties in Vincent's old neighborhood where they danced the salsa under the stars.

Knowing these characters as well as she did, Claire found herself on an emotional roller coaster with each new chapter; one moment feeling their elation and then in another, feeling their intense sorrow. For Claire, learning about her sister's innermost thoughts and feelings was at times heartbreaking. No other reader could understand the author as well as she did. For anyone else it was a stranger's tale, but Claire knew her sister was baring her soul with each truthful word :

As I waited for Vincent and my father to return, I paced the kitchen expectantly checking on Christmas Eve dinner preparations. I thought how wonderful it was that Vincent always seemed to be around to lend a hand. Even though they were generations apart, Vincent got on very well with my father. Having never had a son, I think my father appreciated Vincent's gestures to help him with some of the heavier work that often needed doing. Vincent was thoughtful and respectful that way, much more so than most young men who were generally awkward around their girlfriend's parents. Vincent related to Thomas on his level it seemed, and Thomas began to treat Vincent like a member of the family. I think he and Claire assumed that Vincent would inevitably be part of the family, or at least they hoped so.

Looking out the front window I saw Vincent and my father coming down the street with a huge Douglas Fir, Vincent bearing most of the tree mass on his shoulders while my father guided the way through the snowy streets, carrying the tip of the tree under his arm. They were covered in snow and apparently happy for it. They waved and called out to me as they saw me in the doorway.

"Make way, get the door Bridge," father said.

"Ho, ho, ho...tree delivery ma'am," added Vincent.

"My gosh, it's tremendous," Claire exclaimed.

The rest of the evening was spent decorating, noshing on treats, and sipping mulled cider. Having Vincent spend Christmas Eve with us made the night seem all the more special. It had always been just the three of us before, but with Vincent here it really felt like a holiday. Maybe it just felt that way for me because that was how he made me feel. When neighbors stopped by, Vincent greeted them and easily struck up conversations. I was proud to introduce him as my boyfriend. He was charming and people took to him right away.

As midnight approached, we opened our gifts to each other. Thomas had given Vincent a wallet and Claire had bought him a wool scarf. It was just a gesture on their part, but Vincent was so appreciative, assuring them that he would certainly use these items. As for me, I couldn't wait to surprise Vincent with his gift. I had been saving since the summer to buy Vincent a dress coat. He had started to feel uncomfortable wearing his leather jacket with his better pants and shirts to the architectural office. Working part time and living in Manhattan, money did not go very far, especially with Vincent's taste for fine restaurants.

Vincent opened the large, heavy box and pulled out the long, black cashmere coat.

"Oh, my God, Bridge...what did you do?"

He held it up for everyone to see.

"Do you like it?" I asked.

"Like it? I don't know what to say...it's beautiful."

"Try it on Vincent," Claire suggested.

It was a perfect fit and he looked more dapper than I had ever seen him look. We draped Claire's wool scarf around his collar and commented on how it complimented the coat. He didn't look like he was only 22 years old, he looked so much more mature than that, but then, he always did.

After we picked up all the wrappings, Vincent coaxed me outside to steal a moment alone. As we stood on the steps looking out on the street, the neighborhood seemed quieted by a blanket of fresh fallen snow, except for the occasional person who passed by on their way to midnight mass.

"It's beautiful out here Vincent, but I'm cold."

"I'll keep you warm," he said, running his hands up and down my back.

"I am so glad you could spend Christmas Eve with us."

"I'd like to spend all my Christmases with you," Vincent said, gazing into my eyes.

He ran his hands through my hair and kissed me passionately.

"You're so beautiful," said Vincent filled with emotion.

We held each other and he rocked me a little from side to side, swaying in the quiet cold.

"I have something for you, you know." He said in a coy way.

"I was starting to wonder about that," I teased him just a little.

Then, from out of his pocket, he pulled a small gift-wrapped box.

"Merry Christmas," he said.

I looked at the tiny box, then back at Vincent for an inkling of what it might be, but all he said was, "Open it."

Under the wrapping was a black, velvet ring box. I suddenly felt nervous, thinking this could be a gift I hadn't anticipated. Opening the box, I saw a petite, platinum band, delicately carved. Set within the band were several small diamonds that made this little ring sparkle as I turned it in the box.

"Oh, Vincent..."

"It's an antique," he said.

"It's beautiful."

"When I saw it," he explained "I knew it was meant for you, delicate and one of a kind."

I turned the ring in between my fingers to study it. "I love it."

"I know it looks like a wedding band, but you can wear it on whatever finger you'd like," he said.

"I'll always wear it," I said, slipping the ring onto my right hand-ring finger.

Vincent was pleased by the way it looked on my hand. He took my hand to his mouth, and kissed it gently.

"Wear it knowing that my heart is always yours, and as a promise that someday I will marry you...if you'll have me," he said.

"Vincent, I don't know what to say..."

"You don't have to say anything..."

But I felt like I should say something. Why wasn't I sure of what to say? It was clear that we loved each other, so why couldn't I find the right words. We stood there in silence for a few seconds, each of us I think cherishing the night. As Vincent held me, I think we both felt assured of the future he so believed in. If it wasn't already a perfect moment, the nearby church bells ringing out a Christmas carol made it wonderfully magical. Vincent looked at me and smiled.

"C'mon, let's get you inside," said Vincent as he put me down and ushered me through the door. We were giddy with happiness.

Claire thought back to those days when Bridge and Vincent were together and happy. She remembered how much she liked having Vincent around, as sort of an older brother, a very good-looking older brother. She supposed now, that at 16-years-old, she may have had a slight bit of a crush on Vincent herself. But what she recalled clearly was the feeling that with Vincent around, they seemed to be more of a complete family. It was as if he made them each forget how lonely they all were, despite their living together. Thomas came out of his usual shell when Vincent was around. He made Claire feel special, too. Vincent took an almost protective interest in Claire, much like a big brother would. And, of course Bridge was never happier. Perhaps that was what Claire remembered most about those times; the house seemed alive with happiness in those years, so of course she would remember them fondly.

In the pages that followed, there would be many more memories for Claire, but now she would have a different perspective, a deeper understanding of the events that would forever haunt her sister.

The spring semester of my junior year was a particularly difficult one for me, not academically, there I was doing fine. My advisor at Parsons had recommended me for a special design program abroad. The program consisted of a "study while you work" in an apprenticeship under some of the most well-respected designers and teachers in Paris. It was an opportunity that few would pass on, but the thought of leaving Vincent for a year was crippling. Sure there would be breaks and phone calls, but I wondered how well we would fare apart from one another. As for Vincent, I knew it would be a situation he wouldn't care for, but one that he would not deprive me of either. I hadn't even discussed it with him yet, but I knew it would hurt him beyond belief. Most of that spring semester I agonized over my decision, torn between the only world I had known, safe and sure, where I had the love of Vincent and my family, and a world yet to be discovered, full of opportunity, new people and foreign places. For once I would be totally independent, with only myself to consider and to care for. As the weeks passed on, I realized it was something I wanted for myself.

When the term was over, I couldn't wait any longer to tell Vincent. Students were making plans for their senior year, arranging their fall schedules and getting summer jobs. We had always had such great summers, Vincent and I. I wondered what this summer would be like once this discussion was between us. Would he think I was leaving him? Would he start to doubt our love? Would he start to distance himself from me so as not to hurt so much when the time came for me to leave. I knew it was going to be hard, I just didn't know how hard.

On a cool, late May evening as we sat on a bench over looking the river, I told him of my decision.

"Vincent, there's something I need to tell you...and I don't want you to get upset."

"What's the matter?" he asked, concerned.

"I've been selected as one of the top design students eligible for an elite internship."

"That's great Bridge! I'm so proud of you...what...what's the problem?" he said as he saw the doubt on my face.

"It's in Paris...for the year."

"Paris? Wow...Paris...is....is great." Vincent stared out across the river. "Design capital of the world, right?"

"There would be breaks of course, we could see each other a few times over the year."

"A few times..." he repeated, the stinginess of the phrase hung in the air between us.

"You want to go?" he asked but didn't wait for a reply. "Of course, yeah, you should go...you should do it."

"Is that really how you feel?" I asked as Vincent stared first at his hands, then back out over the river.

"What do you want me to say? Don't go? Of course I don't want you to go. I want you to stay here with me, but that's selfish. You'll always wonder if you don't go."

"We have all summer before I have to leave in September. It's only for a year Vincent, not even a full year, two semesters," I said, trying to downplay the significance. But it was sure to all sink in over the next few days and weeks.

"Okay...Okay," he said as he put his arm around my shoulder

and we sat side by side, looking out into the distance, into the future...in silence.

For the first time ever, I was suddenly uncomfortable sitting there with Vincent. I was aware of his hurt, his panic, all the doubts and fears that must be running through his brain. Ordinarily, at such a moment, you would think we would seek to comfort each other. And yet, we could not. He, I suspected was too worried to give any comfort to me. Although he contained it well, his mistrust of the whole situation permeated the air. As for me, I felt it too unnatural to try to reach out for him now after creating what felt like this huge chasm between us. How could I pretend that nothing had changed? Everything changed in that moment. I was changing.

I remember feeling very odd in the days that followed. A combination of fear of the future, sadness for the few, precious weeks I had left with Vincent, and guilt over my decision, which was clearly weighing on Vincent, heavier with each passing day. The oddity of it all was that along with these feelings, there was a certain sense of relief. Part of me was secretly excited to be going away. For the first time ever, I would be completely on my own. I was excited about going to school and living in Paris, although I dared not show it, not now anyway. I guess deep down I really wanted to escape my fairly predictable life and what I saw as an almost certain future, working in New York and marrying Vincent. Not that those things wouldn't have made me happy, but I really had no other experiences on which to base that on. I suppose it had to do with the lingering doubts of a young, inexperienced girl. It was a time when women were finding new roles and opportunities for themselves. People were dating without commitments, and I had hardly dated at all. Although I loved Vincent, another part of me wondered if he was "the one." How could I be sure? This was my time to find out. Of course, I couldn't share these doubts with Vincent. What would be the point now? To do so would mean risking the love I had with Vincent altogether. I just needed a little bit of time to myself to work a few things out.

We spent the rest of the summer trying to make each day special. Some weeks we'd go for days without talking about the move to Paris, and life seemed much the same. Vincent and I would get off from work and we'd spend the night out at a cafe, or a movie. Other weeks, the inevitability of our impending separation wore on our nerves, causing doubt and insecurities, tension and squabbles. There were many late nights spent in his apartment, too much unsettled emotion between us to say goodnight. Vincent was growing increasingly more intense. He never wanted to be without me and his passions turned to jealousy and mistrust, wanting to know where I was at all times. He talked more and more about our future together, saying things like "he would just have to get through this next year somehow," like it was just another obstacle which he would have to overcome. The notion that this was an opportunity for me, one which I wasn't sure where it would take me, was downplayed...no, dismissed in Vincent's mind. The more he planned, the more uneasy I got.

One Saturday in August, Vincent and I were walking in the park. I knew we had to talk about the situation and I was determined to be very clear about what our separation would mean. Strangely enough, it was Vincent who started the conversation.

"Listen sweetheart, I know I've been a bit of a jerk lately," Vincent said.

"It's hard to get used to the idea of being apart, I know," I offered.

"Well, that's just it," he said. "I wouldn't mind so much if I knew we had something to look forward to."

"What do you mean?"

"Bridge, you know I love you and I know you love me. It would be a lot easier for me to let you go off to Paris knowing that when you come back for Christmas break, we'll get engaged."

"Oh, well...I don't know..." I trailed off reluctantly.

"What's not to know? You love me, right?" Vincent asked.

"Yes, I love you..."

"...Then that's all that should matter. You're the only one for me. You're the woman I picture having children with, growing old with. This I'm sure of, that's not going to change."

We stopped for a moment, then moved under a shade tree and sat on the small grassy mound that covered its roots.

"It's just that you're asking me to make this commitment right before I go away for a year...and well, it's just that a lot can happen in a year," I said, leading us slowly into the conversation I knew had to come.

"What do you mean...like what?"

"I don't know, Vincent...I can't say right now. You say your feelings for me won't change, but what if I change? I mean, as a person. I want this time to become the sort of woman I'm trying to be, independent, experienced and sure of myself...like you."

Vincent was slightly taken aback. He was trying to make sense of my argument.

"Vincent, you are the person you've become through the experiences you've had. I haven't had any experience yet."

"But you're already perfect just the way you are." he said. He was not making this easy. I had to tell him.

"You're sure of us and our future because...you've dated before...a lot...I haven't."

"I can't believe what I'm hearing," he said, stunned.

"It's just that I think since we're going to be apart for a year, we should probably have an understanding..."

"You want to see other people?" he asked through a pained, tight brow.

"I think we should have the option...to make sure."

"I am sure! I'm sure that I would marry you in a year, I would marry you today!"

"I'm not...as sure...," I said, slowly, deliberately.

There it was. It was out there now. Vincent stared at me for a long time as if trying to figure out who this person was. I felt like an imposter myself. All this time telling him I loved him, which I did, and now saying I just wasn't completely sure. I tried to soften the blow with assurances.

"I love you Vincent, it's just that..."

He shook his hung head back and forth. "You don't love me."

"I do," I pleaded.

"You can't. If you're not sure after all this time, then you can't love me the way I love you."

That was always true. He had always been the one who was sure, who loved me completely, without doubt.

"I just thought if I used this year to see other people, I could come back to you certain..."

"Or not at all...," he said, verbalizing what we both knew was the other side of that risk.

"Try to understand...," I said.

"Understand? I don't understand," he said rising to his feet and pacing around the tree.

"The only thing that made this separation bearable was the belief that you were committed to me and to our future together. How am I supposed to handle this situation now, knowing you might be with some other guy?" he said, running his hands his through his dark hair.

I couldn't say anything. I sat there waiting for the impossible. Had I really believed that this could all work out somehow? What could I say now to make it right? Right enough for us to be able to walk out of this park together with a new arrangement, a new understanding. Vincent walked over to me with his black and white mind resolved.

"I can't do it Bridge," he said. "I cannot live without you for a year knowing that I'm going to have to share you with God knows who else you're going to meet over there."

"So what are you saying? Are you breaking up with me?" I asked unconvinced by his all or nothing position. He wouldn't give up on us so easily, would he?

"I am saying that if you need to see other people, you do it, but I can't stand by like the booby prize you settle for if nothing better comes along."

"Vincent! That's not what this is," I persisted.

"Well, that's how I feel! How else do you expect me to feel, Bridge?" he said his voice escalating.

"Why can't you just give me this time as a gift, Vincent...don't you want me to be sure?"

He looked out over the lake with his hands on his hips. He thought for a moment, but his emotions got the better of his judgment.

"I would give you anything Bridge, anything, but this. I can't do it. I know myself. I would go crazy. No...I just can't do it, I'm sorry," he said and he began to walk away.

"Vincent, where are you going? Wait, let's talk about it," I said, still trying to hold on to a compromise that was not to come today.

"There's nothing more to say Bridge...you do what you got to do," he said, his voice trailing off a mix of anger, hurt and disbelief.

It was the first time Vincent ever left me to walk home alone, by myself.

Over the next couple of days, my disbelief turned to anger. As I packed for France, I resented the fact that I now did so with a heavy heart. This wonderful opportunity had been tarnished by this heavy emotional burden, and feelings of guilt. But I was more angered by Vincent's unwillingness to bend on this issue. He had given me an ultimatum and expected me to yield. It made me even more determined in my position. Besides, how could he let me leave like this?

All these thoughts ran my through my head, and tumbled out of my mouth in a stream of consciousness for my sister to grapple with. Claire sat at the side of my bed, trying to reassure me that it would all work out for the best somehow and I should make the most of this year away.

No one, including myself, could really believe that Vincent and I had broken up, and in my heart I knew this could not be the end of our story. He would surely come around. Why wasn't he calling? How long was he going to wait…I was leaving in a few days.

But his call did not come. Instead, I received a letter. It was clearly written carefully and with much forethought. It was not angry. It was not demanding. It was filled with beautiful, loving sentiment, but not with which to reconcile. He was letting me go:

August 15, 1985

My Darling Love,

I walked to the park tonight and sat there alone, dazed and bewildered. I keep turning our conversation over and over in my mind.

You have been the best part of my life and I have many beautiful memories of us, but I don't want to be left with those memories, I want us to be together for the rest of our lives. I want to grow old with you, watch our children grow, and I thought that was what you wanted too.

You said that if I truly loved you I would understand

why you thought it would be best for us to date other people. Perhaps I am not being fair to you, but I know for sure, for myself, there could be no other. It saddens me that you need to tempt fate.

You tell me that you love me, but you owe it to yourself and to us to date others. You say you don't want to marry me because I am the only one you have ever known. You say you need time to grow and if you find your way back to me than you can always be confident in our love. If you truly mean that, then you have my blessing. I only wish I could believe that things will work out. It is just every fiber of my being is terrified of inevitably losing you someday. The thought of you with someone else makes my blood boil.

I will give you your time and I will promise to love you always, but I cannot do both. When you know it is me that you want, I will be here for you. There will never be anyone else for me, you alone will have my heart forever. I hope you find the happiness you're looking for. I can only hope and pray that you will find your way back to me.

**Forever,
Vincent**

I read the letter over and over again. He had accepted my reasoning and my feelings and was not trying to deprive me of them. Now, I had to come to terms with his position. Although the letter made me understand that he simply could not deny his feelings or live with anything other than what he knew to be true, it did not make it any easier for me to accept. Before I left, I put the letter in my drawer with the other letters I had kept from Vincent. But I could not put Vincent away, or behind me. He would stay with me...forever.

The ringing of the phone seemed so far off in the distance, Claire almost did not answer it. She only realized it was her phone when the machine picked up and she recognized her own voice on the greeting. Throwing the covers off, she leaped out of bed and into the living room where her phone sat atop an antique writing desk. It was the call she had been waiting for to confirm their Christmas plans in Vermont.

"...Yes, adjoining rooms would be perfect...and another room for my sister. And it's okay if we get there late Christmas Eve? Well, we'll have two sleepy children with us...yes...oh, that'll be great, thank you. Then I'll expect the room keys in the mail, then? Wonderful! Thanks again."

Claire realized she was still holding the book in her hands. She laid it on the desk as she wrote a check to the Inn. She had wanted to get away this Christmas. They had always spent Christmas at their father's house, and last year without him, it just didn't feel right. She was hoping that the beauty of Vermont with its New England charms would somehow ease the transition of spending Christmas without Thomas. Perhaps it would even become a new tradition.

As she sealed the envelope, Claire imagined her Christmas plans would be enjoyed by all. Tomorrow, she would take it to the post office, but right now she had to eat something to satisfy that queasy, mixed with hunger, sensation that Claire recognized all too well. Besides she only had a few more hours before the kids got back, and she wanted to read some more, maybe even get in a nap before she would have to start getting ready for the opera tonight. As Claire finished snacking and walked back to the living room to get her book, she noticed the sun was starting to brake through, and a November wind was blowing the dark clouds away.

But back in the book it was September in Paris:

My first few weeks in Paris were a whirlwind of activity. Despite the years of French I had taken in school, finding my way around and getting myself settled in was more than challenging. I would have been totally overwhelmed if it were not for the quick friendships I made with my classmates, who helped me maneuver my way through the university system and Parisian life. We were all on our own for the first time in our young lives, and with so many of us having similar interests and classes, camaraderie came easy. Though mostly French, there were many foreign students at the college. Somehow we all managed to understand each other.

Once settled in, it didn't take long before I started missing Vincent. After the chaos had passed and I had time to breathe and to think, my thoughts often drifted to him. At times, I felt like I was on an extended vacation, and I would soon be home. But then, the reality of my situation and my decisions became perfectly clear in the dark, at night, when I was alone. Luckily, my roommate, G, short for Gisella, was a huge distraction. G thought girls were crazy to pine away for anyone. Having G for a roommate was like getting a daily dose of vitamin Freedom. She was a constant source of optimism and vitality, whether you wanted it or not. Plus, wherever G went, there were sure to be men who followed. She was the walking, breathing image of French chic, oozing sensuality. Luckily for me, G always insisted we go out, for that was the essence of French life, to be out, to see and be seen. During the days, there was plenty enough to keep us busy between classes and assignments, but our evenings almost always involved the nightlife. In the Latin Quarter, where most of the college crowd lived, there was always someplace you could go. With the Sorbonne, Lycee, and the Universite de Paris, the Boulevards St. Michele and St. Germaine were always alive with throngs of young people.

Our apartment on the Rue des Carmes was small, but the location was ideal. Apparently, G and I were lucky to have gotten it, for we were the envy of other students who lived on much louder streets with dirtier apartments in less convenient locations. Flanked by the Boulevard St. Germaine on one side and the Rue des Ecoles on the other, ours was a pretty little street whose 17th century buildings had fancy ironwork rails, painted shutters and flower boxes decorating their six story fronts. From the bottom of our street, one can look up the hill and see the Pantheon. I especially came to appreciate the early mornings in our neighborhood where the smell of fresh baked bread permeated the air. The morning markets had everything from fresh fruits, vegetables, and baked goods to linens, wallets and all kinds of assorted items. Everything was within a few blocks and it became easy to befriend the vendors and store owners we'd see everyday. From our apartment, we could hear the bells of nearby churches and schools that still practiced the ringing of the bells to call the children to classes. It seemed to me, that wherever I went in Paris, there were always bells ringing. It reminded me St. Xavier back home, and it made me think of Vincent.

As September quickly turned to October, I became fairly familiar with the city. Occasionally, G and I would spend Saturdays in the shopping district, strolling along Saint Honore, with its fashionable haute couture shop, their new designs displayed in the windows. We weren't there to buy, but to admire, to learn. We all had the same adolescent dream-- to be a famous designer someday, mixing with first ladies, princesses and movie stars. These excursions through the designer district only fueled our hopes and aspirations. It was one of the things I loved to do most on the weekends with G.

Other times, I'd leave G off at the metro stop to meet friends while I went off in search of some solitude. I found many little quiet, green getaways off the boulevards, which I began to frequent often. Of course, there was the large Luxembourg Gardens nearby where you could walk among the formal rows of manicured hedges. But I preferred the smaller, more intimate courtyards and gardens, like the one that surrounds the Hotel de Cluny, a sixteenth century monastery built by the abbots that still retains an eerie, almost holy mystique. Or, the Jardin des Plantes, with its botanical gardens and hot houses. The Paris mosque had a sunken garden and patios you could walk in, and was usually fairly empty. It was not my beloved Cloisters, but it had a peaceful aura to it that was serene. These became some of my little sanctuaries in and around Paris, but it was the museums and the architecture of the more famous buildings, steeped in history, that was the most awe-inspiring.

The Louvre, formerly the king's palace, is an experience in visual overload, not just for the art it contains, but for the sheer size of the building and its ornate design from the Renaissance architectural period. The Grand and Petit Palais with their neo-classical design and railroad station roofs, stand out amongst the stretch of green that leads to the Champs Elysee. Of course, the Eiffel Tower stands seemingly forever over your shoulder, a constant reminder of Parisian sentiment. Because Paris is such an old city, it was amazing for me to see buildings that had been built in the 12th and 13th centuries. The Sainte-Chapelle, built by Louis IX, is a testament to its French Gothic period with its huge expanse of ancient stained glass. And of course, Notre Dame, the cathedral immortalized by Victor Hugo, with its mix of Gothic and Romanesque ancestry built into every detail, from the flying buttresses to the imperial purple rose windows. Once inside, I could not help but contemplate the many people who have used this holy place for purposes of their own, from kings and queens to peasant revolutionaries. And once again, the ringing of the bells. Vincent, would love it here. I wished I could share this with him because I knew how much he would appreciate all the artistry of the architecture in these historic, old buildings.

The weeks passed quickly and the autumn air turned colder. By November, our small circle of friends from September grew a little wider as someone would introduce a new friend or invite a classmate over to our cafe table. G was very selective about the boys she dated; she preferred graduate assistants or the occasional professor. As for me, my dates were few-- not for lack of invitation, but for lack of substance. Most male students, if not gay, weren't looking for friendship or romance as much as they were for a good time. Many of them, like myself, were exchange students, only there for a short time. For now, the friendships I had were fine for me, and if anything else developed I might consider it then. I still loved Vincent and had not fully reconciled all of what had happened yet in my mind.

I hadn't written or heard from him since our parting and I began to fear that perhaps I had walked out on my one, great love. As the holiday season approached and memories flooded my mind I began to panic. I sent Vincent a birthday card; a wonderfully romantic Parisian scene, with a long letter I had written and tucked inside. I wrote him that I missed him terribly and was miserable over the way we left things. I told him that I still loved him, and that I hoped he hadn't forgotten me already. Recalling that moment now, it was a blatant attempt on my part to hold onto the sure thing, the only love I had known. Though all the feelings I conveyed in that letter were real and truthful, I was, in all actuality, trying to have it all my way—the independence and freedom I wanted to date other people, but the security of Vincent waiting for me back home. I wondered how Vincent would see it.

I didn't have to wait long. About two weeks later I received his response. In Vincent's beautiful pen, his letter reassured me of his undying love, but it did not indicate any movement from his original position.

It was December now, and winter break was only a few final exams away. We all had started making our holiday plans and were looking forward to a long break. G was heading up to the Italian slopes to go skiing and was begging me to go with her. Claire had asked if she could visit. But suddenly, I was anxious to get back to New York. If Vincent was so resolute in his all or nothing position, then how long would he wait for me? We had not seen each other since that awful parting in August. Perhaps some time together would help us sort some things out. The truth was, I felt he was coming to terms with the situation. There was no mention in this letter that he was still waiting for me, only that he would love me forever. What did that mean? I had to see him again. I was not ready to let him go.

The day after I received Vincent's letter, I wrote him back, telling him of my plans to come home for Christmas and hoping that they would include spending time with him.

It scared me that I was relegated to a memory and told him that his staunch ways would only drive us further apart. I pleaded with him to think about changing his position temporarily so that we could have the benefit of some quality time together, and for a quick reply so that I would know if I had reason to come home for the holidays at all, for what would Christmas be without him?

Paris was especially beautiful at Christmas time. But the lights and decorations that should have made one merry, only made me a bit sad for not having anyone to share it with. It was an emptiness that I had not experienced yet in my young life. Although there was G and the boys, who were always up for frolicking about the city, the site of young couples enjoying the romance of the season made me miss Vincent even more as I awaited his response. Each day, I would anxiously check the post. As final exam week drew to a close, I finally received the envelope with that small, precise, familiar, handwriting.

Vincent's letter brought me the news I was hoping for. He had conceded to see me, however, reluctantly. It was apparent from his letter he was denying his own inherent nature and his better judgment just to please me. He made it perfectly clear that he felt he had no other choice, but I saw it as the start of a compromise. My anticipation grew as I boarded the 747 bound for JFK. Visions of Christmases past raced through my mind and I wondered if this year could be as wonderful as others I had spent with Vincent, even with the new stress that I had added to our relationship.

Returning to New York felt particularly reassuring to me, especially after being away for the first time. It's a feeling that I still experience today. For despite where your life or travels may take you, and however much the experience is enjoyed, landing in New York still feels like coming home for me. And home was where I desperately wanted to be...but would I still be able to find what I was looking for? After settling into my old room and catching up with my father and sister, I was anxious to see Vincent. It was nearly three o'clock and Vincent was sure to be coming home soon from work. My family didn't really question what was happening between us. They were just glad to know they'd also be seeing him. They had missed him as well and were hoping I would bring him to dinner tonight. I dressed for the evening, hoping Vincent would go with me to the restaurant where we had made reservations. I brushed my hair, put on some lipstick and my beige wool coat and hat and headed over to Vincent's apartment.

When I got there, I didn't find him at home and wondered where he might be. How long should I wait here? What if he was out with friends...or worse? I sat down on the concrete steps outside the walk up and waited. After fifteen minutes, I started to think that perhaps I had been too self-assured. He wasn't really expecting me. Maybe he would even be annoyed that I was so presumptuous. I didn't know what to think, or expect. But the next five minutes would change all that, as Vincent rounded the corner. It took him a moment to notice me, but I recognized him right away. His straight black hair was a little longer and the wind blew it back off his face as he made his way down the street. If his distinct walk wasn't easy enough for me to spot, the long, dark cashmere coat I gave him was. My heart raced at the sight of him and I began to rush towards him, my pace quickening; I was almost running in my heels. The moment Vincent saw me, he slowed his pace, as if to focus on someone you hadn't expected to see. Then, I saw the smile I had hoped for as he began walking quickly towards me. We walked directly into each other's arms and held each other for a long time.

"Hi," I said finally, barely able to get it out.

"Hey stranger..."

"I missed you...," I said.

"Oh, you don't know how much I've missed you. Look at you, you're so beautiful."

"I like the hair," I said running my hands through it and laughing a bit.

"You like it? It's my rebel look...but I'll keep it if you like it."

"I like it..." I whispered back.

"How long have you been sitting out here?"

"Too long, I'm freezing."

"C'mon, let's go inside."

The apartment was reassuringly familiar and once again I was surrounded with Vincent's things: his white starched shirts hanging from the armoire, his sketches scattered about, his weights in the corner, the cigarettes on the table. I looked around as Vincent took my coat and hat, searching for tell-tale signs of another woman. But there were only some new items of Vincent's that hinted of a maturing mans purchase: a silk robe, some new books, a new lithograph from the recent Art Expo.

"I can't believe you're really here," he said, laying my things over a kitchen chair. "And you're all dressed up."

"Well, it is Christmas...," I said.

"Oh yeah," he said remembering to turn on the tree lights. "I forgot to turn these on."

"You put up that little tree I bought you?" I asked, surprised with delight.

"I love this little tree!" he said, smiling as our tabletop tree lit up with color as he plugged it in.

My heart welled up with sentiment. He had kept our tree.

"I guess I should put the rest of the lights on; it's getting pretty dark out," he said.

I walked over to him and took his hand.

"Don't put the lights on...I like it just like this, with only the lights of the tree," I said.

Then I put my arms around him, hoping he would let go of all the issues we knew we would have to deal with eventually. I didn't have to say it. Vincent understood.

"I love you...," he said between kisses.

"I love you, too," I said. I hoped he believed it.

We spent the rest of the afternoon in bed, loving, talking, laughing, careful not to bring up anything that was taboo. Not today. I told him of the sights, sounds and smells of Paris, and how I thought he would love it. We talked about school and what we were learning. He had met some new friends who told him about an opportunity at a more prestigious firm. Vincent was considering following his friend Sammy to a new, up-and-coming company. His friends were graduating and getting married, and I could see that Vincent was considering his future too. I wondered if his new friends knew about me. For the first time, I could see how our uncertain relationship was completely frustrating from Vincent's perspective.

When we became hungry, we realized the whole afternoon had gotten away from us and it was nearly time to meet father and Claire at "One if by Land." In a matter of minutes, we were dressed and on our way.

The landmark restaurant, got its name from a code devised by Revolutionary war patriots whereby a lantern was hung out in front of the place to warn soldiers, one lantern indicating if the Brits were coming in by land, two lanterns if by sea. Vincent and my father loved the historic nature of the place, and my sister and I basked in the glow of Christmas cheer provided by the myriad of lights and fresh flowers the restaurant is famous for. There was no discomfort between us as the four of us got caught up with each other, only genuine pleasure at spending this evening together. I couldn't help but stare at Vincent through dinner. How handsome and charming he was. I studied his mannerisms as he spoke to my father. I watched how he listened attentively, how he folded his hands, how his quick smile softened the intensity of his piercing gaze. Occasionally, he would catch me staring at him and give me a knowing smile.

When dinner ended we parted company with my father and sister and Vincent and I headed uptown. We didn't plan on it, but as we approached St. Patrick's Cathedral, agreed that midnight mass here would be special. It was something I had always wanted to do, and Vincent indulged me the more than two hours we knew it would take. It was only 11:00 and people were already filing in. And so we passed the time, sitting in the pews of St. Pat's, watching families come down the aisle, pointing to little girls dressed in Christmas dresses or boys in suits.

For long stretches, we would say nothing; we just listened to the organ music and stared at the altar. Vincent took my hand and held it in his lap. Then he turned to me. He didn't speak, but his longing gaze told me everything I knew he wanted to say.

"What is it?" I asked.

Vincent shook his head. "Nothing."

I squeezed his hand.

"What are you thinking about?" I whispered.

"The future...," he said, staring straight ahead at the altar. "I'm praying for our future."

Then he kissed the back of my hand.

CHAPTER THIRTEEN

As the three o'clock hour closed in, Claire roused herself from the bed, leaving the book on the end table. She had just enough time to pick up the children, make them a snack, and get ready for the evening. The two hours passed by in a whirl of activity. If not for the almighty power of television to hold the children's attention, Claire would have never been ready in time. Jack came home early since he knew Claire would be leaving by 5:30pm.

Bridge had arranged for an early seating at Picholene, one of her favorite restaurants, which also happened to be located conveniently close to Lincoln Center. They would have plenty of time since the performance did not start until 8:00 pm. When Claire emerged from the bedroom, she captured her children's attention. They had never seen their mother look so dreamy, except for what they had seen in their parent's wedding pictures.

"What do you think, kids?" Claire did a twirl in her chocolate brown silk gown, which made her full skirt rise and swirl around her. Its tightly fitted sleeveless bodice, accentuated Claire's slender figure. The matching silk stole, which wrapped around her bare shoulders, added a regal elegance.

"You look like a fairy princess Mommy," Livy said breathless.

"Why don't you dress like that every day?" James wanted to know.

Claire laughed as she walked over to the mirror. The folds of the sweeping skirt, starting at the small of her back, converged into a gentle train as she moved through the room. It made it impossible for Jack to take his eyes off of her.

"Wow, honey you look great," he said as he approached her from behind, sliding his arms around her waist. Staring at herself in the mirror, Claire tightened her antique crystal earrings, their amber colored glass seem to match the color of her eyes.

"It's hard not to in such a beautiful dress," said Claire. "It's all Bridge's doing."

"But it is you who makes the dress," Jack whispered as he nestled his nose into the nape of her neck. Their eyes met in the mirror briefly and they shared a secret smile.

"I'm afraid it's a bit tight in the waist...," Claire worried.

"Oh? No more bon bons for you, my little chocoholic," Jack joked.

Claire shooed him away just as the doorbell rang.

"That's Bridge," Claire said, quickly powdering her nose.

"I'll get it," said Jack, pretending to pry himself away from his wife. He opened the door and smiled at Bridge who was beaming expectantly.

"Claire, your date's here...," called Jack across the room.

"Very funny," said Bridge as she walked in. Bridge went over to her sister with open arms.

"You look gorgeous," exclaimed Bridge.

"You too!" Claire said. "Have I seen that dress before?"

Bridge had on a black, silk gown with long sleeves that just sloped off Bridge's straight shoulders.

"No, I don't think I've worn it before."

"But I know I've seen those hairpins before, although not for a very long while," said Claire. "I didn't know you still had them after all these years."

"Yes, I know," said Bridge gently touching her hair where the pins laid. "I found them in my old room some time ago, but haven't had cause to wear them until now."

"What made you decide to dig them out tonight?" asked Claire.

Bridge hesitated for a moment. "I thought they went well with the dress."

The colorful jeweled hairpins, held back some of Bridge's hair, which was piled loosely atop her head in a mound of hanging curls.

"Well, they look lovely in your hair," said Claire.

"Shall we go?" Bridge asked.

"Ready, sista," Claire said excitedly.

As they hurried out of the building, a driver in a navy blue suit approached them, and ushered them into a Lincoln town car. It had been some time since Bridge had cause to celebrate, so she made sure this evening was full of luxuries, from the car, to the champagne that flowed over the gastronomic delights during dinner. By the time they arrived at the Met, they were already giddy with indulgent delight. The lights from the Opera house illuminated all of Lincoln Center, providing a backdrop for which ladies and gentlemen, clad in their evening attire, quickly strode past the plumes of water fountains.

Once inside, Claire and Bridge checked their coats downstairs in the patrons coat check on the Orchestra level.

"Do you want to get a drink?" Bridge asked.

"No, I don't think so," Claire said evasively.

"Are you sure? You hardly had any champagne at dinner," Bridge commented.

"No, I'm actually quite full and this dress is a little snug," explained Claire.

"Really? Sorry about that. Well, we might as well find our seats then."

They ascended the red, carpeted marble staircase to the Grand Tier and made their way through the crowded bar area. They arrived at their seats, and soon afterwards the house lights went down. A hush fell over the crowd. In the darkness, you could almost forget the other people around you. Bridge and Claire were quickly lost in the story unfolding before them. Occasionally, Bridge would sneak a sidewards glance at her sister. She was glad that she could share this experience with her. They were both enthralled by the music, the story, and the sheer delight of being whisked away to another place in time through the magic that is opera.

When the lights came back up for intermission break, Vincent stayed in his orchestra seat for a moment, undisturbed by all the people around him looking to get to the lobby quickly.

"Puccini writes the most moving arias, don't you think?" Vincent asked no one in particular in his party.

"Having a good time, honey?" Anne asked, patting Vincent's shoulder.

"Yeah, it's great. Thank you."

It was typical of the kind of responses Vincent had come

to expect from Anne. She was a considerate wife who kept a considerable social calendar and attended all the events she was expected to. But they never did have the same kind of appreciation for the arts. It was not something he could truly share with her and many of their experiences together felt so hollow now.

"I feel like champagne," announced Sammy. "Shall we make our way to the Grand Tier ladies?"

"Sounds good," Lisa responded.

On the way out, Vincent and Sammy walked side by side as the women led the way.

"How you doing?" Sammy asked, putting his arm on Vincent's back.

"Good," Vincent said. "How about you? You enjoying yourself?"

"Yeah, this is nice," Sammy said. "We should do this more often."

"We should," Vincent agreed.

Upstairs, the crowd had already started to grow. Vincent and Sammy made their way to the bar. As Sammy sidestepped his way through the sea of tuxedos, Vincent stepped on something underfoot. Bending down to see what it was, he retrieved what appeared to be a bejeweled hairpin. Vincent moved to a less crowded spot at the end of the bar to look at it more closely. Tucking himself into a well-lit corner, Vincent studied its unique design and thought he recognized it. It was not the kind of accessory you would find everyday, and it seemed to him that this was the second time he had stumbled upon something so rare. Although it had been years since he'd seen them, he could swear this bore a remarkable likeness to the hairpins he had bought for Bridge years ago. He remembered them distinctly, having picked them out himself with such care. The longer he held the pin in his hand, the more sure he became that this was, indeed, the very same one.

By now, Vincent had lost Sammy in the crowd. Vincent felt flushed as his pulse started to race. His eyes darted across the room, scanning the crowd, looking for a familiar face. Was it possible Bridge was here? Would he recognize her? He began moving through the crowd.

"Excuse me...excuse me...," he said, as he began combing the Grand Tier, searching for his past. A sense of urgency began building inside him. He moved quicker, turning his head in all directions. He was sure he would know her. He concentrated on faces. Hair could change, but faces, no. Without a thought for his party, he ran down the stairs one level to the Parterre. Perhaps she would be there? He walked quickly around. There were some people, but no one that he recognized. He continued down to the Orchestra level. As he searched, an overwhelming certainty came over him, as if with each step he drew closer to her presence. He hurried past the TV monitors and the Texaco Gallery with its display of famous costumes. There were a few people walking the gallery; most were returning to their seats. He ran back up to the Grand Tier, to the spot where he found the hairpin. Maybe she was looking for it there. He stood for a moment, watching people pass by, trying to compose himself.

"Hey good looking," the familiar voice came from behind him. It was Anne, wondering what happened to their drinks.

"I don't know...I lost Sammy at the bar," Vincent muttered.

Reaching for his hand, Anne noticed that Vincent was holding something.

"What's this?" she asked, taking the hairpin from his hand.

"Uh, I found it, I stepped on it," Vincent said reluctantly.

"It's beautiful," Anne commented. "Someone will be missing this. You should take it to the lost and found."

Taking the hairpin back from Anne, Vincent fingered the piece carefully.

"Yeah, that's a good idea," he said.

"Look, there's Sammy with our drinks," Lisa said.

"Why don't you girls meet up with him," Vincent suggested. "He looks like he could use a hand. I'll be there in a minute."

Vincent inquired as to where the lost and found was. It occurred to him that its owner might also be there looking for the lost item. But when he arrived, the attendant was alone. Vincent lingered there for a few moments, but no one appeared.

"Excuse me, did a woman inquire about a lost hairpin?" Vincent asked.

"No sir," replied the attendant.

Vincent was about to give the hairpin to the attendant, but suddenly changed his mind. He put the pin in his pocket and made his way back to the grand tier.

"Here he is...the birthday boy!" said Sammy, handing Vincent a champagne glass. "A toast! To my best buddy on his 45th birthday."

"Happy Birthday, darling," Anne said. She thought she detected a curious uneasiness about Vincent tonight. She stared at him while he graciously accepted toasts and a kiss from Lisa. When the bell rang, they made their way back to their seats. Vincent was quiet, but fidgety, looking over this shoulder, then the other.

"Are you alright?" Anne asked, a little concern creeping into her voice.

"Yeah, fine. Why?"

"I don't know, you look a little pasty."

"I'm just a little warm, that's all," Vincent explained. "The stairs..."

"Okay," said Anne, sitting back in her seat. But even as the lights went down, Anne could still see the unsettled look on her husband's face and his moist brow. Why was he sweating? He never perspires. As the curtain rose, and all eyes were fixed on the stage, Anne thought Vincent looked a million miles away.

Unable to see anyone in the dark, Vincent could not help but be lured back into the story of *LaBoheme*. The third Mimi's distress over her lover Rodolfo's excessive jealousy, which plays a role in the lovers parting from one another, only to be reunited again at Mimi's deathbed. Vincent could not help but think of the parallels between this timeless story and his own ill-fated relationship with Bridge. As he held the hairpin in his jacket pocket like a talisman, he wondered about his lost love. He thought of his own jealous obsessions and his need to keep Bridge with him at all times. Perhaps he, too, like Rodolfo, had driven her away from him to seek the freedom she found in Paris. He was so controlling back then, everything so black and white. And now, as a mature man, he saw how the inflexible ways of his youth had been a mistake.

As the last act came to its finale, the crowd cheered. The whistles and bravos increased to a near fever pitch as each of the performers walked out from behind the curtains, hand in hand, taking their long, deep bows. Bridge and Claire were not exempt from containing themselves either, especially for the leads, as they came forward to graciously accept the flowers thrown about the stage.

When the house lights came back up and the ladies reached for their bags, Claire noticed Bridge's hair had come undone.

"Bridge, some of your hair came down in the back."

"Oh, that's alright," Bridge said.

"No, one of your hairpins is missing."

"Oh no…," Bridge gasped, feeling around the top of her head for the second pin.

They searched their seats and the floor beneath them, but found nothing.

"I could have lost it anywhere," Bridge said, obviously deflated by the loss.

"We might as well sit in our seats for a while until the crowds clear out, so we'll have a better chance of finding it," suggested Claire.

"That's probably easier, I guess…," said an unsure Bridge.

"Well, we're not going to get very far at all right now."

"You're right."

They sat back in their seats and waited until the lines from the back and upper sections began to make their way through the exit doors.

Meanwhile, Sammy was ushering his party out as fast as he could.

"C'mon, let's go folks."

"Honestly, what is your rush Sam?" Lisa asked.

"I'm starving!"

"Oh, you're always hungry," she said.

"I'm going to use the men's room," Vincent said. "Where should I meet you?"

"Aw geez, Vincent…can't we get out of here first? We'll be at the restaurant in five minutes," pleaded Sammy.

"Relax," Vincent said. "Why don't you get the coats and I'll meet you there."

"Ok, but hurry up," said Sammy.

Vincent headed back to the lost and found, hoping someone would be looking for a hairpin. Standing aside to watch for any activity, all he noticed was a gentleman who claimed a white silk scarf. He supposed he should turn in the hairpin. Whoever it belonged to, they would be looking for it.

And she was. As the crowd dispersed, Bridge and Claire began searching for her pin, first in the area immediately around their seats, then they moved out into the Grand Tier, all the time with their heads down, their eyes on the floor. They retraced their steps from the Belmont Room, to the ladies room. They stopped at the coat check and asked the attendant if anyone saw or turned in a hairpin to him.

Anne, who had just gotten her coat on, couldn't help but overhear the inquiry. While Sammy helped on Lisa with her coat, then his own, Anne approached Bridge.

"Excuse me, did I hear you say you lost something?" Anne inquired.

"Yes, a hairpin," Bridge answered. "Why, have you seen it?"

"As a matter of fact, my husband turned in a hairpin to the lost and found at intermission. Try there."

"Thank you so much," Bridge said, relieved as she and Claire hurried off to the nearest elevator, which was waiting with its doors open.

Taking the pin out of his pocket, Vincent looked at it again and smiled. He began to walk slowly towards the attendant when he heard Sammy call out his name. He was headed towards him with his coat. Vincent folded the pin back into the palm of his hand and put it back in his pocket.

"Hey, there you are. What are you doing here?" Sammy asked. "I thought you were going to the men's room?"

"I, uh...I just came to see if that pin found its way back to its owner."

Sammy rolled his eyes and threw his head back a little as he grabbed his friend's arm and walked him back to where their wives were waiting.

"You're such a good Samaritan," Sammy said. "Can we eat, now?"

As Sammy and Vincent headed back up the staircase, the elevator doors opened at the lower level. Bridge ran over to the attendant.

"Excuse me, someone handed in a hairpin during intermission tonight. I would like to claim it please."

"Pardon me, madam, but I am not in possession of a hairpin."

"What? Are you sure?" Bridge asked.

"Yes, madam, quite sure."

"Perhaps another attendant...?"

"I've been on duty here all night."

"But a woman just told us that her husband found a hairpin tonight and brought it here," said Claire, a hint of suspicion in her voice.

"A gentleman inquired if anyone was looking for one... that's all."

Claire and Bridge looked at each other, not knowing

what to think. Claire pulled Bridge away to confer with her in private.

"Someone's not telling us the truth here," Claire whispered.

"What do you make of it?" Bridge asked.

"That woman told us that her husband turned it in!"

"Yes, I know, but…"

"I bet this guy pocketed it!" Claire said with suspicion.

"Oh Claire, what would this man want with a hairpin?"

"I don't know! He probably has a girlfriend!"

"But why would he say someone inquired about the pin?" Bridge asked.

"Who knows? Maybe he's just trying to cover his tracks," Claire reasoned.

"Unless…," wondered Bridge aloud "the man never turned it in?"

"Why?" asked Claire.

"Claire, we did our best," said Bridge. "It's just a pin. Forget it."

They walked back to the patrons' coat check to get their coats, the Met almost empty now.

"Well, it was still a lovely evening," Bridge said.

"Yes it was," agreed Claire.

CHAPTER FOURTEEN

"Wake up, sleepy head," whispered Jack carrying a tray of juice and a few slices of cinnamon toast.

"What time is it?" Claire asked.

"It's 9:00," Jack said. "The kids and I have been up a couple of hours already."

Smiling, Claire was thankful he had not let them wake her. She didn't get in that late last night, but was unusually tired nonetheless.

"Isn't this nice!" Claire said, reaching for the tray. "What are they doing?"

"They're just watching TV," Jack said.

"Again? We should really take them out today," Claire stated.

"Ok, if you're up for that," Jack said. "It's pretty chilly out."

"I know, but I don't want them watching TV all day."

"I'll tell you what…I'll take them somewhere for a little while."

"You will? Thanks honey. Oh, make sure they're bundled up, Jack."

"OK, you rest," he said as he kissed her head and took the tray out of the room.

After a few moments of commotion, in which she

thought she heard pleas from her little ones as to why Mommy wasn't coming, Claire was left with a perfectly quiet, sunny morning.

She reached for the book she had left on the side table, and as she found the place she had left off, she thought about the evening before. How odd it was that Bridge had wore the hairpins from Vincent, and how one disappeared the way it did. Claire took it as a good sign that Bridge had come to terms with her past by the way she was willing to let it go. Claire, herself, returned to that past while reading the next chapter.

Although Vincent and I spent a wonderful holiday together, we both knew I'd be returning to Paris soon to finish my year abroad. Our unspoken agreement to see other people was a subject neither of us could broach, and so we didn't. Vincent had made a huge concession in seeing me; all he asked was that I come back to him surer about our future. If it meant seeing other people, he'd have to accept it for now, but he certainly did not want to know about it. The strain of our arrangement showed at times in his jealous explosions or in the awkward silences between us. I knew it was a constant struggle for Vincent to try to live in what must have seemed like a most unnatural situation to him, fighting for control of his emotions. It was painful for me, too, watching him go through this, and frankly, although I loved seeing Vincent, I was secretly glad to be going back to Paris to escape this mess that I was responsible for. In Paris, it was easy to forget the decisions that awaited me back home.

In a matter of weeks, we were each back to leading our separate lives. Paris was colder, but no less lively than before. Students held parties all over the Latin Quarter to pass the long winter weeks. G was surprised at how many of them I went to, with or without her company.

"You know Brigitte, you should really be more selective about which parties you go to," said G.

"I do believe you are a snob, G," I teased.

"Who do you think you're going to meet at these college parties?"

"I would suspect other college students," I said sarcastically.

"Exactly my point! Boys. Silly, little college boys."

"I'm only going to be in Paris for another few months, G. I'll probably never have this opportunity again...to just go out, without a care."

"OK, my sweet American girl. You have your fun," said G, giving me a hug as if to say I forgot your time here is limited and I'm going to miss you. "And by the way, I'm not a snob. I just have incredible standards!"

I laughed as I put my coat on.

"You're sure you won't come?" I asked.

"No, you go...I'm going to work on these sketches."

It's true, I was unlike the Bridge G had known only a few months ago. I was feeling more at home in Paris these days, and more sociable too. Phillipe and I met over a bowl of tapenade, each of us spooning mounds of the olive paste onto slices of bread.

"This is definitely one of the better food groups I've had at a college party," I said, surprised by the interesting array, not your usual college party snacks.

"You like tapenade?" asked Phillipe.

"Like it? It's wonderful!"

"I'm so glad that it pleases you. I'm Phillipe," he said extending his hand. "The tapenade and socca were my idea. Those idiot roommates of mine don't know how to feed their guests."

"But you obviously do...," I said, wiping my mouth with a napkin. "I'm Bridge. You have a nice party here. Are you from Paris?"

"Provence, actually. My parents own an olive farm in Haut-de-Cagnes"

"Ahh...that explains the food," I said. "Where about, exactly?"

"It is a small village just north of Cagnes-Sur-Mer near the Mediterranean."

"It sounds lovely," I said, not having a clue as to where he was talking about.

"It is, but for now, I live the Parisian life while I'm here at school."

After a few minutes we had exchanged all the essential information of what year we were in, what we were studying, where we lived and what we planned on doing upon graduation. Phillipe was supposed to be studying business and economics, at least that's what his parents thought he was doing. It was their intention that he manage the farm and the production and distribution of their olives. But Phillipe had an artist's heart and a gourmand's stomach. His dream was to decorate his own small, exclusive restaurants where, as the chef, he would create art on a plate.

He was intrigued with the fact that I was from New York and wanted to know what the best restaurants in Manhattan were doing. I could only tell him about my limited exposure to places I had been with Vincent or with my father. We talked about life in Paris and he told me about some little known places around town and how I could eat like a king for practically pennies. Then, pretending to be my personal waiter, Phillipe put a dish linen over one arm and showed me into the tiny kitchen where he had a few bottles of wine on the counter.

"May I suggest a wine for madam?"

"I'm sure whatever you suggest will be wonderful," I said playing along.

He opened a bottle and poured a bit into a wine glass. I reached for the glass. I knew I should smell it, but didn't know what I was supposed to smell. I sipped the wine and smiled.

"Just as I thought," I said.

"It is to your satisfaction, madam?"

"Oh yes, but won't you join me, garcon?"

"It is highly irregular, but how can such a beautiful woman be denied?"

When we had finished the bottle of wine, I realized we had been talking for over two hours.

"I've been rude...you have other guests to see," I said.

"No, no, they are the rude ones...being so loud when they can plainly see we are trying to have a conversation in here."

"Phillipe...," I said, looking at him as he had misbehaved.

"Say my name again?"

"What? Phillipe?"

"Ah...when you say it, it takes on a whole new feeling."

"I'm not saying it correctly?"

"No, you say it perfect...Brigitte," he whispered. Then he leaned across the table and gave me the softest kiss. Hardly a kiss really, more a gentle brushing of his lips across mine.

When he pulled his face away, his large green eyes twinkled with mischief as he smiled like he had just gotten away with something. Perhaps it was the wine, or this carefree, flirtatious conversation we had been sharing, but something made me get out of my seat and stand next to him. He put his hands on my hips and I ran my one hand through his long, loose curls of soft brown hair. I bent over and kissed him! It was a suspended moment in time, a stolen kiss in the corner of the kitchen. Then I sat back in my chair. We stared at each other for a moment, each of us grinning and playful.

"Well?" he said. "What now?"

"What do you mean?" I asked.

"Well I can't let a kiss like that just die here! You must agree to see me again."

"I just wanted to see how you kissed."

"So you were using me then?" he said sarcastically.

"Using you? I thought you enjoyed it, too," I said.

"Oui, but it is like the tapenade...you can't have just one, eh? There must be another!"

"Perhaps...," I said, laughing.

"Come," he said standing up and putting his arm around me as we walked to the door. "You will let me walk you home and we will discuss the matter further, yes?" he said.

He was funny and adorable and easy to be with. I thought about it for a split second.

"Oui," I said.

When I was with Phillipe, I was happy. When I was not with him, I was miserable, mostly because I spent those times questioning my every action, every feeling, comparing him to Vincent. And then there were those letters, those wonderful love letters that would arrive from time to time, reminding me of Vincent's steadfast commitment. The end result was always the same, feeling torn between a life and love back in the states and a life I was trying to live here in Paris. There was always an overriding guilt that came over me and it pervaded my ill-fated relationship with Phillipe. I'd tell myself not to get too close, only hurt could come of this for everyone involved. Then, Phillipe would ring me and I would find myself turned around, reasoning that this was my time to see other people and that I should give Phillipe a fair chance; afterall, I did so enjoy his company. Just to be on the arm of an attractive man, walking through the streets of Paris, made me feel alive and free. Shopping together, cooking together, eating together, and always the music playing--it was wonderful.

There was only one thing missing. Poor Phillipe. He was a patient gentleman. Although I'm sure he wondered why I always pulled away at a certain point. Our kisses were sweet, and his embrace was warm and comforting. I could lay with him in the firelight for hours, snuggled up together, talking. But for all our romance and sharing, we never actually made love. There were plenty of other girls who would gladly sleep with him. I suppose Phillipe was waiting for the right moment, when I wouldn't tense up or change my mind. That moment was never to come. It wasn't that I wasn't attracted to Phillipe, I was. But I was still struggling with the reality of letting myself be with someone other than Vincent. Phillipe, was in the tenuous position of being the first person with whom I was trying to test the waters. It was my head that stopped me from diving in...until I met Henri.

It was a cool, Saturday morning in April when G and I stopped at a cafe on Rue de la Montagne St. Genevieve. It was a favorite gathering place for locals as it was ideally located near a charming little place, with a fountain in the center, around which friends often met before deciding on the cafe or eatery they would patron. We took a table facing the sun and ordered our croissants and coffee. A few tables away, a young man sat reading the paper. G and I both noticed him. He was very good looking, with sharp, cut, distinct features. His light brown hair blew slightly in the morning breeze, even though it was meticulously cut and styled. He wore a turtleneck and wool blazer with a scarf around the lapels, giving him an air of suave sophistication, yet he didn't appear to be much older than G and myself. He looked over the top of his paper at us.

"Don't look now, but someone is staring at you," said G.

"Well, maybe he's staring at us because we've been ogling him."

"He's coming this way, Bridge!"

"No?! What do I do?"

"Act casual…"

He approached our table and introduced himself.

"Bon jour mademoiselles, would you mind if I joined you?" he asked confidently.

Standing there, looking down at me, his large, light blue eyes, fixed on mine. He was gorgeous and I was tongue-tied!

"Certainly," responded G.

"It's such a beautiful day and now I have beautiful company in which to enjoy it, eh?"

"I'm G and this is my American friend Brigitte…"

"Bridge," I said as I extended my hand.

"So tell me Henri, how is it that we never noticed you here before?" asked G.

"I usually work in the mornings," said Henri with a touch of sarcasm.

"Oh…right, of course," we said somewhat embarrassed.

"What type of work do you do?" I asked, thinking how typically American the question must of sounded, but he didn't seem to mind.

"I am an electrical engineer," replied Henri.

"Really?"

I would have never guessed him to be an engineer with his athletic build and charming smile.

"Yes, it is terribly boring," he said. "And what brings you here from America?"

"I am studying fashion."

"Ah….then it is our good fortune that you chose to study here, eh?"

I blushed.

"It is such a beautiful spring day. Do you have any plans?" asked Henri.

"Unfortunately, we have a school project we need to work on," said G.

"Oh, that's too bad," said Henri. Turning to Bridge, he leaned forward a little, his gaze was mesmerizing. "Are you sure you don't have time to walk with me a while?"

It was impossible to resist the charming way he seemed to be completely disappointed.

"We really do need to do some work, but perhaps I can meet you later?"

"I would really like that," he said, smiling at me, all the time looking deep into my eyes.

I found it hard to look away. I had never seen such watery blue eyes, sexy and yet so hard to read. It was a little unnerving, but I liked the way it made me feel. I told myself it was risky to get involved with this gorgeous, self-assured charmer who I knew nothing about. And yet I was drawn to him.

I spent the rest of the day thinking of Henri. I did my work with a disinterested quickness, all the time distracted by thoughts of the charming stranger. As day turned to evening, I grew more excited with every passing hour. Even G noticed the time and care I put into primping for my date. I had hot rollers in my hair and more makeup on then she had ever seen me wear.

"You're really nervous about this date, aren't you?" asked G.

"It shows, huh?" I said.

"Only to me," she said.

"I don't know what it is about this guy G, but...yeah, I'm a little nervous."

"It's that you don't trust yourself to be with him," she said. She was wise beyond her years.

"What do you mean?"

"I mean the attraction between you is so strong, you're afraid you'll go to bed with him."

"I will not!" I exclaimed. "I don't even know him!"

"Ok, we'll see..."

"I will not go to bed with him."

"Well, maybe not tonight, but he is very good looking," she said.

"He is very handsome, isn't he?"

We laughed, delighted by what we knew to be true. There was no arguing that fact. I pulled the rollers out of my hair as he knocked on the door. A last minute check in the mirror...I wiped a bit of lipstick off.

Henri and G were talking as I entered the room. He had on a black leather jacket over a pair of tight blue jeans, and black leather boots. He looked different than he had at the cafe earlier. His hair was tousled and he was holding a bike helmet. Was this to be my fate tonight?

"No, no, don't worry," Henri reassured me. "I thought we would walk. I just came back from a ride. It was such a beautiful day."

"Oh, where did you end up going today?" I asked, a bit bothered by the fact that he hadn't even bothered to change, almost as if our date were an afterthought, an appointment he had just remembered he had made.

"I rode around the countryside...out to Barbizon...you know it? It is a really lovely little town, quaint. If you'd like to go for a ride sometime, I would gladly take you."

"I believe I would like that," I said, staring at his figure in the doorway. He had turned back to the door, his hand extended behind him for me to take it. I looked at G who just shrugged. Then he looked over his shoulder and grinned.

"Let's go?"

I grabbed his hand and he pulled me up along side him.

"I've been looking forward to this all day," he said. "Are you hungry? I'm starved," he said without waiting for my response.

Over dinner at a small bistro, I began to fall for Henri. I don't remember much of what we talked about, I only remember being completely captivated by his presence and lost in his eyes. The longer I looked at him, all I could think about was what it would be like to kiss him.

We drank wine and reached for each other's hands, caressing the other's fingers and palms as we waited for the check. He noticed the antique ring I still wore from Vincent, and as he turned it on my finger, I could tell he wondered about it and was looking for the right words of inquiry. I told him the truth.

"What an unusual ring," he said. "Was it your grandmother's?" He smiled.

"No, there's someone back in New York who gave it to me," I said.

"And he loves you?"

"Yes."

"But, of course. Beautiful women always have men who are in love with them," he said.

I thought it was a very modern attitude, refreshing actually.

"And you are in love with him?" he asked.

"I thought I was, but now...I'm not sure," I said.

"I see...and so you experiment a little. Lucky for me," he said with a flirtatious grin.

He did not seem affected by this admission at all. In fact, it was easy for us to talk about. He had half expected that there would be someone else. In minutes we had moved beyond the issue of past relationships and resumed our intent on starting a new one with each other.

It did not feel like a first date. It felt like several weeks of dating all rolled into one night—the night a couple knows will be the night they become lovers. It was all so intense for me. I assumed, from his behavior, for Henri as well. For as soon as we left the restaurant, we had only walked a couple of feet when he pulled me into the nearest doorway. We were still catching our breath when he kissed me, and kept kissing me, as our warm breath met the cool night air.

"I had to kiss you," he said between kisses.

"I was hoping you would," I said.

"We can't stay in a doorway all night," he said.

"There's probably more privacy in that small park a little ways up," I said, not catching his meaning at first.

We walked through the park a bit more comfortable in the knowledge that we both felt the same way. He kept his arm around my waist and our shoulders rubbed against each other as we walked. Under the leafy overhang of an old shade tree we stopped to kiss some more. This time we took our time for there was no one nearby. His lips moved from my mouth to my shoulder and I threw my arms around his neck. I tightened my embrace as if to steady myself for what was to come. I was falling fast, and as I stood there in that embrace I felt as if I was holding on for dear life. I was at a precipice, and he was just the thing that could pull me over the edge.

"Come home with me," he said, urging me on with kisses.

"I don't know...," I hesitated, pulling back just a little.

"Come home with me, Brigitte..."

"I think we should call it a night," I said, finding my wits in a brief moment of clarity.

"No! No, don't say that."

"Yes, yes...," I returned, determined to cool things off a bit.

"Ok, I'll take you home, but only if I can see you again tomorrow."

He was clearly surprised by the rejection. Had I led him on? Or was he just used to getting his way? I decided to make it a bit difficult for him.

"Maybe during the week, Henri?" I put him off just a couple of days. I needed the time to put my own feet back on the ground.

"The wait will surely kill me," he said.

But it was I that couldn't wait to see him again. I knew that whatever was happening between Henri and I was something unique, and certainly something I had never experienced before. I wondered if this was what people meant by chemistry. Maybe this was love at first sight? You always hear about it, but how do you really know? It was too soon to tell. And I was too young to know the difference. One thing was sure; something powerful was drawing me to Henri-- a physical pull that was more powerful than my ability to control it. It was irrational what was happening. I couldn't explain it and I didn't want to try. I just wanted to be with him again. I knew we would make love soon; there was no denying our attraction. And for once, I wasn't thinking about Vincent.

During the following week, Henri and I could not seem to get together. I was somewhat disappointed by the fact that his other plans took precedence over seeing me, but tried to act as though I was busy, too. There was something I knew I had to do before I saw Henri again, and that was to have an honest discussion with Phillipe. My feelings for Henri showed me that Phillipe and I were not meant to be. It was something I think we both could have predicted, so it did not come as a surprise to Phillipe when I told him I had met someone I thought I could be in a real relationship with. He confided that he hoped when I was ready, it would be with him. But by then, Phillipe and I had settled into our warm, but platonic relationship. It was never going to be him. In the end,

Phillipe and I parted friends. We continued to talk and see each other from time to time. Next to G, he turned out to be one of my closest friends.

Henri and I, in the meantime, finally settled on the following Saturday and I wondered if the heat between us had been cooled by the week apart. Perhaps I had let myself get carried away. Maybe he was just as passionate with other girls. I couldn't wait until Saturday to see how Henri would act. I felt a little better when he told me we could spend the whole day together.

Luck smiled on us, for an unusually warm spell came through that spring weekend in late April. Henri showed up with a picnic basket and a spare helmet. Our day was set.

He handed me the basket.

"It's empty!"

"Yes I know. We will fill it up as we go along," he said. "Some of the best markets are on our way."

I still remember it as one of my most fond memories of my time in France. We rode for miles, my arms hugging Henri around his waist, the wind and sun on our face. We passed glorious rolling countryside and stopped in tiny, picturesque villages along the way, walking hand in hand, laughing and kissing. Villagers smiled at us and spoke to Henri in French. They seemed to approve of our happiness, making comments about how wonderful to be young and in love. Were we in love? It certainly felt like that it day, and we certainly acted like it. I was enthralled with him, and was glad to see he seemed just as interested in me as he had been that first Saturday night.

Later, we parked the bike by the side of a road. We found a spot heavy with scented flowers, their perfume mingled with the salt air from the river. We spread our blanket, and started on our feast of fruit, bread, cheese, olives, dried sausage, and of course, wine. Henri had thought of everything. Lying under the sun, we quickly became warm. Henri took his shirt off and lay back with his hands folded behind his head.

"You look comfortable," I said, leaning over him.

"You're blocking my sun," he said dryly.

"I'm what?"

He laughed and pulled me towards him. Together we rolled off our blanket, in a playful tumble. When we stopped he was looking down at me, his wavy hair hanging in his eyes. He kissed me softly, at first. The skin on his back was smooth and my hands instinctively pulled him towards me. He let more of his weight down on me, so that there was no space between us anymore. We looked into each other's eyes and knew immediately that this was the moment. There was no one around for miles. Even if there had been, we were so completely caught up in each other it wouldn't have mattered. Neither one of us hesitated.

It was the perfect moment, in a perfect day. Afterwards, we joked about what we would have done had someone wandered along. The only shelter we could come up with was under our picnic blanket. We rode back through vineyard country as the sun was setting and went straight back to Henri's apartment.

The rest of April and May brought Henri and I even closer. So much was happening all at once. It was nearing the end of the semester. There were final exams and projects to be finished. Some students had been offered apprenticeships in Paris; other students were making plans to go home. But I just wanted time to stand still. I wanted to go on feeling the way Henri made me feel. Henri and I had spent so little time together, I couldn't think of leaving him now.

Besides, I wasn't completely sure of how Henri felt about me. I knew that when we were together, his feelings were genuine. You couldn't fake passion like that. And yet, he had this ability to totally detach himself, sustaining a social life with his own friends that did not include me. He was very independent and secure with himself. I had liked this quality so much at first, someone who did not need me or depend on me, or expect me to be there for him. But it was this same quality that kept me a little insecure about our relationship. I didn't trust these mixed signals, but didn't know how to deal with them either. I only had our time together on which to gauge our relationship. And our time together was pure magic. Henri never asked me about my plans or spoke of a future together, per se, so when he suggested I stay in Paris, at least for the summer, I naturally took this as a sign that he wanted me to stay with him. It made me deliriously happy that he wanted me as much as I wanted him. But before I could make any plans or accept any apprenticeship, I would have to go home first, at least to attend graduation. There were people expecting my return.

Saying good bye to G and Phillipe was made easier by their assurances that we would see each other again. G had taken an apprenticeship in Paris and Phillipe was going back to Provence for a few weeks to break the news to his parents that he was starting a new semester at chef school. Henri, on the other hand, made it much harder for me to leave. He was not happy that I was going home to another love, another life. I had never seen him jealous before. I remember thinking this was a new emotion for him and he dealt with it by retreating into his quiet aloofness. His pulling away only made me want him more. But I knew I could not reassure him of anything for I truly did not know how I would feel when I got home. Before I left, I looked to Henri for some last-minute affection I could hold onto. He looked at my face for a long time, as if trying to commit it to memory. His only words were, "Come back to me, Brigitte."

That plane ride home was excruciating. The last few weeks I had had to put thoughts of Vincent away in order to be with Henri. Now I would have to figure out my feelings. In a few hours

I would be reunited with Vincent; all his letters spoke about how he had been looking forward to this day. All kinds of questions ran through my mind as I tried to compare relationships. I think I truly believed I loved them both, in different ways and for different reasons. I wondered what I would tell Vincent. Should I tell Vincent about Henri? How could I begin to explain that I had met someone else? It was Vincent's greatest fear.

If only I had more time. More time with Henri. More time to make sense of my feelings. I had, after all, known Vincent for four years. I had only just started a relationship with Henri. But how could I possibly ask Vincent for more time? Vincent, who had waited for me, planned a life with me, was so sure and loyal in his devotion. How could I betray that? How could I give that up? And yet, I did not want to let go of what I had with Henri. They were totally different relationships. With Henri I had passion, an aliveness with a sense of my own freedom. We were two individuals who came together and enjoyed the moment with one an other, experiencing it fully with no expectations. But with Vincent I had a true connection, deep affection, and admiration. Which was real and which would last? I still didn't know what love was.

Just as his letter had promised, Vincent was waiting for me at the end of the gate with a bouquet of roses. Seeing his expectant, smiling face in the crowd made my heart swell. He cut through the crowd, making his way toward me. I tried to put aside all decisions and worries at that moment so I could return the smile and big hello I knew he was expecting. As he reached me, he threw his arms around me and squeezed me tight. There was his familiar embrace, familiar smell, and the familiar way our bodies seemed to fit together, to know each other.

"I'm so glad you're home," said Vincent as he held me, our heads buried into each other's neck. "You have no idea how much I've missed you...but that's over now," he said. When we finally separated, his smile was jubilant and his eyes were alive with excitement.

"C'mon, let's get your things."

It became obvious to me over the next few days, that Vincent felt we were starting our life together. He had not asked about Paris, or if there was anyone else he should know about. He had weathered the storm and passed the test. It was clear that he thought my coming home meant that I had decided to marry him as well. For my part, I struggled with what to tell him, how to tell him. I put up a fairly good front when I was with him. That was easy. Vincent was still as romantic and fun to be with as ever, and the ties that seemed to bind our lives together were still strong. But not strong enough for me to forget about Henri.

By the end of that first week, questions naturally came up about what my plans were, would I be looking for a job, and where. But I couldn't even think about starting a career in New York when my thoughts kept wandering back to Paris, and Henri. Nothing had been settled. I was hoping that spending time with Vincent again would help assure that my place was here, with him. But I was more confused than ever. I loved Vincent and being with him again felt right in many ways. I respected him more than ever now, his loyalty, his honesty, his integrity. But how could I love Vincent and feel the way I did about Henri? What was it about Henri that made my head spin and heart race? It was all I thought about when I was not with Vincent. With each passing day, these thoughts weighed heavier on my mind. The more time lapsed, the more I felt like I was lying to Vincent and losing Henri. Claire was one of the first people to notice the change.

"You want to go shopping today?" Claire asked. She was now a student studying journalism at Columbia.

"Don't you have school today?" I asked.

"Bridge, it's Saturday."

"Oh, wow, I guess I've totally lost track of my days. No, I don't really feel much like shopping."

"You okay? You've been kind of spacey lately," she said. Even at 19 years old, Claire was extremely intuitive.

"Yes, I guess I have a lot on my mind," I offered up a vague response.

"I thought you'd be happy to be home...but you're not, are you?"

She had seen right through me and my silence only confirmed that something was wrong. There was no point trying to hide it from my sister. She was definitely in the right field because she had a journalist's instincts, a nose for news. She honed right in on the human-interest story brewing right under her own roof. I flopped onto my bed with a sigh and Claire curled up sitting Indian style on the foot of the bed.

"Ok, spill...," she said.

I proceeded to tell Claire all about Henri and how my feelings for him further complicated matters with Vincent, which were already complicated in the first place. If I wasn't sure about marrying Vincent before I left for school in Paris, I was even less sure now. The last few months seemed to only prove that I was right to hesitate, to take some time for myself.

But now...

"Do you love Vincent?" Claire asked pointedly.

"Yes, I love him...but..." I couldn't quite define it.

"But you have feelings for someone else?" Claire filled in my blank sentences.

"Yes, I do and I don't know what to do about it."

"These feelings you have for Henri...do you think you could love him more than Vincent?"

"It's not a question of more...it's just different...," I said, not knowing how to begin to explain.

"So you think you love this guy?"

"I think I'm falling in love with him."

"But how can you love two people?" Claire wondered innocently.

It was such a sensible question, one that I grappled with myself. Was it possible to love two people? Surely, one love must be real, but which one?

"That's just it, Claire...I don't know. I thought I loved Vincent... no, I do love Vincent...I just don't know if I'm 'in love' with Vincent."

I had said it. Silence.

"Wow. What are you going to do?" Claire asked.

"I don't know," I said at first. "I'd like to find out if I'm really falling in love with Henri or if it's just a passing phase, a wild physical attraction I needed to get out of my system or something."

"You're thinking about going back to Paris, aren't you?"

I paced the room.

"I just need more time...oh, how can I ask Vincent for more time? How am I going to explain this to him?"

"It's going to kill him you know," said Claire. "He thinks you're going to get married."

"Don't you think I know that?"

"You can't ask him to wait for you while you go off to Paris to be with someone else. It's not fair."

"I know, but I don't want to lose him either. What if Vincent really is my one true love?"

"It seems to me you've got to be ready to lose him if you decide to go back to Paris. Why don't you stay a while and see what happens? Maybe you'll forget about Henri."

"I was half hoping that myself, but I don't see that happening."

"You're that crazy about this guy?" she asked. I guess it was a little hard for Claire to believe.

"Yes...," I answered reluctantly, surprising even myself.

"He must really be something to give Vincent competition."

"The thing of it is, Claire, I know in my heart Henri is not half the man Vincent is. He doesn't have Vincent's heart, or Vincent's depth, and yet...when I'm with Henri..."

Claire watched me blush.

"Well, it's not like you have to decide today, do you?" Claire asked.

"Yes, I do. I hate lying to Vincent like this. I feel as if I'm living a charade."

"He certainly wouldn't lie to you," Claire reminded me.

"No, no he wouldn't. That's why I'm trying to do the right thing. I thought of telling him I was going to take a position in Paris...just for a little while...so I can decide..."

"You can't do that," said Claire, slightly offended on Vincent's behalf.

"No, of course not...," I said, hanging my head for the shame of the thought.

"What would Vincent do, Bridge?" Claire asked.

I thought for a long time. I knew what he would do...and then I knew what I must do.

Claire remembered that very conversation. It seemed like only yesterday that she and Bridge had agonized over the decision and struggled to figure out answers to age-old questions. What was true love? What did it feel like? What was most important in a relationship? They had tried to decipher which feelings were true and which would fade. It must have been hard for Bridge in those days without a mother around to talk to about such matters. She liked to believe that they would have had the kind of relationship with their mother where they could have heart-to-heart talks. Bridge only really had Claire to confide in and now Claire wondered if she had helped or hurt her sister. Claire always believed that Bridge had made all the wrong decisions, but for all the right reasons and intentions. Now Claire realized for the first time just how important that conversation had been, how the decisions made that fateful day would forever change her sister's life.

CHAPTER FIFTEEN

Sherman had invited Ester and Bridge out to dinner to celebrate the success of the book; apparently it was selling well already. But that was of no concern for Bridge. She already knew that her own profits from the book would be earmarked for some local charities. The three had become fast friends and Bridge felt just as comfortable with Sherman as she did with Ester.

At the Union Square Café, Sherman ordered champagne and they spent several minutes toasting each other, first Bridge's book, then Ester's keen eye, and Sherman's fast-acting genius. What fate it had been that they all came into each other's lives. As dinner came and went, the champagne flowed along with the conversation as the three regaled each other with relationship stories, some sad others simply hysterical. Sherman was always good for a little drama and a lot of dishing.

After they had gotten a little heady from their celebrating, Ester broached the subject she had long avoided.

"You know Bridge, you never told me about Vincent," said Ester. "What ever happened to him?"

"You know as much as I do," said Bridge. "You read the book."

"But didn't you ever run into a mutual acquaintance or hear anything through the grapevine?"

"No, once I married Neal and moved to Brookville I lost all contact with anyone that might have known him."

"You never thought of looking him up? You were never curious?" Ester persisted.

"Of course I was curious, but I was married after all and I assumed Vincent was as well."

"You're not married now…," said Ester with a curious kind of meddling.

"Oh, what's the point?" Sherman piped in. "What's past is past. Besides you can never go back. And you can never predict what the fates have in store for you."

There was a long pause. Each of them seemed to be considering Sherman's words, until Ester changed the conversation.

"So, how's the vintage couture shop going?"

"Great," said Bridge. "I think I might have found a few places that could work as the store front. I have to check them out."

"What's this store front idea?" asked Sherman. "I'm going to need her to write another book."

"Oh no, Sherman," said Bridge. "That was really never my intention. You know that."

"That's a shame," said Sherman. "Then I guess I'll just send you my best gal pals to outfit."

"It's for charity," said Ester. "Not for those clothes hounds you like to hang out with."

"Ester, dear," said Sherman, "we live in New York City and we work in publishing. Trust me, we are charity." Then turning to Bridge, Sherman had one more request.

"Well, before you embark on your next venture, I do

have one little request. I had been keeping it a secret because I didn't know if it was actually going to happen. But I did book you into a book signing event at Barnes and Noble Christmas Eve day."

"Oh, no Sherman," said Bridge. "I couldn't possibly. I'm leaving with Claire and the kids for Vermont that evening."

"I'll have you out by three or four the latest. I promise," said Sherman.

"How did you…why…? They don't give book signing events to unknown authors!"

"Ordinarily no, not at the big bookstores," agreed Sherman. "But there's a general lack of famous authors on the road Christmas Eve. Besides, it's good for sales. They generally draw people into the store."

"Wow, he even kept this from me!" said Ester. "You must owe someone a big favor."

"Again, Sherman," said Bridge, "I appreciate everything you've done, but…"

"Look, you simply have to do it, darling," said Sherman.

"Ok…," conceded Bridge. "I owe you at least that."

"Good," said Sherman. "You can get the check too, if you like!"

They laughed and raised their glasses again. After dinner Ester and Sherman went onto a little club downtown, but Bridge walked the short distance home to West 16th Street. As she passed through the neighborhood that was long familiar to her, Bridge thought about the evening and the odd turn of events in her life these past couple of years. Leaving Neal, her father's death, moving back to the neighborhood of her youth with all its memories of Vincent, writing the book and its subsequent success, meeting Ester and Sherman, and now a new business she was thrilled to be starting. She remembered Sherman's comment about everything working out because of fate and wondered how much of that was true. At any rate, *Vincent's Gifts* was a one-time effort. Writing it had been a gift to herself and though she was happy the book was selling, Bridge had no intention of embarking on a profession as a writer. Fashion was one of her first loves and now she could do something truly rewarding with her talents.

Bridge also thought of Ester's remarks about Vincent. How she would have loved to have contacted him so many different times over the years, but Bridge knew that was not an option. Even though she had longed for him, and loved him still, their fates had been sealed long ago. Besides, she had spent all these months trying to go forward by coming to terms with the past. Sherman's comment about not being able to go back had given everyone something to think about. She wondered if they all had a Vincent in their lives. It seemed so at that moment.

Tonight as Bridge thought about Vincent, she did so with a hopeful heart. She wished he was happy with the choices he had made. She smiled as she thought about what he must look like, or if he had children. What a wonderful father he would surely be. She hoped that when he thought about her, if he thought about her, that it was with the same good will and affection.

CHAPTER SIXTEEN

Claire's week was a busy one. With last-minute shopping, writing out Christmas cards, wrapping gifts and planning for their trip to Vermont, she had hardly had a moment to herself. She was anxious to finish Bridge's book, which she saw displayed now in the windows of most booksellers. She could hardly believe it. And here she was, having been given one of the first copies, still not finished. Even though Claire thought she knew how the book must end, having been privy to the real life details, she still felt caught up in the drama of these characters. Secretly, Claire hoped that she'd discover something unexpected. Today she would do just that.

I started for Vincent's apartment with a heavy heart. I had played the conversation over and over again in mind, but now was unsure of what I would actually say. Would I have the nerve to go through with it? As I got closer to Vincent's place, I wondered if I was doing the right thing. It had been so clear before. I had told myself it was the honorable thing to do, something Vincent himself would do, but with each step my courage faltered.

When I arrived at Vincent's, he was glad to see me, until he really looked at me.

"What's the matter?" he asked, as he came over to me and

rubbed my arms and shoulders. He looked into my face as if trying to see if I felt okay. I did not. I felt sick actually, my stomach in knots and a lump in my throat.

"Let's sit down, Vincent."

"Are you sick?"

"No…"

"What is it?"

I paused for a long time. All the words, all the preparation flew out of my head.

"I'm thinking about going back to Paris," I said.

At first he must have thought for a short trip, something I needed to take care of.

"For what?" he asked innocently.

"For a job…," I offered up a feeble excuse, unable to get the truth out at first.

"What?!" he exploded. "You just got back."

"I know…I didn't want to tell you right away…"

"This is something you've known about? Planned on?"

I wasn't sure what to say, the lie was getting complicated.

"Actually…"

"I can't believe this," he continued on. "For how long Bridge?"

"I…I don't know."

"You don't know?"

Vincent paced around the room. He was trying to make sense of it all. When he stopped and looked at me, he was angry. He was seething.

"I don't understand you Bridge, you know that? I don't understand…you say you love me, you wanted time for yourself, I gave it to you. You went away, I waited for you. Now you want to go back to Paris, live there, work there. What about us Bridge? What the hell am I supposed to say to that?"

Make it easy on me Vincent, I thought. Get angry, get fed up with me. Tell me this is it, you don't want to do this anymore. But he didn't. He raged on:

"What am I supposed to do? Wait indefinitely? When are we going to start our lives? I'm ready to start our lives now. I thought that's what you wanted too."

"I thought I did, but …"

"But what?"

"I'm not sure…I don't know what I want."

"You don't know if you want to be with me?" he said softer, hurt for fear of the answer.

I just shook my head. I couldn't speak and I couldn't look him in the eye. He collapsed on the couch next to me and wiped his hand over his face.

"I don't understand this," he said. "Bridge, please, sweetheart, talk to me, explain this to me."

But I couldn't find the words. He turned to me and grabbed my shoulders.

"Look at me! Look at me and tell me why you're doing this!"

"Vincent…I…I'm just not ready to commit to you…"

"Why? Why…is…there someone else?"

Silence. Then the realization registered on his face.

"Bridge? Is there someone else?"

"Yes."

He let me go. He rested his elbows on his knees and hung his head, as if defeated by love.

"Do you love him?"

"I don't know…"

"When…how long…"

"It's only been a couple of months."

"But you're going to Paris to be with him, right?" His anger started to build again.

"Vincent, I have to find out what my feelings are for him."

"What about your feelings for me?"

"I'm torn between what I feel for you and these new feelings for him."

"Bridge, don't do this to us...don't throw what we have away for a dalliance with this guy."

"I don't know if that's what this is...I don't know...and I need to find out for myself."

"Bridge, there's always going to be people who turn your head, people whom you're attracted to, but what we have...we have a once in a lifetime love..."

I remember believing that what Vincent said was true. And yet, I could not explain away the passion I had with Henri-- feelings that made me question love itself. It was incredibly painful to go on arguing with Vincent, trying to get him to understand, and my every response hurting him more and more. How easy it would have been to stay with Vincent, agree with him, tell him I must have been out of my mind and promise to be true for the rest of my life. But that would not have been a fair act, and I would have never settled the questions in my own mind and heart. I would never really know what love was supposed to feel like. I would never be totally sure of my decision. I could not live with that, nor did I want that for Vincent. I held my ground.

"That may be true Vincent...but these other feelings I have for..."

"I don't even want to know his name," he said disgusted.

"I have to go back. I have to find out."

More silence. He was controlling his anger. It must have been so hard knowing how intense Vincent felt about everything.

"I know this is a terrible mistake you're making," said Vincent "and I know you will come back to me. There's obviously nothing I can do or say to persuade you not to do this. You leave me no other choice than to wait for you. Wait for you or lose you...and I can't lose you."

I wondered how he could be so sure for the both of us, when I wasn't sure of anything, but there was something comforting in the fact that I knew his love would never die. Still, I couldn't allow him to wait indefinitely on me when I could not offer him any guarantees of returning. I knew what I must do in order to set Vincent free. It was the only way he would get on with his life. And so the lies fell from my lips.

"Vincent stop," I interrupted. "I can't do this anymore. I... I must not love you."

"You just told me you love me..."

"Yes, but I was wrong. I thought I did...I told myself I did, but I don't."

"No...I can't believe this," he said in disbelief.

"It's true Vincent, I don't love you. I can't continue pretending that I do."

Those words were suspended in the air, both of us paralyzed, staring at each other.

He didn't say anything. He just stood there motionless, swallowing hard, choking back the tears. Finally, he just turned and walked out the door.

I sat in the silent room for a long time, as uncontrollable tears flowed down my face, neck and chest. My only solace was that I had stopped inflicting the pain that he would have otherwise gone on enduring had I been selfish enough to let him wait for me. When I finally rose to leave, I looked around the apartment so full of memories and wondered if I would ever see it, or Vincent, again.

I got home and walked directly past my father and Claire who were getting ready for dinner. I walked straight up to my room and closed the door. I lay there all night, my heart breaking, my mind racing, trying to comfort myself thinking I had done an honorable thing. I stared at the ceiling for hours.

I told myself that this might only be temporary. Soon, I would surely discover who I was meant to be with. But Vincent had left so utterly distraught. It was clear that there was nothing left for him to say. It seemed so final. I couldn't quite convince myself that I might never see Vincent again. Sometime late into the night, I must have finally fallen asleep.

In the morning, I woke teary eyed and began packing for Paris. Before I left, I took off the small, delicate ring that Vincent had placed on my finger a year ago. I put it away, safe in my jewelry box. I could not wear it now certainly, but I hoped that if it was meant to be, I would return to wear it knowing that I was confident in my decision, in myself, and most of all in my heart.

The following week I was back in Paris. I was anxious to see Henri, to let him know what I had done. But he was not home when I arrived. He must have already gone to work. I scribbled a short note that explained where I was staying and slipped it under his door. I had already arranged with G that I would return to the apartment and she immediately started investigating job possibilities for me. Of course, that was not going to be easy now. I was no longer a student and visas were hard to come by. I really didn't have a very good plan, a lot depended on Henri. G was supportive, but couldn't believe I was sacrificing so much for Henri. Frankly, neither could I. But here I was, nonetheless, determined to settle my romantic triangle once and for all.

Later that day, Henri arrived at my front door holding a bottle of champagne. His smile said everything he did not.

"You've come back to me?" he said, leaning on the frame of the doorway. His head cocked a little to one side, his blue eyes staring up at me from under his bowed head. I had almost forgotten how blue his eyes were.

"Yes," I said. I wasn't about to try to explain everything at that moment, and it seemed enough of answer for Henri.

"Then that is reason to celebrate," he said as he opened his arms wide and walked towards me. His kisses were electric. I held onto his neck as he slammed the door behind him and we moved together, locked in a kiss, across the living room.

"I'm so glad you're back," he said between kisses. "I didn't think you would come."

"I missed you...I had to come."

We left the champagne on the counter and stumbled over my bags as we made our way towards the bedroom. There he uttered the words I had hoped to hear, the words that justified my being there. "Brigitte, I love you..."

Later, we emerged to find that G had been home and gone. A discreet note on the counter read: Went out. Champagne in icebox. -G.

"Excellent," said Henri. "Chilled to perfection."

He opened the champagne and searched the fridge to make us a quick snack. After a while, G returned, hesitant at first as she came through the door. We were there to greet her.

"Are you decent?" she called in from the door.

"No, cheri, we are terribly indecent, and we plan to be for a long time," joked Henri.

"Come have some champagne with us, G," I said. "We're celebrating."

"Alright, to your return then Brigitte?" asked G.

"To love..."

We drank champagne and lounged around in our robes, seeming not to have another care in the world. It was a bittersweet reunion for me though. Although it was a wonderful night, I had had to leave one love for another. But now, I felt that Henri and I had made a new start and everyone seemed to be on a high. Even G, who had had her doubts about the sometimes aloof Henri, seemed happy to have me back and have him puttering around our small kitchen again. But, it wouldn't last long. In two weeks time, I had moved in with Henri. He had wanted me to from the beginning, but I was busy trying to sort out plans for myself. There was a job to consider and rent to be paid; I still had the matter of my visa. Henri argued that that was all the more reason to come live with him. And so I did.

I went back to Parsons to see if the school had any job leads for recent graduates, but all the jobs in Paris required a visa. There was an opportunity for me to work at the school itself. A sort of teaching assistant's position and since it was an American school, they would arrange for a visa for me to work there for a year. It wasn't what I had hoped for, but it was a job and I liked being around other designers and students.

In the weeks that followed I felt more and more comfortable with our situation. I'd often pick up things to spruce up the apartment so that it became our place. I spent most of my money on the gorgeous fabrics G and I would find on Saturdays. They became our bed linens, pillows, curtains and tablecloths. I started thinking that this must be what married life with Henri would be like. Romantic dinners, and talks about our respective days. I'd usually do the shopping, and we would cook together. Occasionally, we would eat out. There were so many lovely summer evenings we spent about Paris, where you could eat very inexpensively and still go to a club or cafe later. This was part of the Parisian lifestyle. There were nights too when Henri would go out with his friends and I would see G, or Phillipe, who had also got back into town that summer. We both thought the space was healthy. After all, it was an adjustment to go from living alone to living with someone all the time, and neither one of us thought that meant having to give up our social nights with friends.

Those first couple of months with Henri were exciting, sharing intimate details, finding out about each other's past and supposing about our futures. But by that September, as summer whimsy turned to fall routine, the reality of everyday living gave us an opportunity to see each other in a more realistic light. Not just as a new lover with whom you are infatuated, but as a man, and a woman. As individuals, we would discover we were different in many ways. Henri was a person who liked to be by himself, and I was a person who liked to be with him. It became obvious that Henri started feeling a bit penned in by our living arrangement and it came out in small, selfish acts. Like the nights I'd come home late from work, and he had only thought of dinner for himself, letting me fend for myself. Or, other nights that he would not be there at all, then come in late from having been out with his friends. He was not without his flaws, which in the beginning were easy to forgive.

But as the months passed by, and our passion began to cool, our routine comfort turned to discomfort. I had expected that chemistry like ours could not continue forever. I suppose I thought it would mellow into a warm, loving and affectionate intimacy. Instead, I felt Henri growing restless with our relationship. The newness was gone and there was little we could actually do together. We tried doing things the other liked, but all our efforts were in vain. And I became increasingly disappointed with Henri. His lack of thought or effort became more apparent. For Christmas, he gave me money in a card, saying I should pick out a nice dress for myself. We had drinks with his friends Christmas Eve instead of going to any sort of services. For my part, I had put so much effort into making our first Christmas together special, but discovered Henri and I had different sensibilities about the holidays. It was just another day for him, a reason to miss work.

It was impossible not to start comparing Henri to Vincent.

Christmas with Vincent had always been so magical, a time we both looked forward to and reveled in the spirit of giving. Only the year before, Vincent and I had sat in St. Pat's together, humbled by the solemnity of the holiest night of the year. I remembered how moved Vincent was as he prayed for our future.

Suddenly, all those things that seemed so confining and intense about Vincent, the things I tried to escape from, were now the things that I missed most in my relationship. His assuredness and steadfast commitment to working at our relationship, his constancy and loyalty, his decisiveness, his depth of emotion. And the things that I loved about Henri when I met him, the free-spiritedness, independent air and devil-may-care attitude, now seemed like an empty promise. But of course, Henri had never promised me anything.

And yet we went on, Henri and I. We did care for each other and we were loving, but we could not connect on any other level except the physical. For his part, he thought me to be a dreamer whose lofty ideals were not only unattainable, but naive. I thought him to be too grounded in the mundane. Our conversations went nowhere. Our expectations of a relationship could not be more different. And apparently, we operated by a different set of values as well.

By spring, Henri went out by himself more and more and I heard that Henri was seen at the cafes with other women. I never knew for sure if he was unfaithful, but his wandering eye and alarming good looks made for a risky combination. With the end of the spring semester coming, I was feeling the need to know where I stood with him. In May, I confronted him with questions about his intentions and our future. I argued that we lived together like a married couple, but hardly spoke about specific plans for our futures. I almost think had I not confronted Henri, he would have been content to go on the way we were. At first he was evasive, as if he really hadn't thought about any other plans. But when I was specific about where he saw our relationship going, he admitted that he did not see a future for us. In fact, it had been some time since he felt like he was in love with me. He assured me that he loved me, but that he just didn't feel the same way about me. I was hurt at first, but not surprised. In truth, the more I came to know the man, the less in-love I felt as well. I had traveled far and risked much to follow my heart, to find out what true love felt like. I had found my answer.

Luckily, I had G and Phillipe who rallied around me. G insisted I move back with her, and Phillipe did his best to mend my aching heart. Every time I talked of moving back to the States, they would convince me to stay, saying that summer was coming, or that I was making good contacts through the school and something would surely come my way soon. It was easy to let them care for me, easier than uprooting myself again and returning to more uncertainty back home. Besides, I was numb. I was not thinking very clearly. Staying took the thinking process out of any decisions. And so I stayed on in Paris with my friends, watching them make their dreams happen. G was working with a design house and Phillipe had finished his culinary training program. The summer months went by uneventfully for me. There were occasional dates and whispers about an opportunity in Milan. I chose to pursue neither. I functioned marginally, only by the comfort and familiarity of what had become my routine. I was lost, as if in a haze, not being able to see my way out. Months went by...

The haze lifted one early November afternoon. I was lunching by myself at a nearby cafe. From my window seat, I was staring out at the square, though not at anything in particular, until a man caught my attention. He was very well dressed with dark hair and he carried a bag of groceries with a bouquet of flowers peeking out over the top. He had a sense of purpose to his walk and seemed to be smiling, maybe he was singing; I don't recall. But what struck me most about this man was that he was happy and on his way to meet someone who apparently made his heart sing, hence the flowers. Across the square, opposite the man, a third- story balcony window opened and a woman appeared in it. He spotted her as she waved to him. His pace quickened as he looked up at her. He was more than happy; he was a man in love. In seconds, he was in the building and up the stairs. I could see them embrace as he reached her on the balcony. The scene moved me to tears for it so reminded me of Vincent. Deep inside, some old, familiar feelings stirred and struggled to the surface. I had known love like that.

And yet here I sat, a shell of myself with no love and no career. What was I doing here in France? Why had I stayed so long? With the tears, came the release of all the emotions and all the questions and all the failures I had not faced before. Conversations played out in my head and I saw my actions for what they were: innocence maturing.

Like fog dissipating, I suddenly began thinking very clearly. It was like emerging from a long, deep sleep; my night of indecisiveness had ended. I wanted to act, throw off the sad and lazy malaise, and kick start my own determination. Now I was making quick, instinctual decisions, not stopping to reason them out. I headed out to the University and gave them two weeks notice then booked a flight back to New York. This time, G and Phillipe could not dissuade me. I was intent on winning back the love of my life.

I was back home in time for Thanksgiving, where I dominated the conversation with talk of my plans to recharge my career efforts. I was a different Bridge, with a new focus to get my life on track again. They were careful not to ask, but I knew my family wondered if those plans included Vincent. I wondered the same myself. It had been a year and a half since our awful breakup and I didn't know how to approach him, or if I even had a right to think I could. But how could I not at least try? Now that I knew what we had was true love, how could I not do my all to mend a great wrong.

All that week, I thought about how to approach him, what I might say, what he might say. I had to anticipate that he might be dating someone else. Still, I had these dreams of us flying into each other's arms, letting go of any obstacles or leftover anger that might still be between us. I wouldn't even need to explain. Vincent would take one look at me and understand; he would see that I was ready now, that I was sure now. He had always known my heart. He was my soul mate. This was what I told myself. I believed that despite all that had passed between us, Vincent still loved me and this would be the time we would finally get it right.

It was easy enough to find Vincent. After graduating, he took a full-time position with the same architectural firm that he had worked at with his friend Sammy. By Friday of that week, I could no longer contain my anticipation. I timed my arrival to coincide with what I assumed would be Vincent's lunch hour, thinking we could use the time to talk. The fifteen minutes I spent waiting outside the office building seemed endless. It had a large entry enclave and its cement walls offered only a little protection from the wind. I paced initially, then settled into a spot, leaning against the building, far left of the sets of glass doors. From there I could easily see any one who left the building. Every time the doors opened I steadied myself, listening to the voices engaged in conversations, then searching for his familiar face.

Finally, as a group of people passed through the doors, I thought I heard Vincent's laugh. It sounded wonderful. He was joking with his friend Sammy, and I was glad they had stayed friends through this whole ordeal. My heart raced as I took a few steps forward towards the doors. When Vincent and Sammy emerged from the building, Sammy automatically turned to his left, walking away from the building. Vincent stopped to hold the door for a woman behind him, creating a lag between him and Sammy. It was then that I called his name. His eyes first went back to the doors, but then he looked to the other side of the building. He was more handsome than I had remembered. I must have been smiling, but my feet seemed unable to move. He too seemed paralyzed at first. He stared at me for a long time as if in disbelief. I was unable at that moment to read his expression or perceive what his emotions were. Then, he moved towards me briskly. I stood motionless, not knowing if I was going to be on the receiving end of a soon to ensue tirade or tearful embrace. It was neither. Instead, he came in close, his face very close to mine. But he never touched me.

"What are you doing here?" he asked in an almost breathless whisper.

"I came to see you," I said, thinking the answer should have been obvious.

"Why?" His voice took on a stern tone.

"Why? Because...I'm back, I've come back."

"That's nice. But why are you here at my office? How did you find me?"

"It wasn't hard, Vincent."

"So, what do you want?" He sounded guarded, defensive.

"I wanted to tell you that I finally realized what you've always known," I said. "That we love each other and we should be together."

He paused, not knowing what to say at first. Then the angry words came. It wasn't the reaction I had hoped for.

"Oh? You realize that now, huh?"

"I know how crazy this must sound to you Vincent, but let me explain..."

"No, let me get this straight. You show up here after a year an a half, after not hearing from you in all that time, and you expect me to believe that you're ready to be with me now?"

"Well...I wasn't sure then...but I know now..." I was getting upset.

"What do you know now?"

"That I love you, Vincent."

"You love me?"

"Yes, I've always loved you, now more than ever."

"Why now? What's different now?"

"Because I understand now what love is, and it's you, it's us..."

"I wish I could believe that you mean that Bridge."

"It's true!"

"Why should I believe you now? Why did it take you so long to see?"

"I don't know Vincent, but I do see now. You've got to believe me..."

"It doesn't matter now anyway; it's too late!"

"It's not too late, Vincent. We can start again," I pleaded.

"No Bridge, we can't. There's someone else in my life now. I've moved on."

"But can't we try again? I know, you probably don't trust me anymore...but I can win your trust back, just let me..."

"Bridge, stop! I'm getting married to someone else."

Shock. Disbelief.

"What? Married?" I stammered. "So soon?"

"I met her several months ago. She loves me."

"I love you!"

He was still angry. I was crying. The more I pleaded, the more frustrated he got. Even in the state I was in, I was sure he still loved me. Why else would he be so angry?

"Please Vincent, let's go somewhere and work this out," I said as I reached for his hand.

But he pulled away.

"No, Bridge! Don't do this to me again!"

"Vincent, I came back for you. For us…"

"There is no more us!" cried Vincent. "You told me you didn't love me. You told me it was over. I had to get on with my life, Bridge!"

I wanted to tell him that it was all a lie before. I wanted to explain why I said those things, but he was so angry I doubt he would have comprehended it all. He pulled away, trying to convince himself and me of his argument.

"How long did I wait for you?" he went on, pacing, angry. "How many chances did I give you Bridge? You still walked out on us… you weren't sure…you weren't sure."

"But, I'm sure now…"

"I can't take that chance again Bridge. What if you decide next year that you don't love me after all?"

"That won't happen."

"I don't know…," he said frustrated. He ran his hand through his hair. He was visibly torn. "God! I can't believe this!" he shouted.

"Vincent, please…I know you still love me."

"It doesn't matter…"

"It's all that matters!" I shouted. "We can work this out."

"I can't. I can't do that to Anne. I made her a promise."

"You made me a promise!"

"Yeah and you threw that away! No, no, it's too late Bridge."

"Vincent, you're angry, you're making a terrible mistake…"

"I can't do this with you anymore, Bridge…I can't…"

He walked away. I stood there crying, watching him disperse

into the crowded street. As he caught up with Sammy and they got further from me, Sammy looked back over his shoulder, but Vincent did not. He just walked away.

Claire had to close the book in order to catch her breath. Besides she could no longer see the print through the cloudy pools of tears welling up in her eyes. She reached for the tissues and wiped her face. It was a part of the story Claire had never known. A tragedy of errors compounded by lies and pride. Each had acted out of their sense of what was right, what was the honorable thing to do, and each had paid a price. Claire understood and respected Bridge's choice of taking the time to experience love, to find out for herself what was love. Most people would have never taken the chance--to stretch one's wings and risk a sure thing. But Claire hadn't known how Bridge set Vincent free. She hadn't known about the lie that would be their downfall in the end. In Bridge's mind, she had done it for all the right reasons. But Vincent would never know the truth. Perhaps if he had known the truth, things would have been different. Perhaps he would have waited for her. Perhaps he would not have hardened his heart towards Bridge or plunged into a convenient marriage. Perhaps. She would never know. Instead, both Bridge and Vincent would have to live with the consequences of their actions, a terrible twist of fate. She had gambled on love and lost. He had turned his back on it.

  Now the rest of Bridge's life made more sense to Claire. She understood for the first time how this had changed her sister and why Bridge would go on to make the decisions she did.

The days that followed were dark. I had written Vincent one last letter, hoping that he had time to calm down and consider all that had transpired. The letter tried to explain all that I had not been able to at the time, and ended with one last plea to come back to me. I anxiously waited for his reply, but none came. It was as if all hope of ever being happy again had gone. I spent many solitary hours reliving all those crucial moments with Vincent. I knew he must have been getting married soon. Sometimes I let myself fantasize that he would show up on my doorstep saying he couldn't go through with it, that he wanted me back. But as the months passed, reality confirmed my worst fears. I had really lost him forever. To live with the knowledge that I would never see him again was unbearable. I had lost him through my own actions.

I recalled the words from that famous quote, whose words hung on a popular poster in many a young girl's room in those days. "If you love something set it free...." Those words had once seemed so right to me, words that had guided my actions with Vincent, now seemed to mock me. I had learned that they were not true, at least not for me. They had cost me everything.

Nothing else seemed to matter much. I knew there would never be another love like Vincent's and mine, so dating seemed pointless. The only thing that kept me from falling entirely into an incapacitating depression was the lure of work. Parsons had a job bank program for all its graduates. After a few weeks of talking with my contacts in Paris and in New York, I followed up on a lead they had for an assistant designer's position with a well-respected formal wear house. This particular position was in the sketching department, what I loved to do most, and I actually started to feel somewhat excited by the promise of designing.

It was also through this same company that I met Neal. It was the week of the famous Seventh on Sixth, an extravaganza of fashion shows where designers, top models and celebrities from around the globe were known to attend. Invitations, although much sought after, were hard to come by, only the most elite professionals in the industry were invited. Luckily, one of the designers we had worked particularly hard for surprised us by giving us two tickets.

I was so bedazzled by all the goings on, the news crews, and of course, the often outrageous displays on the cat walk, I was unaware that I myself was being watched. Neal was standing nearby with a couple of other investors when we caught each other's glance. He smiled and then walked over to us. He was very charming and very well dressed. It struck me that perhaps he might be a designer himself. He assured us he was not, although he did have an interest in some of the design houses from an investment perspective. Then he joked with us, saying he was really there to meet a super model and did we know any of them. We pretended to be offended and he insisted on making amends by buying us a drink. Four of us ended up having drinks together, but Neal and I broke away for dinner.

Away from the crowds, Neal's voice had a smooth, deep quality to it. He had a kind of polish about him, the manicured good looks that came out of wealth and position, and the confident air of experience. He was very sure of himself and it showed in the way the corner of his mouth curled when he smiled, like a coy smirk. It showed in his light blue eyes that had a way of fixing their gaze upon you so that it was difficult to look away. I found him intriguing.

We started dating fairly regularly. At first, it was a pleasant distraction for me. We both had an interest in the design world, although for different reasons. I was in it for the art, and Neal was an investor. At first I didn't understand. On the surface Neal appeared to be a conservative businessman, but I would come to understand that Neal liked the glamour of the fashion industry, the attention it received from the media and the social status conferred onto those who followed the trends and were wealthy enough to actually purchase the designs.

Neal had come from a wealthy Long Island family. He was twelve years older than me and together we saw and tasted the best of New York. For me, it was entree into a new world, a world where all the beautiful things I had long admired, the performing arts, fashion, elegant furnishings, now became available to me. I was living the life that G and I used to dream about. Through Parisian windows, she and I had admired the designs and decorations we could appreciate, but never afford. Now, Neal was bringing me into his world, a world that exceeded my dreams, going from one social event to another. It kept me from thinking; it kept my mind off my wounded heart.

Before I knew it, a year had passed. When Neal proposed, I had the strangest feeling that I hardly knew him any better than I did than when we'd first met. Everyone told me I was crazy to hesitate. He was handsome, smart, cultured, and could provide me with a lifestyle that most women dream about when they think about their someday. But he did not have my whole heart. There were things that I noticed about Neal that made me uncomfortable, perhaps things that kept me from falling in love with him. He was short on patience at times and could have a biting, sarcastic sting in his retaliations. His answers were always of premiere authority, and he used his matter of fact attitude to control almost every situation. Sometimes I thought he was just a spoiled boy, always having to get his way. But then, Neal was used to getting his way.

There were always plenty of excuses made by Neal's supporters, people who advocated for our union, who chalked up his bad behavior to the stress of business, or managing the family's finances. People said I just didn't understand the demands of

Neal's many obligations and that if he was curt with someone now and again it was surely excusable. Now I understand why people were so willing to forgive Neal's shortcomings. I've learned that people tend to overlook someone's faults when that person is wealthy. Somehow, the money compensates for behavior that they ordinarily would not tolerate from the average man.

But back then I listened to the excuses. I told myself that his good qualities outweighed his bad and that for the most part, Neal was good company, generous, and considerate of my needs. He seemed interested in my design aspirations and had considerable connections that could open new doors for me. He thought we made a good team, that we could be helpful to each other. I had to admit, he was a very enticing package, all in all. He always treated me well. I wanted to believe that the way he treated me was indeed his true character and the way he treated others was a mere aberration. However, I would discover after we were married that the exact opposite was true.

As for love, I was sure I would never have the same kind I had with Vincent, the once in a lifetime love, so I reasoned that perhaps this was the next best thing. It was easier than facing the truth that I had known great love and had lost it through my own fault. How could I live with the pain of that knowledge every day? It was much easier to hide from it by throwing myself into a life filled with grand distractions.

It took me more than ten years to come to terms with the truth. I was emotionally numb when I met Neal, never having a chance to heal. I had hoped that a life with Neal would help me to forget, but I was wrong. It only served as a way for me to bury a huge part of myself. And I suppose it worked for a while. But with every passing year, the numbness wore away and I began to know my heart once again. Over time, I realized I had made a mistake by marrying Neal. I had not followed my heart, but had let reasoning prevail. Eventually, I realized I missed being in love. It was not that Neal did not love me, I'm sure he did as much as he could love anyone. It was I who could not love a man I no longer respected. Our marriage had become a convenience and it was costing me more than I realized, until the moment I decided I could not live the facade another minute.

It wasn't until after I left my husband, that I finally had the opportunity and the solitude in which to begin my long overdue healing process—a period of mourning for the love and for the woman I had lost. The former I would never be able to recapture, but the latter I was determined to get back. For so long I had buried the pain of the past, but now I was facing those memories and reliving the raw emotions as if they were all new again. Incorporating all of those bittersweet feelings into my life once again, although painful, awakened the best part of me. Like the dormant rose given new life from the spring sun, a part of me which was forgotten is now revived. Only by living with the pain of the past, was I able to go forward, for in the past was where I found the key to my future.

My years with Vincent yielded one great truth: That once you have experienced true love, you never forget it; you carry it with you forever. Whether you hold onto it, or lose it, you are somehow better for having known it, for at least you have had the honor of its company, have felt its warm presence and have walked in its light. Although I lost that love with Vincent, I now see that those who have experienced great love can be forever transformed by it. Those who choose to live with its memory, are endowed with a great gift, a unique capacity to reach into the innermost part of themselves, to feel love deeply, and to be able to pass it on to someone else. Almost as if part of some bigger divine process, we become vehicles for love first by receiving it, then by giving it to another. Now I realize that this was Vincent's greatest gift to me. Knowing that, gives me great hope for the future.

❦ **The End** ❦

Claire closed the book, holding it against her heart. She sat in the almost dark room for a few minutes and thought about these events and had how they had derailed a good part of Bridge's life. Claire had never really known the kind of heartbreak her sister did, but imagined there must be other women who had suffered the same cruel fate. But now it seemed to Claire that Bridge had made a kind of sense of it all, a reconciliation with the past that opened the door to a truer, happier future. She wanted it to be so for Bridge. So much time had gone by now. They were not young girls anymore, but still young enough to follow their hearts desires, to not compromise, to hold out for the real thing.

When Jack and the kids came through the door, Claire was miles away.

"I'm hungry, when's dinner?" asked James. Claire did not answer for a minute.

"Honey, you okay?" Jack walked over to her and put a hand on her leg.

She paused for a minute. Then looking at Jack and the kids, Claire smiled.

"Never better," she said.

CHAPTER SEVENTEEN

It was after 11:00 p.m. when Vincent arrived home. He had been out to dinner with a client then had gone back to the office to revise a contract. The living room floor was covered with shopping bags from Anne's favorite stores. She had mentioned she had a few more Christmas presents to get and she had obviously succeeded in the task. Vincent went into the bedroom where Anne was already half asleep. He turned on a small bedside lamp and took his shirt and tie off.

"It's late," Anne said.

"I know," he said. "I got involved with some changes to a client's job."

"Long day…"

"Yeah, you too? You went shopping I see?"

"Finished, finally," she said.

"That's good. Did you get anything for yourself?"

"Of course…," Anne said sleepily, smiling.

"Of course," said Vincent. He kissed Anne's head. "Go to sleep…I'm just going to take a shower."

On the bedside table lay a new book that Anne must have just purchased. Something about it caught his eye. A familiar title? No, just a familiar name. *Vincent's Gifts.*

He smiled to himself as he walked into the bath,

wondering if Anne had purchased the book because of its name.

The shower washed some of the stress from the day away, but left him strangely refreshed. Not ready for bed, Vincent remembered the new book that bore his name. He reached for it off the night stand and noticed the author's name. Bridge Hamilton. Strange. Another reminder of the woman who had been on his mind lately. As he opened the book, a bookmark fell to the floor. A cardboard angel, obviously provided with the holiday purchase, lay on the dark, wood floor staring up at him, its traces of gold foil shimmering in the dark. He picked up the bookmark, inserted it back into the book, then quietly made his way to the living room with the curious little book that now piqued his interest.

After checking the mail and pouring himself a cognac, Vincent settled into a leather chair and casually began flipping through the pages. He noticed that some of the pages were printed differently from the others. They were indented and in a handwritten style font. Then he realized there were letters within the book. He breezed over the first letter, a short piece, without any real cognition, and flipped around to another letter. This one he read.

He recognized it right away as being strangely familiar. The more he read the long, impassioned pleas of lovers parting, the more shocked he became. His eyes flew across the copy, sure of what would come next. The words came rushing up from the recesses of his memory like a tide washing over a conscious mind. He knew the words, for he remembered writing this very letter. He flipped to another letter. Again familiar. Again his. Each of the letters the author had included in the book, was his own. As he read each one, every familiar event, Vincent was transported back to his days with Bridge. He relived all the emotions penned by the young writer. Vincent's mind struggled for some explanation. How could the author have gotten hold of these letters? Then he remembered the author's name. He turned to the cover. Bridge Hamilton. It must be Bridge. Bridge Adair. How else could it be so? Vincent closed the book, then rose from his chair. He paced the living room as a thousand questions ran through his mind. What had possessed her to write this book? Why now? Why had she used his letters? Vincent poured himself another drink, steadying himself over the cabinets that served as a bar area. He closed his eyes for a moment and let his head hang with the weight of his thoughts.

 He didn't have to try very hard to see her face. It was always there in his memory-- when he let himself remember. He had seen her a thousand times over the years, pictured her in the park, at a downtown market, a playground, passing one of their favorite restaurants. He always imagined her looking much the same. Vincent thought about the last time he saw Bridge. He remembered how beautiful she looked, and how her deep blue eyes pooled with emotion as she pleaded for him to be reasonable. He remembered how angry he was with her, furious that she had left him, and that it had taken her so long to learn what he had always known. But mostly he was upset because she had come to him too late. Anger was the only emotion he could show her at the time, even though his heart was torn. It was the only way he knew he would be able to walk away from her forever. Years later, he wished that things hadn't ended that way.

 Now, it was as if his past was trying to find him. But

why? The angels in the promenade, the hairpins at the opera, and now this book! This was just one coincidence too many, and Vincent started to feel as though the fates were demanding his attention. But what was their intent?

Vincent returned to the little book. Perhaps the answers could be found in its contents.

He sat down to read it from cover to cover, unsure of what he would find. At first he thought it might be fiction, a story loosely based around two central characters named Bridge and Vincent.

But a few pages was all it took for Vincent to realize that this was their story. Although it was written with a mature perspective, and from an author who had a hard-learned lesson to share, there was no mistaking the historical accuracy of their years together. Vincent knew in an instant that this was indeed his Bridge. As he read, he recalled moments and memories that he had buried long ago, but not completely forgotten.

The tightness in his chest he felt when he first saw the letters had eased now. Instead, his body warmed as he read how the author first described her Vincent. He flushed from her teenage description of his physical appearance. He smiled as she recalled their Christmases together and what his gifts had meant to her. He felt the old familiar pain of jealousy rise up once again as the writer described her other lovers, each one teaching her something about herself. But he was moved to tears as the author explained how she had lied when she told him she did not love him in order to set him free before returning to Paris. He read the passage twice, recalling the scene as if it had only been recently.

"Why Bridge, why...," Vincent cried silently to himself.

It had always been hard for Vincent to accept Bridge's

argument then, but it was the reason he was able to move on as quickly as he did. And now to learn that it was a lie. A lie made with the noblest of intentions, but a lie nonetheless. Vincent used the cardboard bookmark to hold his place as he recalled the exact conversation. As he laid his head back on the chair and closed his eyes, he felt his heart ache again. He had never expected her to lie. How the truth might have changed the course of both their lives. All these years...

When Vincent opened his eyes it was almost morning. Anne would be missing him. He slipped into bed and lay there silently beside her, exhausted, but awake. He could not sleep.

When the alarm went off, Anne began her morning routine, but Vincent remained in bed.

"You getting up?" Anne asked.

"You know, I think I'm coming down with something," said Vincent evasively.

"Well, I'm not surprised with the hours you've been keeping," Anne said. "Why don't you call in sick and rest?"

"We'll see...maybe I just need a little sleep."

"OK, call me later. I've got to run."

After Anne left, Vincent jumped out of bed and returned to the book. He was almost finished, and besides he was in no condition to go to work.

In the last few chapters, Vincent learned more about how Henri, then Neal, would disappoint Bridge, and how she came to understand what love was too late. Bridge described her last attempt to save the love she finally realized she had all along. But Vincent had turned her away, not trusting her intentions. She described how her heart broke, and how her hope died with every passing day that she did not hear from him.

As an older man, Vincent could now understand what he could not as a younger man in love. As he moved through pages in time, one thing stood out so clearly for Vincent; this woman had always loved him. She had loved him despite misplaced intentions, intense emotion and hasty actions. Through time, marriage, divorce, she had still loved him and had credited him with the gift of knowing true love.

Vincent also learned of his own part in their downfall. He had been too passionate for his own good, too impetuous. There was never any gray with Vincent, only black or white, and he was always forcing Bridge to choose, to see things as clearly, or as simply as he did. In the end, it was Vincent who had hardened his heart on that fateful day. He could not let himself take a chance on Bridge once more. It was too much to risk. His pride would not let himself get hurt again. Or, perhaps some overdeveloped sense of duty to Anne won out over the truth he knew his heart held. That he loved Bridge. He would always love Bridge.

But it was all so long ago. Still, Vincent could not think of anything else. So now he knew the truth. What of it? He was consumed with mixed emotions, first anger, then sadness, then frustration. Vincent had always been comfortable with his emotions stored away. He had settled his past long ago and kept certain disappointments in a manageable place. Until now. Suddenly, Vincent questioned everything, his marriage to Anne, their childless lifestyle, their comfortable, but passionless living.

Vincent thought about the man he had become and wondered what had happened to that man who used to dance the salsa at neighborhood block parties? Or, the Marine who hauled Christmas trees on his shoulders for neighbors and friends? Here it was, almost Christmas in Manhattan, yet there was no tree in this large, well-appointed apartment. He and Anne had stopped that tradition years ago. They had used the excuse that they were both so busy and were hardly home to appreciate it. Now airline tickets lay on the desk, ensuring that Anne would not have to spend another holiday with his family. Like so many other decisions Anne had made, he hadn't even remembered agreeing to these plans. His life was full of compromises now, it seemed. Funny, the very thing he had always had trouble with in his youth, was now so easy. Why? Vincent suspected it was because a part of him just stopped caring so much. He had learned to negotiate with Anne; it was easier than facing their differences yet again. But it was costing him more than he realized. Looking around him, Vincent started to wonder what was real. He had to get out of the apartment.

CHAPTER EIGHTEEN

After a long, hot shower, Vincent dressed to go to the office. He remembered he had left the book in the living room. He thought about taking it with him to show Sammy, but Vincent decided Anne might miss it. He wasn't sure why he didn't want Anne to know he had read it. She would never suspect that he was the Vincent in the book. He had never shared that part of his life with her. Still, he didn't want to take any chances. Vincent got the book from the living room and returned it to the bedroom. He was careful to lay the book on the end table just as she had and even thought to make sure the bookmark was placed on the inside cover.

When Vincent arrived at the office, Sammy had just gotten back from lunch.

"Hey buddy, what are you doing in?" asked Sammy. "I thought you were sick?"

"I couldn't stay home."

"Well you look like hell. You alright?"

"I didn't sleep at all last night," said Vincent. He closed the door to Sammy's office.

"What's going on?" Sammy asked, concerned.

"I'm not sure…you got a few minutes?"

"Always." Then using the intercom Sammy instructed Nancy to hold all his and Vincent's calls.

Vincent wasn't sure where to start. He paused for a moment, then ran his hands through his hair, taking a deep breath.

"Okay, you know how I haven't been myself lately?"

"Yeah..."

"Well, strange things have been happening to me."

"Strange things? Like what?" Sammy asked.

"Well, the morning of my birthday, I thought I saw someone through my window who looked like Bridge."

"Bridge? Your old girlfriend from like twenty years ago?" Sammy asked.

"Yeah, she was moving through the park below and there was just something about this woman in this red cape that reminded me of her," Vincent explained.

"So?" That's what had you so weirded out that day?"

"Well, it wasn't just that...," said Vincent. "But let me finish. Then, that night at the opera, I found a hairpin."

"Yeah, I remember."

"It looked like the same hairpin I had bought for Bridge years ago."

"Vincent, it was a hairpin," said Sammy, "it could have been anyone's."

"No, not this hairpin," insisted Vincent. "I'm positive it was the same one I gave Bridge."

"So, what if it was? Which it probably wasn't."

"Ok, wait, it gets better," explained Vincent. "Then Anne comes home with this book last night. It's called *Vincent's Gifts*."

"Cute, a book with your name."

"Not just my name, Sammy, my life!" shouted Vincent, becoming more and more excited. "My life Sammy, my life with Bridge..."

"What? What are you talking about?"

"…My letters, my stories…my life!" exclaimed Vincent.

"Slow down Vincent…"

"She wrote a book about us, Sammy…"

"Who?"

"Bridge!"

"Bridge wrote a book about you? You're sure it's your Bridge?"

"Well the author's name said Bridge Hamilton, but I'm sure it's Bridge Adair," said Vincent. "The details of our lives…it's all there Sammy. There's no mistaking it."

"Ok, calm down Vincent."

"Why is this happening?" Vincent asked himself out loud as he walked around Sammy's office. "I don't understand…"

"So Bridge wrote a book," said Sammy. "Why has that got you so unhinged?"

"Why has it got me so…?" Vincent grew more agitated. "What's the matter with you? Don't you see what's going on here?"

"Yeah, I see what's going on here, do you?"

"What? What do you think is going on here Sammy, because I would really like to know? Please tell me!"

"Ok, I see a guy going through a rough patch with his wife, so now he's thinking about the one who got away."

"Oh, I'm just imagining all this, huh? The hairpin, the book…"

"First of all, you don't even know it's the same hairpin, and second of all, you can't even be sure it's Bridge Adair."

"Then how do you explain the letters in the book? How do you explain whole conversations I remember having?"

Sammy paused.

"Ah ha! You see? You can't explain it...," Vincent said, pointing a nervous finger at Sammy.

"I'll admit it's strange..."

"Strange? It's more than strange Sammy. And everywhere I look...angels. Angels in the promenade, angel book marks flying out at me..."

"What?"

"Bridge, she had this thing with angels...I don't know what to think," said a bewildered Vincent.

"About what?"

"About what all this means..."

"Why does it have to mean anything? It's just a couple of weird coincidences, Vincent."

Vincent stood for a moment and looked at Sammy. He caught his breath.

"Yeah, you think that's all it is?" asked Vincent.

"I do," said Sammy. "But you obviously don't."

"I don't know, maybe you're right...," Vincent slowed his pace and walked around the office. "...It's just that I've been thinking about her a lot lately."

"Well, with this book and all...," Sammy said.

"No, even before all this started happening," confessed Vincent.

"You never stopped loving her, did you Vincent?"

Sammy, who had been there through his break up with Bridge, and who had introduced him to Anne, knew him better than anyone.

"Thanks for listening...," said Vincent as he turned towards the door.

"Wait a minute," said Sammy, "where are you going?"

I don't know," said Vincent "I'll see you later."

Vincent walked as if in a fog. He wasn't sure where to

go or what to think. He instinctively headed in the opposite direction, away from his home and office. Even though mid-town was always so chaotic with throngs of tourists Christmas week, he nonetheless made his way through the sea of pedestrian traffic. He should have been exhausted from his sleepless night, but the thoughts in his head and pieces of conversation played over and over again in his mind. The brisk weather helped to spur him on. Block after city block, Vincent recalled those letters and conversations. He could return there in his mind, but could he return there now?

Vincent had walked through the tourist zone, past the station, down past Chelsea and was now coming into Gramercy Park. The crowds had thinned and he began to recognize just where he was. He instinctively walked towards Union Square, then west, counting off the streets in his memory. When he saw St. Xavier's at the corner of W. 16th Street, he stopped and paused. It would be silly to think that she would still be here; the book had not said much about the author except that she lived in New York and that this was her first book. He thought of Thomas Adair and wondered how old he would be now?

He slowly walked towards the brownstone. His heart raced a little. Even while his reasoning mind told him how far-fetched this was, another part of him, the piece of him that carried him here, pushed Vincent forward.

As he approached the house, uncertain for a moment which set of stairs had been the one he had carried those Christmas trees through, a door flew open unexpectedly and startled him. He jumped back a little as a grey-haired woman came out of the door next door. She too was a little surprised to find a handsome man standing out on the sidewalk looking up at the addresses. They startled each other.

"Oh! Can I help you?" asked Ester, as she looked over the rim of her glasses.

"I'm sorry," said Vincent. "I didn't mean to scare you."

"It looks like I'm the one who gave you a scare!" said Ester. "You look lost?"

Vincent smiled a little. He felt lost.

"Maybe I am a little...," said Vincent. "I used to know the people who lived here, and was just wondering..." He trailed off.

"Well, I've lived here a while, but not that long. Who were you looking for?" asked Ester. She was not about to give out any information to a perfect stranger.

"Well, this was a long time ago," said Vincent. "Thomas Adair? Did you know him?"

"Oh, well I'm sorry to tell you he passed away," Ester revealed.

Vincent silently mourned Thomas' passing and bowed his head for a moment. "Oh...that's too bad."

"Were you a friend of his or a colleague?" asked Ester.

"I guess you could say a friend of the family," said Vincent. "I knew his daughter."

"Oh well, I know the daughters," Ester offered cautiously. "Who should I say was inquiring?"

Vincent suddenly brightened. If this woman was in touch with Bridge, he could have a means of reaching her. He wasn't sure what to do. In the same instant, he considered his choices. He could leave now and not give his name. He could give his name and contact information, then the next move would be up to Bridge. Vincent reached in his coat pocket and pulled out a business card.

"I'm sorry," said Vincent extending his hand to Ester. "My name is Vincent. And you are?"

Ester shook his hand, but stared at him in disbelief. She looked at his card and the name, Vincent Valez, and then looked back at Vincent. It only took her a second to realize Bridge's main character from *Vincent's Gifts* had materialized right in front of her. Vincent smiled at Ester, wondering what had come over her. "And you are....?"

"Uh, I'm Ester...," she said still holding onto his hand. She thought quickly, wondering what she should say or do. Here was an opportunity, she thought, but Ester didn't want to overstep her bounds with Bridge. Ester knew Bridge was out looking at retail space and would probably be home in a little while. She blurted out the next thing that came to mind.

"I'm a friend of Bridge's," she said. "You've only just missed her!"

It wasn't like Ester to give out personal information, but she had said it, she wasn't even sure why, and now the truth was out.

Vincent stood quite still as the realization came to light.

"She's here?" he asked. "Bridge lives here?"

"Do you want to come in to my place and wait for a bit?" Ester couldn't believe the things that were coming out of her mouth! What was she doing?

Vincent was suddenly frightened. He hadn't really expected this.

"Oh, no, thank you. I have to get back to work...," he stammered, "I...I was just passing by and wanted to say hello..."

"I'll tell her you called," said Ester as Vincent started off. "It was nice meeting you, Vincent!"

"Yes, thank you! You too," said Vincent as he hurried down the street.

As Ester watched Vincent walk briskly away, he turned

back once and saw her looking after him. He waved again and then kept walking, back to the corner, and then out of her sight. She stared at his card in her hand, then turned and slowly made her way back up the stairs and into her own brownstone. Funny, she couldn't even recall why she had opened the door and come outside in the first place?

Ester waited the rest of the afternoon, checking for Bridge's return. But Bridge did not return. She had spent the afternoon with a realtor, signing a lease for a storefront. Afterwards, Bridge had been so excited, she took a cab to Claire's and stayed there, dining with them until very late. Before bed, Ester placed Vincent's card in Bridge's empty mail slot. And there it sat.

CHAPTER NINETEEN

The next day at the office Christmas party, Vincent could not bring himself to feign merriment. He kept to himself most of the morning and even after the catered lunch had arrived. Sammy had not spoken to Vincent since their last conversation. But today was Christmas Eve, a short workday, and a day that they always had a few drinks before heading off to their respective families and holiday plans. It had become a tradition over the years, but this year Sammy wondered if Vincent was up to it. Sammy poked his head into Vincent's office just before noon.

"Hey, you gonna come out and join us?" Sammy asked.

"Sure, you bet," Vincent replied. "Just finishing up."

"Are we still going out for drinks later?" Sammy asked.

"You know, I thought I'd go drop these plans off to Barry before they go on break for the holidays. This way they can have the time to mill over them."

"Are you kidding me?" said Sammy. "Walk to Times Square today?"

"Sam, he's an important client," said Vincent. "It'd be a nice touch if we personally delivered them."

"We?" asked Sammy. "But what about our tradition?" What about our drink?"

"Well, if you come with me, we can get a drink afterwards," Vincent persisted.

"I guess we could go to the Renaissance Hotel," Sammy suggested. "Remember, you liked it so much after they re-did it? That will be nice and quiet too, as quiet goes in this city."

"Yeah, that might be alright," said Vincent.

Sammy moved on down the hall, where Vincent could hear the remnants of conversations. People were still exchanging small gifts, and discussing their plans for the holidays. But Vincent was in no particular rush to get home. He only had to pack a few things for their flight tomorrow.

Slowly, the office began to clear out. A few of the younger architects stopped by to wish Vincent a Merry Christmas before they left. When everyone had gone, Vincent put on his camel overcoat and turned off all the lights. Sammy was just hanging up with Lisa, but was ready to go.

"OK, let's go."

From their office on 53rd and Park, the two friends headed to the West Side. As they rounded the corner onto Fifth Avenue, passing the Rolex building, the foot traffic became noticeably thicker with holiday pedestrians. Slow moving tourists lined the avenue, spilling in and out of Salvatore Ferragamo, Versace and Cartier. They did their best to move through the crowds in front of St. Patrick's Cathedral and then again in front of the Saks windows. Approaching the Barnes and Noble on the corner of 46th Street, Sammy was surprised to see an advertisement for the book which bore Vincent's name. Amidst the display window that featured the holiday selections, was the book *Vincent's Gifts*. Vincent was sure to notice it any second. Sammy wondered if it would send him into another tailspin of emotion. But

Vincent seemed more reasonable today and perhaps now was as good a time as any to broach the subject.

"Hey, there's your book...," nudged Sammy.

"Yeah, I noticed," said Vincent

"You okay with all that now? Vincent?"

They had stopped in front of the bookstore window. Vincent did not answer. Instead he was fixated on one of the event posters. AUTHOR SIGNING: BRIDGE HAMILTON, *VINCENT'S GIFTS,* DECEMBER 24, 2:00PM.

The two men stood silent for a moment. Then Vincent turned to Sammy, his index finger pointing at the window.

"You see this?" said an exasperated Vincent. "This is exactly the kind of thing I've been telling you about."

"What? You think this is another sign or something?" asked Sammy, his arms flailing wildly.

"Well, what else would you call it?" Vincent demanded, his voice rising the way it always did when he became excited. "Signs, signs, everywhere I go! All those things the last few weeks, now this?"

"Vincent, believe what you want. The fates are playing some weird, cosmic joke with your head. Is that what you want to hear?"

"You know what?" said Vincent, frustrated and throwing his hands up in the air. "I don't need to hear it from you or from anybody. It's right in front of my face!"

"What is?" asked Sammy.

"The truth, Sammy!" shouted Vincent.

Sammy had not seen Vincent this worked up in a long time. He didn't know how to reason with his friend. Vincent paused for a long time before telling Sammy of his actions and what he now knew.

"Sammy, I...," started Vincent more quietly. He was still

looking at her name on the posters. "...I went to Bridge's old neighborhood last night."

"You what? Why?" Sammy asked in disbelief.

"I was walking and just kind of found myself there," said Vincent. "She's still there, Sammy. I found her, I found Bridge."

"Did you see her?" asked Sammy.

"No, no...I met a neighbor who told me she lived there," said Vincent. "I gave her my business card."

Sammy walked in close, right next to Vincent as if anyone on the street might care what they overheard.

"Ok, Vincent...even if it is true, even if something has caused you two to trip over each other again in this city, what are you going to do about it, huh? Have you thought about that? What's supposed to happen now? She calls you? Or you show up on her door again? Or stalk her at this book signing?"

"I don't know...," said Vincent. "It just seems as if I'm destined to see her. What's the harm in that?"

"Just see her?" asked Sammy, not trusting that Vincent was being completely honest with himself. "OK. And then what?"

"I don't know..."

"Well, you gonna talk to her? Maybe go for coffee?"

"I hadn't really thought about it."

"You hadn't really thought about it?" asked Sammy, who knew Vincent better than that.

"Of course you've thought about it Vincent," said Sammy. "It's all you've been thinking about.

So, what are you thinking? You could be friends with her? Or maybe something more? What are you gonna do, leave your wife?"

Sammy had played out all the options Vincent could not. There was an awkward silence between them. Sammy had either gone too far, or struck a tender chord. He tried a different line of reasoning.

"Besides, you don't know if she even wants to see you… people do move on with their lives, Vincent."

"But the book…," Vincent said, almost to himself.

"The book was a sweet sentiment based on something that happened a long time ago," Sammy reasoned.

Vincent looked down at the pavement and then around at the myriad of shoppers passing them by.

"Yeah, I guess you're right…" He realized how he must seem the sentimental fool to Sammy right now.

"Listen Vincent," continued Sammy, "if she really wanted to find you, it wouldn't be so hard. You've got an architectural firm with your name on it."

"Bridge wouldn't want to cause trouble."

"Or, maybe she has someone in her life now…you don't know…"

"You're right, Sammy. I don't know."

"So, what's the point of all this?" said Sammy, sure he had talked Vincent out of any crazy notion to put something in motion he could not finish.

"It's just that I can't shake this feeling…like something is guiding me towards…" Vincent caught himself sliding backwards. "You're right, forget it. C'mon, let's get these plans to Barry and then go get that drink. I'm freezing standing here."

"Now you're talking…," said Sammy with an encouraging slap on the back. "Besides, I'm hungry again."

"You're always hungry!" exclaimed Vincent. "Doesn't your wife ever feed you?"

"Yeah, about as much as your wife feeds you," Sammy quipped.

"Let's go," said Vincent, as they turned to make their way into one of the high-rise buildings. It didn't take long for Vincent and Sammy to make some small talk and leave their client with the drawings and with an even better impression. Crossing at 46th and Fifth, they headed over to Seventh and back up the couple of blocks to the Rennaissance on 48th.

Tucked into the second floor of the hotel, was an oasis from the crowded streets below where guests, as well as the public, could dine or drink while enjoying a fantastic view of all Times Square. The Lounge was surprisingly empty, but the crowd from the adjoining restaurant drew them in. Two Times Square was an American restaurant with a modern décor that was warmed this time of year by the red of the holiday poinsettias, lush greens and floral displays. When the waitress arrived to take their drink orders, Vincent and Sammy were able to put their cares away temporarily.

"Good afternoon, I'm Liz...," said the waitress with a distinct British accent.

"Hi Liz," they responded in unison like grinning schoolboys.

She smiled as she handed each of them a drink menu.

"I take it you gentlemen are on holiday already?"

"How are you doing today, Liz?" asked Vincent with sincere interest.

"I'm fine, thanks. A little busy."

"I hope you're not working too late today," said Vincent.

"Not too bad. I'm off tomorrow..."

"Enjoy, enjoy..."

"So what can I get you fellows to drink?"

"I'll have a sidecar," said Vincent, closing his menu.

"Gee, all these girlie drinks!" Sammy joked with a shrug of his shoulders. "How about just a regular martini?"

"We can do that," Liz stated.

"No wait," Sammy said. "Make it a dirty martini." Sammy flashed a boyish look of excitement; Vincent rolled his eyes back and shook his head in embarrassment.

"Please excuse my friend here...," Vincent said.

"I'll be right back with those drinks. Thank you gentlemen, " Liz said.

"No, thank you!" they said in unison.

"Ok, you guys are just a little too happy..."

"You think we're too happy?" asked Vincent curiously.

"It's quite refreshing actually," Liz remarked.

Vincent nodded and smiled at the seasoned waitress. "Well," he offered in his defense, "it is Christmas after all..."

"That's true...," Liz agreed.

"But I don't know what his excuse is," said Vincent pointing at Sammy.

"Hey!" objected Sammy.

"Him, I'm going to have to keep an eye on," Liz said as she turned and walked towards the bar.

"What the hell is the matter with you?" asked Vincent, half kidding.

"What? I'm in a good mood," said Sammy. "Just trying to have a little fun, Christmas vacation and all that..."

"Just try to behave yourself when she comes back."

The hotel had expansive views made possible by a wall of windows that made the city below look almost surreal. It was a relaxing change of pace from some of the more intimate, but confining places they took clients.

"...besides," Sammy kidded Vincent, "how am I supposed to have a chance when you're being so charming?"

"Yeah right, like you ever had a chance with her."

"I could have...," Sammy protested.

"Who are you kidding? You would never..."

"I know. I'm just saying, it's nice to think I still could. You must know what I mean, Mr. 'How you doing today Liz?'"

"What are you talking about?" Vincent protested.

"Oh, c'mon," said Sammy. "You weren't flirting just a little bit there?"

"No. I was just being nice. It's Christmas and she's working."

Vincent's eyes drifted above Sammy's head, where he had a clear view of the Dow Jones zipper.

"What do you keep looking at?" Sammy asked, turning his head to see what was so distracting. "Oh, the zipper... anything interesting up there?"

"No, all the same news I already heard on NPR this morning," Vincent said.

When Liz returned with their drinks, she had brought lunch menus.

"One sidecar, one dirty martini," she said, placing the drinks in the front of them and then handing them the lunch menus.

"We already had lunch..." Vincent started to say, but Sammy cut in.

"But we can eat a little something..." Sammy interjected, shooting Vincent a look. Vincent reluctantly opened his menu.

"What's small and dirty, Liz? I mean delicious? " joked Sammy.

"Oh, boy!" Liz knew she had a jokester on her hands. "Right then, the crab cakes are quite good…"

"That's fine, that's what I will have," Vincent conceded.

"Maybe the sliders for you?" inquired Liz. "We can dirty them up a bit."

"Ha, that's funny!" Sammy said. "I'm in the mood for something hot! How spicy are the chicken wings?"

"Really spicy…" Liz stressed the word really, her accent lingering on the two syllables.

"Really?"

"Very, very spicy," she continued. "We dare people to try to finish them."

As Liz and Sammy each tried to get a sense of the others opinion of just what "spicy" means, Vincent's attention drifted back to the news zipper. Vincent could not believe what he was seeing. The zipper seemed to be experiencing a technical glitch! A message parked, then flashed in front of Vincent's eyes that read: …BRIDGE THE GAP…

"Are you quite sure? They're really pretty hot," Liz warned.

"The hotter the better," Sammy grinned. "Besides, a dare's a dare."

Something caught Vincent's ear. "What did you just say?" he asked to no one in particular. Vincent continued to stare at the zipper as Liz answered his question. Sammy noticed Vincent's face held the same distracted look of disbelief as from before at the bookstore.

"A dare's a dare…?" said Liz, somewhere in the background. But all Vincent could hear was her name, Adair.

Vincent rose from his seat, reached into his pocket, and peeled off a few bills.

"Vincent, what's wrong?" Sammy asked. He turned

around to see what had set Vincent off. But as Sammy looked over his shoulder at the view of Times Square, the technical glitch had righted itself and completed the message so that all Sammy could catch was:... TO YOUR FINANCIAL FUTURE...

"I gotta go," Vincent mumbled as he tossed the money on the table.

Sammy didn't understand at first.

"What? Where are you going, Vincent?" shouted Sammy after his friend, already stepping away from the table towards the exit. Vincent shouted back across the crowded room.

"I'm going to meet with destiny...," shouted Vincent as he walked out of the restaurant, that old, familiar bounce back in his step.

As Sammy watched his friend leave the restaurant, he smiled. He knew where Vincent was going, but didn't know what his fate would be.

"Merry Christmas, buddy," said Sammy to the empty chair.

"Was it something I said?" asked a perplexed Liz.

"Cancel the crab cakes, honey. I don't think he'll be coming back."

CHAPTER TWENTY

Vincent moved quickly through the crowded streets, doubling back to the bookstore where he knew she would be. It was almost three o'clock. The book signing started an hour ago. She would still be there, but he couldn't be entirely sure. With every quickening step, Vincent felt his heart racing. What would he say when he saw her? Should he even approach her? Maybe it was enough to just see her from afar. Although questions lingered in the back of his busy mind, there were no clear answers, no set plan; only that he get to her.

As Vincent approached Fifth Avenue, he slowed his step. Taking several deep, steadying breaths, he carefully turned the corner and looked in through the front windows of Barnes and Noble. He could see it was crowded, but didn't know where in the store Bridge might be. He chose the revolving door, and upon entering was greeted by the security guard.

"The author signing?" Vincent asked.

"Upstairs," she responded, pointing towards the turnstile and down escalators.

Only a second or two into his escalator ride, Vincent could immediately see some people around a table towards the back. The line was not considerable, about fifteen people, all carrying copies of *Vincent's Gifts*. He stepped off the elevator and into a crowd of women. He stood for a moment, unsure of what to do. He could not see past the people standing in front of the woman sitting behind the table. He quickly sidestepped to a small display area, hoping to catch a glimpse of her from a different angle within the store. Then, several women who had obviously come together, stepped away from the table and he saw her. It had to be her. She looked at the next woman in line, laden with packages stuffed into a stroller, her baby in her arms, and smiled her radiant smile. Vincent had no doubt, this was Bridge Adair. In the excitement of recognizing her, he took several steps forward before stopping himself from rushing the table. He slowed, and moved up to the line in order to get closer to her. His senses heightened and adrenaline rushed through him. Vincent could feel his heart pounding in his chest.

Bridge looked much the way Vincent had imagined her. As he peered over the top of an open book that nearly covered his face, he studied those familiar features hardly changed by time. She no longer possessed the long, blonde tresses from her youth, but wore a more mature style, swept back to compliment her beautiful face. Her hair was different, the clothes expensive, but other than that little seemed to have changed.

"Excuse me, sir?"

At first, Vincent did not hear the bookstore employee trying to get his attention.

"Sir, if you're planning on having the author sign that, you need to purchase it first."

"What?" Vincent asked, unaware that the book he was hiding behind was *Vincent's Gifts*.

"Oh, uh…yeah, okay. Thanks," said Vincent.

"I can ring you up at this register."

Vincent followed the young man to a nearby register and paid for the book. There was nothing left to do now except get on line. He searched for the right words to say to Bridge. Would she even recognize him? He hadn't changed that much, a little heavier in the face perhaps, a little different hairline. It might take a moment, but she would recognize him, then what would he say? What would she say? Had she gotten his card yesterday? Suddenly, Vincent was filled with doubt. They wouldn't be able to say much with all these people around. They would only have a quick moment to exchange a few words. It might be awkward for her and he didn't want to make her uncomfortable. Maybe Sammy was right, this wasn't a good idea. He took a last look over his shoulder at her. She looked happy. Vincent took his purchase and left the store.

Stepping out into the cold gray street, Vincent felt an overwhelming sense of disappointment. The elation that first filled his heart upon seeing her, was replaced by an anti-climatic sadness. He had come all this way. These last few weeks had taken him on a journey, leading him up to this moment. He had not felt this alive for years. He had not felt his heart reel since he was a young man. And now, to turn back? To return to only half-feeling days of predictable routines? Vincent circled the pavement in a slow, pensive stagger caught between thoughts and emotions. Practical, rational thoughts told him to walk away. Romantic fantasies filled with hope and idyllic love lured him back. To what possibility, he was not even sure. Just to say hello, to have some conversation with her was a chance that was worth taking. He decided he would wait for her.

As the four o'clock hour drew nearer, the city grew noticeably quieter. The bridge and tunnel crowd had long since departed and only the last minute shoppers walked about, who were considerable. Every time someone exited the bookstore, Vincent spun around to see if it was Bridge. He had decided on a few opening lines now. Congratulatory remarks mostly and then compliments about how well she looked. Eventually, he might segue into his leaving his card with that neighbor. Would she think he was stalking her now if she had in fact received the card, but chose not to respond? While Vincent was imagining how their conversation might go, a private car doubled parked in front of the store. Vincent made no notice of it at first, but Bridge had apparently been waiting for her car to arrive from inside the store. When Bridge finally emerged, she was not alone. A store manager walked her out and was talking with her as Vincent waited at the side of the building.

"That went really well," said the manager.

"Yes, I thought so too," said Bridge. "It was fun."

"I'm glad we could arrange it on such short notice."

"Thank you for being so accommodating, and on Christmas Eve!"

"It was our pleasure. You enjoy the holidays."

"You too."

And with that Bridge quickly ducked into the waiting car and its door was promptly closed.

"Bridge! Bridge!" Vincent shouted, waving to the car. He couldn't tell if she had heard him; he could not see her through the car's tinted windows. Vincent stood stunned, waiting for the rear window to roll down, but it did not. As the car began to pull away, Vincent had an unexpected frantic reaction.

"No! Wait!" He looked around for the nearest cab. Just

up at the corner, one was already picking up a fare. He ran and jumped in front of the crowd.

"Excuse me, excuse me!" Vincent shouted, pushing the man out of the way.

"What? Hey, watchit buddy," said the man, struggling to hold onto his ride.

"I'm sorry, I need this cab," Vincent stated with authority, grabbing the man by his coat collar, throwing him out of the way. He jumped in the cab and closed the door, leaving the other man shouting obscenities from the curb.

"Follow that black livery...that one right there...do you see it? It's a couple of cars up now." Vincent was exasperated.

"Yes, yes...I see...you want me to follow?" asked the alarmed driver.

"Yes, please, just don't lose that car," instructed Vincent. He leaned against the plastic divider, also keeping his eyes on Bridge's car.

"You probably think I'm crazy...," Vincent said breathless.

"No, no, not crazy...not my business," said the driver looking wild eyed at Vincent from his rear-view mirror.

"Look, I'm not dangerous," said Vincent pulling out a billfold of money. "There's fifty extra bucks in it for you if you stay with that car, okay...Raji?" said Vincent, reading the driver's ID.

"Yes, yes, I stay with car..."

"It's just that this woman in that car...well...I gotta see her..."

"Oh yes, woman...much trouble...," said Raji.

No, no trouble...just..." Vincent wasn't sure what his point was. He wasn't even sure why he was doing this.

"No trouble? Ahh..." said Raji. "Must be love."

As the cabs jockeyed in and out of lanes, creeping down

the heavily traveled Fifth Avenue midtown streets, they had no problem keeping sight of Bridge's private car. In fact, at the 42nd Street intersection, her car stopped at the light, and they pulled up right behind her. Vincent looked over towards the corner and noticed the time. The old, round clock flanked by two Indian chiefs that hung over the entrance to Nat Sherman's Tobacco Shop read 4:15. It would be getting dark soon.

The further they moved down Fifth, the more traffic eased up and cars sped forward wherever there was a gap. Bridge's car was no exception. As they approached the intersection at 34th Street, the yellow light was just turning red. Bridge's driver ran the red, leaving Vincent and Raji behind.

"Go! Make the light!" shouted Vincent.

"It's already red…"

"So what, go through! Go through!"

"I can't!" reasoned Raji as they came screeching to a halt. "The other traffic was already starting to pull out into the intersection. Are you trying to get us killed?"

As they waited for the light to turn green, Vincent tried to see past the people in the crosswalk.

"Can you see them, Raji?" asked Vincent. "I can't see them…"

"Don't worry, we will catch up to them," assured the driver.

Vincent looked up at the darkening skies. The Empire State Building lit up in its holiday colors.

"C'mon, c'mon," whispered Vincent.

When the light changed, Raji floored it. Neither one of them saw the black livery, but said nothing. Raji raced through the yellow light at the next intersection and caught up with a pile up of cars stopped at the next light.

"There! Is that it?" Vincent asked, pointing at a black sedan parked under the light.

"I'm not sure...you want me to follow?" asked Raji, who, himself had become caught up in the emotion of the chase.

"I'm not sure if that's her car..."

"Light's changing...what you want to do?" urged Raji.

"Yeah, follow it," Vincent said. "Can you get closer?"

"Yes, I think so, hold on..."

Raji cut off a cab on their left, then used an empty turning lane to speed past several more cars, nosing his way back into the lane of cars going straight down Fifth. They were practically next to the car they hoped was Bridge's. Vincent looked for other similar cars, but this one seemed most like the one they had been following. As they approached 25th Street, they wondered which lane they should stay in. Raji knew that 5th Ave. split here, just before the Flat Iron Building, where it intersected with Broadway. They watched to see which fork the car they were following would take. It veered off to the left, luckily, since they were already closest to the left lanes. The car came to an abrupt stop at 21st and the driver emerged and opened the side door to let his passenger out. It was Bridge. Vincent sighed with relief.

"Looks like this is where I get out, Raji," said Vincent. He paid the fare plus the fifty dollars he promised the driver and wished him happy holidays. Raji seemed to appreciate the gesture.

"Good luck!" he shouted after Vincent, already a few paces down the street.

Vincent followed closely behind Bridge, wondering where she was going; she was several blocks from her home. He followed her down 21st Street where Bridge crossed the street and entered Campagna Home, an eclectic little store of European specialties, linens and earthenware. Bridge shopped there often and wanted to stop there tonight to pick up a few things for her family's trip to Vermont. Bridge hoped she would find some chocolates for James and Olivia and some biscotti for the adults who would undoubtedly be up late wrapping presents. Vincent waited across the street not knowing in which direction she would turn when she re-emerged. It only took a few minutes for Bridge to exit with her package. She surprised Vincent by heading back to Broadway instead of continuing down 21st. She would be coming right at him. Vincent looked for someplace to conceal himself. He was able to duck into a freight entrance on his side of the street while Bridge walked past him on the opposite side of the street. When she got to the corner, Bridge crossed left, continuing down Broadway to Union Square West. It was nearing the five o'clock hour when Bridge turned on W16th Street. Vincent suddenly felt the hands of time turn back twenty five years as he entered into this street where he had gone to see her so many nights and had spent so many holidays. Tonight, like so many other Christmas Eves, people were starting to arrive for evening mass at St. Xavier's on the corner. How many times had he and Bridge heard these bells ring out, calling people into the church.

 Bridge was almost nearing the house. Vincent wondered if he should run up to her, but that would surely expose the fact that he had been following her. He could continue walking towards the church and mill in with that crowd. He could not just stand here on the street. He walked very slowly to the opposite side of the street. Bridge walked slowly up the stairs with her keys in hand. She paused when she got to the door then looked up. It had started to snow ever so lightly, and the wetness of it falling on her face must have gotten her attention. Or was it the familiar carol ringing out from the church bells. Bridge turned to watch the Christmas crowd walking up the stairs of the great, old church. If Vincent were looking for an opportunity to approach her, this would be it, but instead he continued his slow pace and began mixing in with the church crowd. He ascended the first few stairs of the church front where convenient marble pillars helped to obscure him. From this angle he could see Bridge's face. She was smiling at first, but then she sat down, almost wearily, on the stoop, listening to the Christmas music and recalling some distant memory.

She had always gotten a little blue around the holidays, she had for years, but now Bridge was surprised by this sudden sweep of nostalgia that overcame her. She thought she was over all the hurt of the years gone by and was dealing relatively well with the loss of her father. But at this moment, despite her recent triumphs, she felt sad and lonely. It was Christmas Eve and she was alone. Sure, Claire would be along shortly to pick her up for their trip to Vermont, but she still felt alone, with no love or children of her own. Here, with the snow falling and carols playing, Bridge could not help but think of happier days with Vincent, when on this same night years ago he had given her a promise ring. She closed her eyes to see his face and her tears felt warm falling down her cold cheeks.

Claire was rounding the corner and looking for a place to park, or double park for a moment if need be. She thought she noticed Bridge waiting for her on the stairs outside, but something about the scene did not appear right. She found a spot not too far from the house and parked the car. What was her sister looking at? She couldn't tell. Looking across the street to the church, Claire did not notice anything that seemed peculiar at first. Then her eye went to a familiar-looking man standing in the darkening winter night. Everyone else had gone inside the church. Lurking from behind a pillar, the man seemed to be watching Bridge. Claire could hardly believe the scene unfolding in front of her. She would recognize Vincent anywhere. Claire turned off her headlights and slumped down a few inches behind her wheel.

Vincent could tell Bridge was crying, yet through her tears she was smiling. He wondered what other sadness she had known or losses she had endured. He wondered if any of those tears were for him. As he watched her wipe her face and start to gather her packages and turn towards the door, he rushed towards her, crossing the street and climbing the stairs. Bridge spun around startled by the stranger on her stairs. It only took her a moment to recognize him.

    Bridge stared at Vincent with disbelief for a few moments.

    "Vincent," she whispered.

    Without a word, Vincent took Bridges face in his hands and kissed her lips softly. For a moment, they were suspended in time. He slowly pulled away to look into her tearful, blue eyes. He was looking for shock, or guilt, or disapproval, but all he got was a dancing sparkle of light as she began to smile with wonder.

    "How did you find me?" Bridge asked.

    "Are you kidding?" he laughed and held up the recent purchase. "I read the book!"

    "I didn't think anyone would read it…that's not why I wrote it…" Bridge began, but Vincent stopped her.

    "Shh…," Vincent assured her, wiping her tears away.

Then he reached into his coat pocket and produced her hairpin, the one she had lost at the opera.

"I believe this belongs to you...," Vincent said, holding out the hairpin.

"My hairpin! How did you know?"

"It's the craziest thing," Vincent started to explain. "Call it fate, but I think I was meant to find this pin, just as I was meant to find you."

"I think I understand," Bridge said, throwing her arms around Vincent's neck.

"You do?" he asked.

"Just listen, Vincent..."

As Bridge and Vincent stood in their embrace, they could hear the muffled song of the church choir singing:

"*...Angels we have heard on high, singing sweetly through the night, And the mountains in reply, echoing their brave delight...*"

"I think we have heard the angels, Vincent..."

"Maybe so, Bridge. Maybe so..."

Then they turned and went inside together.

Claire wiped her eyes before starting the car engine. As she turned on the headlights, she knew they would miss not having Bridge with them this Christmas, but she also knew this incredible gift would be all her sister needed. Besides, Claire had her own Christmas gift to share with her family. She rubbed her small, but growing belly, then drove off down the street.

THE END

CPSIA information can be obtained at www.ICGtesting.com
Printed in the USA
BVOW031927091111
275724BV00002B/2/P